ALTERED

A Psychological Thriller That Keeps
You Guessing Until the Very End!

ALTERED

JUSTIN WRIGHT SUSPENSE SERIES
BOOK 1

ROB KAUFMAN

Altered

Copyright © 2023 by Rob Kaufman

For my readers —
Your encouragement is the motivation
behind this book and all those yet to come.
Thank you all.

PROLOGUE

The frigid breeze whipped across his face. He ran up the city blocks, wiping melted snowflakes from his eyelids so he could see where he was going. By the time he reached 49th Street, he was out of breath and had to stop. He leaned against the steel pole that held both the street signs and traffic lights. After a few deep breaths, he wiped the liquified flurries off his cheeks and walked as quickly as he could until he reached 50th.

He made a right off Park and because the office was so close to the corner, he could see a glow of light coming from the window. Breathing a sigh of relief, he went through the building's glass front door and made a quick left. He didn't stop long enough to ring the bell to let anyone know he was about to enter. Trying to catch his breath, he opened the office door.

The first thing he saw was a man holding a gun up to his own temple.

He yelled, and before he could say a coherent word, he watched the man turn toward him and heard a loud bang. And then another.

His legs wobbled, then his head banged on the wooden floor. He brought his hand up to his throat and felt warm liquid oozing from a hole in his neck. He was surprised at the lack of pain and how rapidly numbness was spreading throughout his body. His throat felt like it was swelling up, closing his airway. He fought out a gasp and heard a soft gurgle. Did he just make that noise? Was blood filling his throat?

He tried to take another breath and heard the same sloshing liquid. His mind went void of thought, his body, frozen.

Suddenly there was muffled yelling, unintelligible screams. Something that felt like a hand cupped the back of his head and soft skin brushed his cheek. As time passed, seconds... minutes... hours... he couldn't be sure, everything faded except a weightlessness enshrouding him, a gentle sense of calm. He closed his eyes and listened to the blood pump, with each heartbeat, through the opening in his neck.

From some obscure corner of his mind, reality edged its way back in and he struggled to open his eyes one last time.

Through the haze of his dissolving vision, he saw a familiar face hovering over him. Anguish twisted it, and as if from a long distance away, he heard the cries and moans falling from the man's mouth.

He wanted to cry, grieve for them both, but once again his heavy eyelids fell down. The weeping and mumbling became a fading hum and then ultimately silence.

His final thought was not about this man who sobbed above him, his killer or the "why" behind what just happened. It was the hope that he'd see the loved one he'd lost — a hope that made him smile inside as a comforting warmth enveloped his body like the most snug of blankets warmed by the sun itself.

CHAPTER 1

The clock read 4:50 and Justin Wright cursed himself as he watched, from his ground-level office, Park Avenue fill with pedestrians leaving work early.

Some of them talked vivaciously on their phones while others smiled as music, a podcast, or possibly an audiobook played through the pods stuck inside their ears. And then there were those wearing a pronounced expression of relief, as though they'd just been released from an eight-hour prison sentence. Others trudged in exhaustion from the tedium of a daily routine they endured to pay their bills and barely survive.

Although he felt sympathy for them, self-induced frustration gnawed at his nerves. The people in the street were in the enviable position of heading to where they wanted to be. Justin was not. More than anything, he longed to be on the New Haven Line train, heading home to Rye so he could sit in the backyard with Mandy, sipping some iced Johnnie Walker Black while the autumn leaves flew off the giant maple trees and into their laps.

But his uncompromising benevolence — Mandy often described it as "you're what's called a soft touch," — had again gotten the better of him. He agreed to meet a new client, Frank Devlin, at 5:00 even though Fridays were his one day to leave the office early.

The man had called two days earlier, sounding desperate and on the verge – of what, Justin didn't know. However, there was something in his gut that made him powerless to say "no" to this guy. So he extended his hours for a man he'd never met and, depending on how today's session went, might never meet again.

As he lowered the delicate muslin shade halfway down the window, his cell phone rang. He walked to his desk and saw Mandy's photo displayed. Blushing, Justin closed his eyes as he answered. After thirty years this woman could still make his heart skip a beat.

"Hey, babe," he said. "Just thinking about you."

"And me, you. That's why I'm calling. I was thinking about those baby blue eyes of yours." He heard rustling in the background and then a file drawer slam. At least *her* workday was over.

"Oh, yeah. I'm sure. My 'baby blues.'"

"And that soft, thick head of salt and pepper hair that makes you look so distinguished and professorial." Silence. "And those chiseled facial features – with cheekbones I'd die for, long eyelashes and a dimpled chin that – "

"Enough!" he said. "If I didn't have a five o'clock, I'd let you go on forever. Especially since you're being so honest and truthful about my looks."

Mandy giggled. "I *can* go on forever and will continue later, but I'll stop now because I know you have a five. I'll make this quick. First, I wanted to make sure that sushi was okay for dinner."

Saliva filled Justin's mouth as he almost tasted the wasabi and felt its burn permeating his nostrils. "Sushi is *always* okay for dinner," he said. "And second?"

"Dylan's coming for a visit. He'll probably be here before you!"

Justin rolled his eyes, the flirtatious mood evaporating. "Well, isn't that nice of him?"

"Justin," Mandy said a bit sternly. "Please don't."

"I'm sorry, Mandy, but you know how I feel. I work in New York City, our son goes to NYU and I never see him. Not even for a lunch or dinner. Now that he's a grad student, is he too much of an adult to spend time with his father? Is he too busy to invite us to his apartment for a visit? It hurts my feelings, you know that. And now he's coming home and didn't even ask me if I wanted to ride with him. I mean…"

"Justin, please. I don't want you getting upset before your session. We'll discuss it when you get home. I'll even have a *pre* talk with him if you'd like."

He could visualize the distress on her face. "No. No. No 'pre talks.' I want to be there for everything. I'm going to get off the phone, take a few deep breaths and wait for my new client to arrive. I love you."

"I love *you*," she said. "And so does Dylan. Now good luck and get home as soon as you can, please. Your spicy tuna rolls, pickled ginger and homemade wasabi will be waiting."

She knows me too well.

"Can't wait to see you both – and those rolls, too, of course."

He heard her laugh right before she hung up and the line went silent.

Sitting in his chair, he picked up the patient intake forms Frank Devlin had completed online. Other than his birthdate, which showed he was twenty-five years old, and the statement that he was working at an accounting firm while studying in a Business Analytics Master of Science Program, it was obvious the man didn't want to provide information – at least in written form. *Paranoia?*

During their call, Frank did admit he'd been feeling a bit "off" lately. No details about what "off" meant, even when Justin asked.

"Not myself," was all Frank divulged. "A little weird, you know, off-kilter. I'd rather not get into it over the phone. I just know I need to see someone, to talk with someone who can help me find out what's going on. My anxiety is getting worse every day."

During their conversation, Frank also disclosed his recent panic attacks and how he'd been experiencing some new obsessive and compulsive tendencies. Yet he didn't indicate any of these issues on the intake forms. The only online feedback that provided marginally more information about the patient were the checkmarks in the "YES" boxes next to "irritability" and "lack of interest in doing things." Justin scratched in his notepad: *General Anxiety Disorder? Depression?*

He read further down the list. Almost all "YES" and "NO" checkboxes that might suggest trauma, bipolar or suicidal tendencies were left blank, as were the spaces for any additional comments. Although Frank did check "NO" to hearing unusual sounds, he didn't answer the questions about familiar surroundings sometimes appearing strange or experiencing peculiar feelings beneath the skin, like crawling bugs – both potential symptoms of psychosis.

Just about every checkbox up and down the forms was empty. And that meant, like the papers sitting on his desk, Justin would have to begin with a close to blank slate. He'd start with the man's anxiety and dive deeper from there. From the minimal information Frank provided, experience told him there was too much to tackle in one fifty-minute session.

Justin glanced at the clock in the upper right of his computer screen. 5:00.

Great. If he doesn't show up and I've wasted my time, I'll be…

The soft ring of the bell from the waiting area provoked a sense of relief. Not only hadn't he wasted his time, but Frank Devlin was extremely punctual. *OCD?* Justin bit his lip. *Slow down, man. People are allowed to be on time without having a condition. Look in the mirror, for God's sake!*

***

Justin offered Frank a seat in one of the two wingback chairs in the center of the room. Covered with an off-white damask for aesthetics and comfort, each held a square black velour pillow – an object most patients cuddled or picked at during their sessions, just one of the many reasons Justin kept a stash of more than thirty pillows in the office closet.

He sat in the chair across from Frank, crossed his legs, clipped his pen to his journal and placed it on his lap. It took less than three seconds to sense the anxiety of the man who bounced his legs so incessantly that the heels of his blue suede Reeboks never touched the tufted wool rug beneath his feet.

His charcoal leather vest with the Ralph Lauren polo horseman logo contrasted with the exceptionally wrinkled, untucked and oversized green and red plaid shirt beneath. His thick chestnut hair, though inherently wavy, was trimmed in a crew cut — styled with such precision, it suggested strength of character which seemed in direct opposition to the expression of confusion and fear on his face. His dark brown eyes darted around the room as though trying to absorb each and every object so he could remember them at a later time, like when journaling or maybe even providing an alibi.

Although his eyes never settled on Justin, he did offer a twitch of a nod every now and again. The young man could have been more handsome if he tried to be, but it seemed Frank didn't care about his appearance. The way he was both disheveled on some levels and very well-groomed on others intrigued Justin, but also confused him. It was as though he had two people in one body sitting across from him. As he tried to pinpoint his initial opinion based on first impression, only one word came to mind: *Nerd.*

He was about to start the conversation when Frank stopped moving and stared directly into Justin's eyes.

"No couch for me to lie down on?" he asked, a slight tremble in his voice. "And where are all your certificates? I thought they'd be hanging from floor to ceiling. You know, diplomas, degrees, affiliations. All I see are creative canvasses and watercolors of landscapes on latte-colored walls – a color, I suspect, that's supposed to induce calm. So seriously, how do I know you're legit?"

Latte-colored walls? Justin was caught off guard, his initial assessment torn apart by the tone and cryptic insinuations of a man he just met – and a person who sought *him* out for help. He pursed his lips and lifted the corners of his mouth. His obligation as a psychiatrist was to show Frank he had control over both his emotions and the situation, and that was just what he intended to do.

"Very observant, Frank." Justin pointed to the empty spot beside them. "I used to have a beautiful, cushy sofa right over there. But to be honest, I felt as if it made me seem *authoritative*. I set up the office like it is now so when I have a conversation with someone like you, for example, we're basically on even ground... a level playing field, if you will."

Frank nodded, continuing to look Justin in the eyes, plainly anticipating the second part of his response.

"As for the diplomas and affiliations, they're all in the closet over there." He nodded toward the storage space by the office entrance, the one that also held the extra pillows. "I don't hang them on the wall because, well, there's no need for me to flaunt my expertise and education. People come to see me because someone referred them or they've done their research and think we might be a good fit."

He waited for a response. Nothing. "I'm sure you did your research, which is how you found me."

Frank barely bobbed his head, apparently waiting for more.

"If you'd like, I can get the certificates and diplomas so you can take a look. They're all framed and ready for showing."

As Justin started to rise, Frank leaned back in his chair and exhaled deeply. "No. Don't worry about it. You're right. I did my research and checked your background. I'm sorry. I just didn't know what to say or how to start the conversation."

Justin smiled. "Frank, that's what *I'm* here for. There's no need to concern yourself with those things. The credentials you asked about? I got them because my calling has always been to work with people and help them lead happier, more fulfilling lives." He looked down and tapped the journal with his index finger. "I know it sounds corny, but it's the truth. Well, it's *my* truth."

Frank placed his right foot over his left knee and fiddled with his sneaker laces. "It's not corny. I get it."

"I'm glad," Justin said, opening up his journal. "By the way, if it's okay with you, I'd like to take notes as we talk. It helps me remember things for future sessions… that is, if you decide you want to have another session."

"I will."

Justin tilted his head. "How can you be so certain?"

"Because I can."

Frank's words and the tone he used made Justin feel uneasy. He was like a human pendulum, swinging from timid and nervous one minute to strong and self-confident the next. Justin held himself back from wriggling in his chair.

"Okay, then," he said. "I have the forms you filled out online right here, but to be honest, there's not much to go on. You left a lot of items blank where you could have checked yes or no. Any particular reason?"

"I don't like to put private things in writing. You never know…"

"You never know what?"

"Who might see it or get their hands on it. Like when I was doing my research on you, I found out a lot about you online. And your son, too."

Justin flinched inside. Why would this guy bring up Michael? It's hurtful, disrespectful and just plain heartless. Justin was about to stop the session when Frank started to speak again.

"Seems like he played a lot of sports in college, hugs lots of girls and is studying to be just like his father."

Christ almighty. He's talking about Dylan, not Michael. His muscles relaxed as the tension in his body spilled like rain from the fullest of clouds.

It took Justin a few seconds to recover from his erroneous thoughts before he could respond.

"I've never been a fan of social media," Justin said as calmly as possible, his heart beating hard against his ribcage. *What else does he know about me and Dylan… my wife… Michael?* He'd have to check Dylan's Facebook page on the train ride home to make sure there was nothing on there that crossed his own personal boundaries. He didn't want current, or future patients for that matter, to know about his private life. "There's way too much personal information shared with the world. But we won't get into that right now. You should know that the portal I use is extremely secure, but I do understand your hesitance. Do you mind if I ask you some questions before getting into what you told me on the phone about your increased anxiety? I'll warn you in advance that they're a little personal. Is that okay?"

Frank nodded.

"Can you tell me about your family? Parents, siblings?"

"Father dead. Don't speak with mother. Think she's shacking up with some guy upstate, like in Schenectady. No siblings. Just me."

Justin made some notes in his journal. "Any blood relatives you speak with?"

"Nope. Not one."

"Do you wish you did?"

"Can't say one way or the other."

"Why is that?"

"Can't miss what you never had, right?"

Can't disagree with that.

Justin tipped his head to the side and scribbled, *no family worth mentioning.*

"I hear you, Frank. I'm not *happy* about it, but I hear you."

Frank turned toward the window. Reflected in the glass, Justin could see his eyes moving, focused on nothing in particular, shifting with any outdoor motion he could find. He clearly didn't want to get into Justin's comment any further.

"Can people see in here?"

"No. These are reflective windows. You can see out, but no one can see in."

Frank continued looking out the window.

"Would it bother you if someone knew you were here?"

He turned to Justin. "Well, I don't want anyone to think I'm crazy or anything. You know, I just want to be able to calm myself down when I feel all jittery from everything."

"When you say 'jittery,' is that what you feel when you say you're having a panic attack? Or do your feelings and symptoms differ during panic attacks?"

Frank sighed and rubbed his eyes as though trying to recall his last bout. "I guess I start off jittery and then things either calm down or blow up."

"Blow up?"

"Yeah, like I'm all tense and nervous and then I start to sweat and can't breathe. I know this sounds crazy, but sometimes I start pulling at my hair. It helps calm me down a little. I try taking deep breaths, closing my eyes and doing all the shit I've watched on YouTube. Usually I just end up taking a Xanax and things slowly get better."

"Are there any specific times, places or circumstances that you find might cause these attacks to happen more often? At school? Work? Home? All the time?"

"No place specific. They can happen anywhere, anytime."

Justin took a breath and thought carefully about his next question. The youth across from him was still very much an enigma. Obviously he was lonely *and* alone, anxious and a worrier. But there was also an arrogance at times, like the challenge over his credentials, an attitude that Justin couldn't yet fit with Frank's character.

"Got it. So you wrote that you have a job, but are also going for a master's. Do you like your job? The people you work with? Your salary?"

Frank smirked. "Worried you won't get paid, doc?"

"Do I look worried?" Justin smiled. He wasn't about to get into a war of words.

"My father's father started a trust for me when I was born. I could only get hold of it when I turned eighteen. It's worth a shitload now and since I'm low man on the totem pole at work, I use the trust to pay for pretty much everything." He looked Justin in the eyes. "And that includes you."

"When did your father pass away?"

"I was ten."

"Did your mother take care of you on her own?"

Without answering, Frank again turned toward the window. Justin let it sit for a few more seconds.

"And did your mother take care of you on her own?" he repeated.

Frank placed his thumbnail under his front teeth and began to nibble at it with great intensity.

"She gave me to her brother for a while," he eventually said around it. "Said she had to 'find her own way first' or some shit like that before she could take care of me on her own."

The mood in the room had changed. Justin felt it as a dull ache in the back of his head. He wasn't sure if Frank sensed it too, but the increased gnawing of his fingernail suggested he did.

"Did her brother have a wife or family at the time?"

"No, just him."

"Where is he now?"

Frank shrugged.

"Is he alive?"

Another shrug.

"You said before that you don't have blood relatives, but this person took you in when..."

"You asked if I have any blood relatives that I speak with," Frank interrupted. "I don't! Can we talk about something else? You're supposed to be helping me and I feel like I'm being interrogated."

The words hit Justin like a jackhammer: *This boy is troubled.*

No father figure; a mother who discarded him at an extremely sensitive time; an uncle who, Justin could only assume, did something to a young boy that scarred him for life. And who knew what else he'd been through? He needed more information to get anywhere with this kid, but he also had to tread extremely lightly. Everyone who came to see him was distressed in one way or another, but his intuition was telling him this situation could turn out to be extreme.

"I promise you, Frank, I am going to help you. I just need to know a little more about you first. I know it'll take time for you to trust me, so you don't have to talk about anything you don't want to. Tell me I'm asking too many questions... tell me you're done with a specific topic... tell me to shut up. I promise I won't take offense. Got it?"

He nodded. "Yes."

Justin glanced at the pendulum clock hanging on the wall behind Frank.

"Out of time already?" Frank asked.

"Wow, you don't miss a thing," Justin acknowledged with playful sarcasm. "And no, we're not out of time already. Now, can you tell me a little about the anxiety you mentioned during our call?

For instance, is it the same as with your panic attacks? Does it come from nowhere and just hit you? Are there certain times of day it's worse?"

"I always feel it." Frank paused and picked at the cuticle of his left pinky. "It's worse after I lose time."

Justin nodded, feigning indifference though pleased that Frank broached such a personal topic during their first session. "Lose time?"

"Yeah. Lose time."

"Can you tell me what you mean by 'lose time'?"

Frank shuffled in his chair, clasped his fingers and clenched his hands. He looked around the room as though someone might be listening.

"That's really why I'm here," he said, just above a whisper. "I definitely have anxiety. Always have. But lately, I've been losing time. You know, like I start off one place and end up in another without knowing how I got there." He looked down to the rug and closed his eyes. "I know. It sounds like I'm a fucking lunatic. But I don't know what to do and you're my last hope."

Justin clipped his pen onto the top edge of his journal. "First of all, Frank, you are not a lunatic. Let's get that out on the table right away. There are millions of people who 'lose time' for thousands of different reasons. So don't think you're so special." He waited for a laugh or smile from Frank, but received nothing other than a glower. "Secondly, I've dealt with this kind of thing before and I'm sure we can work together to figure it out and get you feeling better, okay?"

Frank nodded, still looking down with clasped hands.

"Since you didn't complete this on your forms, I need to ask if you're currently on any prescription medication? You mentioned Xanax earlier."

"Nothing other than the Xanax. My primary doctor sends the script in for me."

Justin wrote in his journal, *Xanax from primary doc.* "Have you *ever* been on any type of psychotropic medication?"

"What's that?"

"It's a medication used to treat…" Justin searched for words other than *a mental health disorder.* Frank's earlier comment about not wanting people to think he was crazy suggested he wouldn't welcome such a term. "…things like depression, anxiety, panic attacks, ADHD. You might have heard some of them referred to as SSRIs or mood stabilizers. Maybe even heard their actual names, like aripiprazole or clozapine. Do any of those sound familiar?"

Frank shook his head. "My doctor once gave me Prozac. I used for a few weeks, but it actually did the opposite of what it was supposed to do. I got so depressed, I thought about jumping off the GW Bridge. I stopped taking it after a week and a few days later it felt like a giant cloud lifted."

Justin noted that down and brushed his top lip with the back end of his pen. "So, is it okay for you to give me an example of your 'lost time' episodes? Just a little more detail so I get a better understanding of what you experience?"

"Yes." Frank opened his hands, studied his palms and then turned them over and examined his knuckles as though seeing them for the very first time. "Last Friday I was on the subway going to Midtown.

I was meeting Becky. She's a girl I'd started talking to online. It's a rare occurrence – meeting a girl, not going to Midtown – so I was kind of nervous."

"Where were you meeting?"

"Anchor Wine Bar. It's a bar-restaurant kind of place on Broadway. Anyway, I chose that place because I figured if things went well after having a few drinks at the bar, we could have dinner there."

"Got it. Okay, so you're on the subway…"

"Yeah. I'm on the subway and look at my watch. It's about 6:30. We're supposed to meet at 7:00, which gives me plenty of time to get off the train and walk to the bar. So I'm sitting in my seat looking around the subway car. The lights, as usual, are flashing on and off like I'm at a dance club or something. There are weirdos hanging on the poles, twirling around and laughing like idiots. Most of the people sitting around me have earbuds in so they don't even know what's going on around them."

"Do you have earbuds?"

"No. I don't like music. Can't ever find anything I want to listen to more than once or twice. So why waste the cash?"

Justin made note of the music comment and remained expressionless, although that point concerned him. He often used music therapy as a way to help patients with emotional, cognitive or social problems. Without an appetite for music, he doubted that mode of treatment would work in this case.

"How about audiobooks? Would you listen to those?"

"No. Bad enough I have to read my books for school. Why would I want to read anything I don't have to?"

"So if I were to ask you who your favorite author is, would you have an answer?"

"No."

"Never interested in reading Harry Potter? Psychological thrillers? Fantasy? Romance? Any genre of book?"

"I already said I don't like to read. Is there something wrong with that?"

"Not at all. Again, Frank, I'm getting a picture of who you are. *You* know who you are, I don't. The more I know, the better and faster I can help you. Okay?"

"Okay."

"How about TV? Do you subscribe to Netflix or another streaming service?"

"Dr. Wright, between work and my — my, well, my issues, there aren't enough hours in a day to handle what I already have to deal with. You think I have time to binge watch some moronic crime series or comedy show?"

No entertainment, amusement, diversions, Justin scrawled in his journal.

"Back to the subway. It's 6:30, you're in a dance club with a bunch of morons pole dancing and…" He tried adding levity to the conversation but by the look on Frank's face, it didn't work.

"That's when it happened," Frank said, now staring out the window into the approaching dusk.

"What happened?"

"I don't know. I can't remember. That's the problem!"

The sudden increase in Frank's breathing and a flush creeping into his face made Justin move. He could recognize the beginnings of a panic attack.

"I want you to take a slow, deep breath and I'll count to four as you inhale. I then want you to hold it as I count to four again. Then you'll exhale slowly as I count to four one more time. Got it, Frank?"

"Yes," he said, his voice quivering slightly.

Together they went through the breathing exercise until Frank's breath was back to normal and the redness had vanished from his face. Justin looked at the clock on the wall – 5:50. Although it was time to end the session and he wanted nothing more than to be on his way home, he couldn't stop things now. An emotional break like this, and any subsequent actions, could tell him more in a few minutes than a full twenty sessions. Still, the boy had to agree to push himself further.

"Frank, do you want to continue or would you like to take a break and talk some more next time?"

"Is our time up? Do I have to leave?"

"Our time *is* up, but you don't have to leave. I am more than willing to extend our time together tonight… if you are."

Frank closed his eyes. Justin watched carefully as the young man's lips moved, just barely, but enough to look like he was talking to someone beside him. And then his eyes jolted open.

"Just a little while longer. I have to tell you what happened so you can figure it out and fix me."

"Then by all means, continue," Justin said softly. He was relieved that Frank wanted to stay but also frustrated that he'd be home late… again.

"Like I said, I was looking around the subway car, and then I looked out the window at the cement wall flying by and then boom!"

"Boom what?"

"The next thing I remember, I'm unlocking the door to my apartment. It was like I woke up from a dream. I had no idea how I got there or where I was coming from. I was all shaky and shit. When I walked inside and looked at the clock on the wall, it was eleven thirty. Eleven thirty! Five hours had passed and I don't remember a thing!"

Justin remained calm even though the story he just heard was very unnerving. He had a few ideas as to what might be the cause of an experience like this. And none of them were good. However, he needed to learn a lot more before making any sort of diagnosis.

"So you don't remember your date… meeting Becky… drinking… eating… the ride home? Nothing?"

"Nothing. Not a fucking thing."

"Okay, Frank. I want you to think back. I want to be one hundred percent sure you don't recall *anything*. And that includes a sound, a smell, a taste in your mouth from food you might've eaten. *Anything.*"

"Did you hear me? I said *nothing!* Don't you think I tried to remember something? I threw my keys onto the dining room table, fell onto the couch and held my head, screaming, 'Remember! Remember!' I kept trying to remember *something*. The bar, Becky's face, food, the noise in the restaurant. But nothing happened. Then I started to wonder if I even *went* to the restaurant. Did I even *meet* Becky? And if I didn't, where the hell did I go? I gotta tell you, I was really losing my shit."

"And I gather that's why you called me?"

Frank washed his hands over his face, then leaned his elbows on his knees. "That wasn't the worst of it." He forced a laugh and fell back in his chair. "While I was lying on the couch, I felt my phone vibrate in my pocket. When I took it out, there was a text from Becky."

He stopped talking, and redness crept back into his face. Justin took a deep breath of his own and exhaled slowly.

"And what did it say, Frank?"

Frank reached into his pocket and took out his phone. He pressed a few buttons, scrolled a bit, looked at Justin and then back down to the phone's display.

"It says, *I had a great time tonight. Thank you so much for dinner. I hope we do it again very soon. You're a very special person –* " He swallowed, then read the final word of the text: "*Nathan.*"

CHAPTER 2

Seated on the sofa, Mandy and Dylan each had one arm stretched across the edge of its backrest. Mandy gazed at her son, taking in every feature of his face while Dylan glanced at their clasped fingers.

"Mom, I've been here for almost twenty minutes. I think you can let go of my hand now."

His words made her squeeze harder and rub her thumb along the soft top of his hand. He was his father's son, for sure. Same deep blue eyes, high cheekbones and the same thick brown hair Justin had before the gray began its uninvited infiltration. She noticed at times he even had the same expressions as his father – a slight raise of his left eyebrow or the pursing of his lips that made him look as though he was hiding something.

"When I want to let go, I'll let go," she quipped. "It's so rare I get to see you, I want to savor every moment."

Dylan rolled his eyes and then offered a smile. "Geez. I'm forty minutes away, I see you guys at least once a month…"

"More like once every *two* months."

"Whatever. It's not like I live in California or something and see you once a year. Plus, I'm a second-year grad student now."

"And that means *what* exactly?"

"Well, it means I'm busier than last year and I'm more... well... more of an adult. I shouldn't have to see my parents all the time."

Suddenly Mandy understood what Justin was talking about earlier on the phone. Dylan had no idea his father felt hurt and offended that he didn't see him more often. He actually thought that not spending time with his parents made him more of an adult.

She let go of his hand and ran her fingers through her hair until she reached the French braid that ran halfway down her back. She pulled the braid over her shoulder, letting it fall onto her arm, and picked at the elastic hair tie. "So are you saying that acknowledging your parents' existence is immature? Juvenile?"

Another roll of his eyes. "No, I'm not saying that."

"Are you saying that recognizing the two people who love you the most in the world, the two people who have helped you get to where you are today, the two people who would give up their lives for you, makes you a child?"

Dylan stood and walked across the room to one of the two brown suede club chairs and plopped down. He pulled the hair on the top of his head and fell back. "No! How many times do I have to tell you I'm not saying that? I'm just saying that I'm busy, this nutty world is affecting my focus and I can't think about keeping you and Dad happy all the time with calls or visits." He took in a deep breath and sighed. "You know I love you both. I always have and I always will.

I'm just having a hard enough time getting through the days without the pressure of constantly keeping in touch with you."

Mandy moved toward the edge of the sofa cushion. Her heart rate sped up, her anxiety level rose. Something was wrong with her son and he was hiding it from her.

"Where is this coming from, Dylan? What's going on with you? I've never heard you sound like this before. Is there too much pressure at school? Are Kyle and Jim causing problems again? I know they've been your roommates since freshman year, but if they're starting their partying and messing around again…"

"No, Mom. First of all, Jim screwed us over and decided to follow his girlfriend to Berkeley this year. He backed out of the lease without any warning. Kyle and I are actually in the middle of trying to find someone to take his place. So we're strapped for cash." Before she had the chance to speak, Dylan put his hand up. "And no, but thank you. I'll make it through without a handout. I've increased my hours at Starbucks and I'm making some great tips. It's helping until we find someone to take Jim's place."

There was an ache in the center of Mandy's stomach, ascending toward her heart. She hated seeing Dylan in such distress, especially when she and Justin had plenty of money to give him.

"Dylan…" she started. "You know we've always believed that education comes first. And if life's crap is getting in the way of that, then you have to do something about it. Your father and I have been putting some money aside each month in a special account for you just in case there was a time you needed extra funds. I think this is the time. Please let us help." His eyes glimmered with what might be the onset of tears. "If it will make you feel better, you can call it a loan."

Dylan shook his head. "I'm sure Dad's pissed that I haven't found the time to have lunch or dinner with him. And I'm also sure he's grumbled about me never visiting him at his office when I'm only a subway ride away. And *you're* already upset that I rarely come home or meet *you* in the city for dinner." He picked at the thinnest of threads sticking out from the arm of the chair. "And now I'm going to take your money? Wouldn't you say there's something wrong with that?"

Mandy smiled, stood and walked over to him. She bent down and took both his hands in hers. "I hope that one day you'll understand what I'm about to say… that you'll have a family of your own and realize your child or children *are* your life. That no matter what they do or don't do, what they say or don't say, how much they call you or don't call you…" She placed the back of his hand on her cheek. "…your love for them never wanes. You will always do anything for them because they are a part of you. *Their* happiness is *your* happiness, just as *their* hurt is *your* hurt. So when I see life taking its toll on you, all I want to do is help you get back on the path to happiness and less stress. And whether you believe it or not, Dad feels the same way. Your success and joy are his number one priority, no matter how many disagreements or cross words might come between you. Please trust me on this." She kissed his hand and stood up. "Your mother is always right. That is one fact you can *always* count on."

"Mom, I hear you and appreciate every word... even if it did sound a bit like one of your closing arguments in court."

Mandy faked a slap at him and as they laughed, the front door opened. Justin walked down the foyer into the living room. They turned toward him, wearing big smiles.

Justin, on the other hand, wore an expression of complete confusion.

"What?" he asked. "Why are you both looking at me like that?"

"It's not always about you, hon," Mandy replied. She glanced at her watch. "Although it's almost 7:30 and the dinner is getting cold."

"Sushi is *supposed to be cold*," Justin and Dylan said at the same time in the exact same tone.

With an expression of feigned annoyance, Mandy walked to Justin and kissed him softly on the lips. "I would think the two of you would know a joke when you heard one. Now let's sit down and eat something. I'm starving."

***

From the moment the three of them sat down at the dining room table, Mandy felt the tension. Justin was obviously upset that Dylan wouldn't find time for him and Dylan felt too much pressure from the both of them and wanted more independence. As always, she tried combining her legal training with her personal intuition and worked hard at keeping all parties happy.

She'd attempt to keep the conversation on light topics or would pass more sushi to Dylan when he was about to reply to one of Justin's passive-aggressive comments. Much of her time was spent as it was in court, twisting another's words to work in her favor. In this case, it was twisting one's words to avoid any sort of conflict.

But this wasn't just today's tension.

There'd been a longstanding strain between the two of them that she could never quite figure out. Was it a competitive thing? A father-son issue all families had to contend with? Or had what happened seven years ago prevented any possibility of a healthy relationship?

She didn't know, and now was not the time to try to figure it out. At this moment, her job was to keep the peace and make sure the three of them enjoyed a meal together.

"It's good to see you," Justin said, dipping his wasabi-streaked tuna roll into the soy sauce. "Will you be staying for the weekend?"

Dylan swallowed his food and took a slug of water. "Wish I could, but I have to get back. Kyle and I are meeting with this guy tomorrow to see if he's a fit to share the apartment."

"What? Where's Jim?"

"He followed his girlfriend to California."

"Did he give you any warning?"

"None."

Mandy looked at Justin and gently rubbed her stockinged foot against his shin. Justin never liked or trusted Jim and had told Dylan his feelings many times. She didn't want the "I told you so" carousel to start spinning as it always did, so she nudged him a little harder. Justin lightly pushed back on her foot, letting her know he'd keep his thoughts to himself.

"Well, *that* stinks. How'd you find the guy you're meeting with tomorrow?"

"We put an ad on a bunch of sites like Diggz and RoomieMatch. I put it on my Facebook page, Instagram, WhatsApp. You name it, we're on there. I gotta tell you, we got loads of responses and we could tell right off the bat most of the people who responded were nutjobs." He looked at Justin. "Sorry. I know you don't like that word. I meant they were not our cup of tea."

Justin pinched another piece of sushi between his chopsticks and swirled it in the creamy wasabi on the side of his plate. "I get it. So why this guy? What made him stand out as non-'nutjob'?"

Dylan peeled the shrimp off the rice of his ebi nigiri, held its tail and stuffed it into his mouth. After dropping the denuded tail onto his plate, he took another swig of water. "He's a grad student at Fordham. I think he's going there for economics or accounting or applied mathematics. Not sure. It's left-brained stuff. Something I have no idea about. Which is good for two reasons… he's smart, *and* he won't be my competition when he graduates."

Mandy waited for Justin to laugh and was relieved when he let out a soft chuckle.

"You're too smart to have competition," he told Dylan.

"Thanks."

The conversation was civil, but tension still lay behind the words and it unsettled Mandy's stomach. She ate what she could, but mostly fiddled with her chopsticks.

"And how's Kyle feeling?" Justin continued. "The last few times we spoke, you said he was mildly depressed. Is he doing any better?"

"Not really. I swear, I'm not sure how he's going to be a psychologist if he can't handle his *own* life."

"Isn't he studying Forensic Psychology?"

Dylan nodded.

"Well, that's quite different than Clinical Psychology like you're studying – at least from a one-on-one, doctor slash patient perspective."

"I know that, Dad. But still, he needs to assess people, evaluate criminals and their cases, serve as an expert witness or trial consultant. How can you do that with a focused mind if you can't get out of bed in the morning?"

Justin let his chopsticks fall to his plate. "Is it *that* bad, Dylan?"

Dylan glanced down and pushed the shrimp tail around his dish. "Not all the time. There are days when you'd never know anything's wrong. And then there are days when I literally pull him out of bed."

"Do you think he'd come to see me? I'd be more than happy to —"

"Absolutely not. He wouldn't do it and I'm not sure I'd really be comfortable with that."

"But he needs to — "

"No."

Mandy's stomach knotted up. "Dylan," she said softly, "is Kyle getting *any* kind of help? It sounds like something he shouldn't be going through alone. Do you know if he's on any medication?"

Dylan slid his fingers through his hair and let out a big sigh. "I think he tried Wellbutrin, but that didn't work. So his GP put him on Prozac."

"GP?" Justin's face flushed. "He has his general practitioner prescribing antidepressants?" Mandy could tell he was trying to restrain his anger, but his expression gave away his true feelings. "Dylan, you know that's not right. He needs to be seen by a psychiatrist or psychopharmacologist. Someone trained in the treatment of these types of disorders. Maybe I should call the Harpers and offer a — "

"Dad, no! Do *not* call Kyle's parents. I don't care how long you've been friends with them or how close you guys are. This is Kyle's business, not ours. And if his parents hear something from you, he will never trust me again. Just leave it alone for now. Can you do that, please?"

Mandy closed her eyes and held her head in her hands. The evening was going the way it always did, and the knot in her stomach untied as she gave in to what was about to happen.

"I probably shouldn't have brought it up at all!" Dylan took another deep breath in an obvious effort to calm himself. "But just so you know, we're both taking this Cognitive Behavioral course and the professor advises his students to go through the therapy process. So we're both going. Not together, of course, but to different psychologists. It gives us an idea of what it's like from the patient's perspective."

Mandy again rubbed her foot against Justin's leg.

"Wow," Justin said. "Okay. Well, I'm glad to hear that. I think it's a great idea. Hopefully this person can direct Kyle to the right doctor." He stirred his wasabi with a chopstick. "I actually went through that process when I was going to school."

"Really?" Dylan sounded surprised.

"Really. Believe it or not, they had good ideas way back then, too. And who are these therapists?"

"There are clinical psychologists on and off campus who work with students in our course of study. The prof gave us a list and we get to choose."

Mandy crossed her fingers beneath the table, hoping that would help stop Justin from asking more questions. Unfortunately, the finger-twisting didn't seem to be enough.

"Do you think it's helping *you* in any way? I mean, from a professional standpoint."

"Definitely," Dylan said. "She's a very intelligent woman and has good intuition when it comes to her patients. I'm learning a lot."

Justin, don't, Mandy thought, almost saying it aloud. *Please don't ask him if...*

"And what about from a personal standpoint? Do you think it's helping you in that regard?"

Dylan fell against the back of his chair and shook his head. "Why? Do you think I need psychological help?"

"I didn't say that, Dylan. I just asked if you thought it was — "

"I know what you asked, Dad. How does the conversation start with Kyle's problems and end up with me having issues?"

"Again, Dylan, I didn't say that. You're putting words in my mouth and that's not fair."

Mandy pulled on her braid as she read the anger on both their faces, heard it in their rising tones. The tension had passed the point of no return. As Dylan was about to respond, a voice came out of her mouth that, at first, she wasn't even sure was hers.

"Why?" she yelled. "Why must the two of you fight all the time? We were having a nice dinner and then… and then… this!" She took the napkin off her lap and threw it on the table. "Well, guess what? I don't want to hear any more. I give up."

She stormed out of the room, leaving the two men she loved the most behind her. Walking down the hallway to the bedroom, she felt a tear fall down her cheek. She wiped it away, more angry at herself for getting upset than sad for what was happening behind her.

When she entered the bedroom, she grabbed the edge of the door, slammed it shut and sat on the bed. The huge mirror in front of her revealed crimson eyelids and smeared mascara that she attempted to erase with the bottom of her black V-neck shirt. It only spread the makeup further across her cheeks.

On the bureau sat photos in frames they'd bought on their last trip to Italy. Left to right, she took them all in: the shot of Justin and Dylan standing arm in arm at the entrance to the lodge atop Sandia Peak in Albuquerque; the silhouetted profile of her and Justin kissing at their wedding; the picture taken three years ago at a family Christmas gathering, all twenty-seven relatives, four generations, squeezed into a single frame. She smiled, remembering the laughter along with the grunts and groans that accompanied that photoshoot.

Her smile quickly disappeared when she reached the center frame. It held the photo of *her* entire family: her husband and two sons, all holding on tightly to one another as the winter wind on the 86th floor of the Empire State Building blew fiercely.

Dylan was eighteen years old, Michael only eight, when a passing stranger with hair shaped like a horseshoe from premature baldness offered to help them preserve a memory on the observation deck. Someone who would never, in his most bone-chilling nightmare, know that the family he'd just photographed would be torn to shreds one day later.

Mandy stood and gently held the frame in both hands. She blinked the tears away so she could see the four of them smiling. She could still feel her cheek against her son's as she zipped up his hood, both of them cold, but his skin so soft. Closing her eyes, she brought herself back to the moment the photo was taken... threads of Michael's hair blowing across his forehead, his shoulder blade beneath her hand, his head nestled inside the curve of her torso.

When she opened her eyes, the tracks of mascara ran from her eyelids to her chin. But this time she didn't care; she didn't want to stop herself from crying. She didn't want to know what was happening in the next room or how Justin and Dylan would sort things out... or not. The only thing she wanted was the same thing she'd wanted for the past seven years: to know, where in God's name was her son?

CHAPTER 3

It happened the first night after his mother dropped him off at his uncle's house and continued regularly until she picked him up four years later.

Frank barely knew Uncle Carl before he went to live with him. He'd met him a handful of times, mostly at family get-togethers where he always had a glass of scotch in one hand and the yellow stain of nicotine on the other. He was the only family member who called him "Frankie," no matter how many times Frank asked him not to.

"Frankie," he'd say, the stink of liquor and cigarette breath turning Frank's stomach, "you gotta come over one night. Just you and me. I have the coolest video games, the ones all the kids are playing. Your mom can drop you off, you'll hang out and spend the night. It'll be so cool."

Frank would wriggle out of his uncle's grasp, away from the vile breath and eerie feeling that crept its way up his spine whenever he was in the man's presence. He'd search the room for his mother only to find her guzzling down her own dose of booze. She'd order him to "find a kid to play with" or lean her arm on his head to help keep her balance.

One gloomy summer Sunday, Frank and his mother attended a barbeque on Long Island. It was held at a relative's house – a cousin "once removed" or something like that, connected to Frank in a way he could never quite figure out. On the drive home, he peered out the window and watched the faster cars pass them by. He was trying to count how many license plates included the number eight when his mother suddenly said something and he lost track.

"What?" he muttered, annoyed that he'd have to start his game all over again.

"Did you have fun with your cousins today?" Her voice was raspy from too much talk and scotch.

"It was okay," he replied. "And why are you going so slow? It's the Long Island Expressway and everyone is passing us."

She sped up and attempted to clear her throat.

"I'm having a hard time here, Frank."

There was an awkward pause and Frank sensed a tidal wave about to hit, a surge of words that would make him want to open the car door and fall into moving traffic. By the tone of her voice, he could tell the news she was about to lay on him was even worse than a year ago when she told him they were moving from Hartsdale to the Bronx.

"Since your father died from smoking like a chimney, I haven't been able to get my feet on the ground. I can't find a decent job, even as a waitress or food runner. The worst thing is, I can't even get a tiny bit of the money that's sitting in your fuc… I mean, waiting in a bank account for when you turn eighteen. I can barely take care of myself, let alone a ten-year-old boy."

For a few seconds, Frank lost his breath and couldn't inhale. He thought he'd pass out when he finally took a gasp of air and felt a little bit better. The tidal wave had turned into a hurricane and he just had to hold on while the full force of its winds blew over him. He gripped the door's armrest for dear life and closed his eyes.

"Your Uncle Carl has a real nice two-bedroom apartment in Queens. There's a good school in walking distance and a lot of kids to play with." She hesitated, apparently waiting for a question that never came. "He's offered to take you in and let you stay there for a while until I get back on my feet again. I swear it'll only be for a little while. I just have to get a good job, save some money and be able to keep our heads above water." Her voice was getting louder. "I'm drowning here, Frank. I swear I'm drowning!"

Frank's head spun and he could barely hear the words she yelled. *Why would she do this to me? What did I do? Why would she leave me with that smelly, weird man? He gives me the creeps!*

His body went numb and though he wanted to scream, his mouth wouldn't open. He looked out the window in silence as more cars passed by, moving shapes as blurry as the thoughts swirling inside his head.

"Aren't you going to say anything? What are you thinking? Talk to me, Frank! Say something!"

As the sun set, the inside of the car turned gray. When he turned to look at her, the shadows emphasized how ugly his mom was: the split ends of her poorly dyed hair framed a face as white as a ghost's and covered with pockmarks like moon craters. Her nose was hooked like the Wicked Witch of the West's and the lack of chin made it look as though she only had half a face. *Is it the shadows or is she that ugly? Has she always been that ugly?*

"Well, Frank?"

I hate you were the only words that came to mind. But instead of shouting them out like he wanted to, he turned to the window and stared into the cloudless, bloody red sky.

"Do I have a choice?" he mumbled.

"Right now, neither of us have a choice." She swallowed hard and kept her eyes on the road in front of her. "I'm not giving you to foster care. I'd give you to my sister, but that fuc… shit-for-brains has three of her own to deal with. She's not going to take in another kid. She's not only a bitch, but she's pretty much already lost her mind."

Give you to foster care? Take another kid?

Geez, what am I? A dog?

"And Uncle Carl hasn't lost his mind?" he asked, looking out the window again, down into the East River this time.

"Why would you say that? He's always been nice to you." She started to yell again. "Frank, why would you say that? Jesus, can't you just give it a chance? You have no idea what I'm going through!"

Frank didn't respond. He couldn't move his mouth, his lips feeling like they did after the dentist gave him too much Novocaine last year. They were numb and paralyzed, unable to spit out the thoughts racing through his mind. A new home, a new school, new kids to taunt him every day. And dealing with whatever was wrong with creepy Uncle Carl. His insides trembled and he wanted to vomit on the dashboard, but his mother would make him clean it up and that would make him puke even more.

He held his stomach and closed his eyes, bringing himself into a deep, dark place where he could hide from the screaming voice beside him and the thoughts that were making him shake. It was the place where the strong boy lived, a space inside where he could be someone else, someone tougher, someone who could deal with life without getting nauseated at the drop of a hat. It was a place he'd visit often over the next few years, an escape from the reality of life and the pain that came with it.

***

"Hey, Frankie!"

"Frank," he responded. "My name is Frank."

"Okay, I hear you. Frank it is," Uncle Carl said as he walked over to the car. He gripped Frank's shoulder with what looked like the devilish sneer of The Martian Manhunter, one of his favorite superheroes. The only difference was this loser drunk was not going to save the world. "We're gonna have lots of fun and you're gonna like it here. I promise you that."

His mother stood in the street, between the car and curb, two suitcases concealing her legs with their razor scars caused by shaving drunk too many times. Frank wanted her to leave without saying anything. What was happening was already so unreal and making him sick to his stomach. He didn't need long goodbyes or fake tears.

All he wanted was to grab the suitcases, pull them up the stairs to Carl's apartment and get a glimpse of what was waiting for him. He was scared that anything more would make him cry, yell or even run away – to somewhere, anywhere other than this ugly brick building filled with people probably as weird as Uncle Carl.

"Are you going to say goodbye to your mother?" she asked, bending down so her knees scraped the curb.

Frank trudged over and stood before her, hands in his pockets. He looked at her face and waited for anything – a pouty frown, an expression of guilt, something that would prove she gave a shit about what she was doing to him. He saw nothing but two holes, two bottomless pits empty of any warmth or emotion. Although he was used to how little she cared about his feelings, just like his father hadn't cared before he croaked, he had hoped that this "goodbye" would show she had some kind of feelings toward him. He'd even take the fake tears right now –an apology, a good excuse – something… anything. But all he got was a dry, chapped-lipped kiss on the forehead and a false promise.

"I'll be taking you back home in no time, okay? It'll be for two months, three at the most. I just have to get my shit together first." She turned to her brother and waved. "You take good care of him, Carl! Don't let him get away with too much!" she yelled as she walked around the car and got into the driver's seat.

With one last glance out the passenger side window, she gave a thumbs-up to Frank, stepped on the gas and took off down the street, carefully avoiding the lines of cars parked on both sides.

Although it was sunny and probably more than eighty degrees, Frank felt a chill throughout his entire body. It was the sort of sickly tingle he'd have right before coming down with a bad cold or the flu.

"You ready, Frankie? Uh, I mean Frank? Let's get these bags upstairs and show you your room."

*****

After climbing the two flights of concrete stairs, dragging his suitcase every step of the way, Frank followed Uncle Carl to the left and inside the door marked 2C. As he entered, he smelled cigarettes and something similar to old bleach. The trembling inside his stomach started again and he imagined his vomit streaking the cracked walls and soaking into the plaster behind them. Uncle Carl would lose his shit, screaming and yelling while dragging Frank into a dark, windowless room, punishing him for something that wasn't his fault. Or was it?

Who would he be able to turn to for help? For a second he felt like he was being kidnapped until he remembered his mother looking out the car window and giving him a thumbs-up. *How could she do this to me? Why does she hate me so much? Am I so bad that…*

"And this is your room," Uncle Carl said, parking Frank's other suitcase against the wall next to the door.

Frank stood in the doorway and scanned the room. Beige chips of paint flaked over the bed, and cracks spread across the bare walls like cobweb tendrils preparing to pull him into an inescapable abyss.

The black laminate desk was splintered on every corner and each of its legs leaned inward. One too many books placed on top of it and it would surely collapse. The chair in which he'd be doing his homework was metal, a "bridge chair" as his mother would call it. Unsure why, he called it the same in his head and did nothing but stare at it as an odd pressure crept up the back of his neck and a heavy darkness slowly filled the inside of his chest. For a second he thought this rising shadow was about to take over his entire body, that he'd have to give in to it and lose total control. He was just about to yell and beg it to stop, when he heard his uncle's voice.

"I took the pictures down off the walls so you could put up things you want, like Superman posters. I have Scotch Tape in the other room."

Superman posters? Really? What am I five?

"That's the closet," Uncle Carl said, pointing to a narrow door at the far corner of the room. "You can hang your clothes up in there. And I slid in this dresser I saw just sittin' on the side of Jamaica Avenue last week. The sign said 'free,' so I picked it up myself and threw it in my trunk. Drove home with the trunk open. Couldn't see behind me, but that was okay. Didn't really have any problems. Now trying to park the car… that's a whole different story."

Frank's stomach churned. He couldn't think of anything to say. Did this guy really want him to put his clothes in a dirty, nasty used dresser? He hadn't said a word since he stepped into the apartment and knew if he said something now, it wouldn't be good.

"I'll tell you about that fiasco at dinner," Uncle Carl continued. "For now, I'll just leave you to get settled in. I'll be in the living room. Got some bills to pay. You let me know if you need anything, okay?"

Frank nodded and wheeled his suitcase into the room as Uncle Carl walked down the hallway toward the other side of the tiny apartment. *This place is crap,* he thought. Not that he and his mother lived in a palace, but for some reason this place felt more closed in, too tight in every way.

He went to the bed and sat down on the pilled blanket. The flannel sheets beneath it still had tags on them. At least there was something new in this shithole. He stood and walked over to the nasty chest of drawers, which looked as old as the one he'd seen at his friend Joey's great grandmother's house last winter. More than that, it looked as though a dog had tried eating its way into the drawers. The light-colored wood on top was scratched with blue pen marks and the mirror was foggy. He could barely see his reflection, but what he did see made him panic.

He looked pale, scared and on the verge of tears. Although he was still in shock at being abandoned, he didn't feel as horrible as the boy he saw in the mirror. It was almost like the kid staring back at him was someone else. What the hell was going on? He shook his head, trying to rid himself of the chaos barreling around his skull like a rollercoaster that had gone off its tracks.

It's okay. Everything is okay.

Frank walked to the window and pushed the wool drapes aside. They were on a main street, 88th Avenue or something, which was a good thing because there was a lot going on. People sitting on front porches talking to each other, kids on skateboards riding down the street doing tricks. There was even a small dog park up the block where he could see dogs chasing balls as they flew through the air. If he ever got bored, which he knew would happen living in this box with Uncle Carl, he'd have something to watch and occupy his time.

The view from his room made him a little more comfortable. Not a lot, but enough to start to soothe the fear that ran through every nerve in his body. Knowing there were other people around, especially kids, made the inside of his new room feel less like a prison. He took a deep breath and held back tears. *Maybe it won't be as bad as I thought.*

***

That night, after a bowlful of Kraft macaroni and cheese, Uncle Carl asked him if he'd like to watch some television. The last thing Frank wanted to do was sit on the sofa with a man who smelled like old socks and inhale cigarette smoke until he went to bed.

"I'm going to take a shower and go to sleep. I'm kinda tired."

Uncle Carl glanced at his watch. "It's only seven thirty," he said. "But I hear you. It's been a long day, I guess. Remember, day after tomorrow we go to P.S. 050 Elementary and get you signed up. We have an appointment at ten o'clock."

"Yeah, I got it. You told me already."

"Okay, just making sure, Frankie… sorry, I meant Frank."

Frank faked a smile and walked down the hallway to his room. He grabbed his soap, shampoo and pajamas and headed to the bathroom.

Once in the shower, he closed his eyes so he wouldn't have to see the missing pieces of pink porcelain tile along the wall or the soil stains at the bottom of the tub. He just wanted to smell his soap that reminded him of home and wash the stain of his mother's kiss from his forehead.

His skin was wrinkly and had red blotches from how long he spent under the stream of hot water. But it didn't matter. He felt a lot cleaner and a bit more free from the memory of being dropped off like an unwanted puppy at the door of a freak show.

Frank walked into his room, closed the door and threw his dirty clothes on the floor of the closet. He'd have to talk to Uncle Carl about some kind of laundry basket or hamper, but right now, he just wanted to get in bed, fall asleep and leave the day behind him.

After turning off the light, he lay on his right side facing the windows and pulled the covers up to his chin. As he closed his eyes, there was a light knock on the door. A pang of fear split open in the pit of his stomach and he curled his legs up into his body. He didn't make a sound, hoping Uncle Carl would think he was asleep and keep his reason for knocking to himself until tomorrow.

There was another short knock before the doorknob rattled and wood squeaked against the hinges.

"Frankie... you still awake?" he whispered from the part-open door.

Frank didn't respond. He just lay silent, motionless, holding his breath until Uncle Carl left.

When he heard the door close, he let out a sigh of relief. He was now safe and alone, ready to sleep until the sun woke him the next morning. Relaxing, Frank turned over and saw the dark shadow of Uncle Carl standing beside his bed.

"I just wanted to say 'goodnight' in my own special way," the man murmured, his breathy voice shaking.

Frank smelled cigarette smoke and brought the sheet up to cover his nose. He turned over again, looking out the window one last time before he masked his eyes with his hands and brought himself deep into the dark place – the space within where the strong boy lived, the boy who would one day be able to fight the demons that took advantage of him from both inside and out.

***

You're such an asshole!

Nathan slammed the apartment door shut behind him and stomped down the entryway. He passed through the dining room, into the living room and then the bedroom.

First, you go talking to this shrink about your horrible problems. What problems? Me? Am I your problem? Are you trying to get rid of me? Jesus Christ, if it wasn't for me, you'd never get out of bed in the morning!

He looked into the giant circular mirror on the wall above the dresser and pointed to the Ralph Lauren leather vest he was wearing. *And what the hell is this? A designer vest with this old-man plaid shirt? What is wrong with you? I swear to God, you are such a fucking loser. Who taught you how to dress? Your grandpa?*

He unbuttoned the vest, ripped it off and threw it on the bed.

Oh, that's right. You never really knew your grandpa. He was dead too soon after you were born. You must have learned how to dress from your dear old uncle.

As he tore open the red shirt, buttons popped out in all directions. *This piece of shit goes in the garbage!*

Nathan opened up the top drawer of the dresser and pulled out a black mock turtleneck. He held it up in front of him, checking for wrinkles. A presence deep inside stirred, protested, tried to stop him from what he was about to do. He pushed it down and pulled the shirt over his head.

And now it's up to me *to go back to that shrink and tell him this therapy shit is over. I'm gonna let him know that* you're *the one we need to get rid of, not me.*

He used the palms of his hands to smooth the shirt over his chest and stomach.

In fact, you know something? I really don't need to go see that head shrinker. None of us do. Nobody's going to show up to that appointment. Next week or ever. He'll forget about you and your lost time crap and we'll just pretend the whole thing didn't happen.

A pressure grew at the base of his skull, the first sign of the presence starting to emerge, heavy and dark, this time with more intensity. Nathan tried again to push it away, but this time it wasn't as easy. It was as though someone stood beside him even though he was alone.

Glancing in the mirror, he tried to distract himself by straightening out his shirt a bit more and finally moved his gaze up to his eyes. Nathan almost jumped backward when the person in the mirror was not the person he expected to see.

He tilted his head. There was a resemblance: the eyes, nose, cheekbones, even the chestnut hair. But there was a difference, too, something he couldn't quite pin down, something that stirred a visceral anger in the cavity beneath his breastbone and worked its way up into his shoulders, neck and ultimately his head.

He gave a hard shove to the unwelcome presence within and combed his fingers through his hair, messing it up so that he looked less timid... so that he appeared stronger, a man who could take charge of any situation. He did an about-face, leaving behind the mirror and the reflection that had looked back from it. No time to concern himself with mind games now. It had been a rough day and he had to get the whole shrink situation out of his head with the help of a few tasty whiskeys and a good lay.

In the foyer, he opened the closet door, grabbed his favorite leather jacket and slid his arms into the sleeves.

"On to Max's," he said, ignoring the rage still swollen inside him. "We're gonna get laid tonight!"

Nathan reached for the doorknob but paused, looking down. He'd forgotten to change shoes and was still wearing sneakers.

I told you you're an asshole!

He ran back into the bedroom, pulled off the sneakers, grabbed a pair of brown Cole Haans from the closet and quickly slipped them on. While retracing his steps to the front door, he kept his head down to avoid all mirrors.

Remember, whoever tries to get rid of me is gonna pay big time! Take something from me, I'll take something from you.

He grabbed the doorknob and before turning it, said aloud, "It's *you* that has to go. Not me. *You! You're the loser!*"

He went out and headed directly to the elevators, holding himself back from yelling "loser" every step of the way.

CHAPTER 4

While Justin waited for Frank Devlin to arrive, he made a few notes in other patient files. Once done with them, he slid the folders inside the filing cabinet. He looked at his watch: 4:50. Pulling Frank's file from the cabinet, he took a glance and slowly shook his head. There was nothing in this boy's file to give him any more information than he already had. Justin felt certain of the problem: it was a clear case of dissociative identity disorder, and he'd be delving a lot deeper into Frank's past to get to the root cause.

He still hadn't made up his mind about whether or not to use medication. Over the years, many of the patients he'd treated with this condition had responded well to SSRIs and antipsychotic drugs. They helped with the anxiety and depression that lay behind the problem, leading to improvement over time. Still, there were other patients he was able to treat effectively without pharmaceuticals by using two specialized phases of treatment.

The first was to develop safety from suicidal and self-destructive behaviors. Most likely Frank grew up in an environment of unpredictable danger. It was up to Justin to help him be safe and feel stable around Nathan. He had to make certain that both of them posed no danger to themselves or others. He also had to determine if there were more than the two of them. After just one session, it was impossible to establish that fact, but after today, he might have a better idea. He crossed his mind's fingers, hoping that Frank and Nathan were the only identities with whom he'd have to work. The more identities, the more complex the solution.

Once safety and stability were developed, he'd then focus on recalling Frank's history. This would be the most painful part of therapy, as Frank would have to relive the parts of his life that he'd worked so hard to repress. Justin would have to heavily integrate the safety and stability aspect into this treatment phase. The safer Frank felt while dealing with the past, the sooner his symptoms would balance out and gradually decrease. Depending on the outcome of this phase, Justin might have to focus on the third phase which was to decide upon medication, hypnotherapy or specialized PTSD remedies.

He stopped himself from trying to forecast the future and looked instead to his previous patients who had experienced the same issue. His hope was that within a few months, Frank would experience a complete merging of his subjective identities and be able to use his energy to better focus on living as himself. If that wasn't possible, Justin might employ functional multiplicity as he did with some of his other patients – helping them live life to the fullest while keeping their independent alters intact. There were a number of ways to go; to decide which, he'd need to learn a lot more about Frank, his past and his current circumstances.

With five minutes left before his arrival, Justin sat down at his desk and closed his eyes. He inhaled deeply and exhaled just as intensely, trying to settle and empty his mind. He didn't want to enter the session with any preconceived notions or agitating thoughts, like memories of the scene with Dylan last Friday night.

His mouth tensed and he closed his eyes even tighter. How had he helped hundreds of patients live fruitful and productive lives, even assisted New York's finest, pro bono, with complicated criminal cases, yet couldn't figure out how to get along with his own son?

They'd always had their differences, even before Michael's disappearance. Preaching would only set Dylan off, so Justin had consistently given him enough rope to almost hang himself. While growing up, Dylan was allowed to fraternize with people Justin knew were just plain trouble, to go to parties the night before an important exam and generally to do things Justin hoped would allow him to make educational teenage mistakes.

Unfortunately, Justin's laissez-faire attitude didn't help their relationship, nor did it help Dylan learn on his own. He'd slip up the way Justin expected, but he didn't take lessons from it. He'd repeat the same mistake as though doing it again would bring about different results. Was he *that* stubborn or *that* stupid? Or was he trying to get back at his father for giving him all that rope? Justin had never figured it out, no matter how hard he tried.

Then came the Michael catastrophe. With eyes still closed, Justin couldn't help but run his hands through his hair and press his palms hard against the sides of his head. How Dylan and Kyle, two eighteen-year-old young men, could lose a boy who meant so much to them... so much to so many people... was still unfathomable.

When it first happened, he blamed the two of them. Not aloud, but to himself and in subtle ways to Mandy as well. There was no excuse for their lack of focus, but placing more guilt on two people going through their own nightmare of regret and remorse would have traumatic effects that might never go away.

Then he wondered if it was his *own* fault for giving Dylan too much latitude, for enabling him to become so careless and irresponsible that he lost his own brother. Was *he* to blame for the worst thing that ever happened to his family?

In time, and through many sessions with his mentor, James Van Sessler, Justin settled on the realization that life brings about disastrous, often tragic challenges. Dealing with what happened to Michael in a practical manner, rather than wasting time playing the blame game, would not only help him work through his own trauma but also help keep his remaining family intact. Changing his way of thinking actually strengthened the connection between he and Mandy. It also made it possible for them to endure their tragic situation together, unlike so many couples that are ripped apart when such a grievous event occurs. Still, two problems persisted: instead of a relationship of benign neglect, he and Dylan now fought on a regular basis, and there wasn't a morning over the past seven years Justin didn't find himself crying in the shower.

He softly cursed when the waiting area bell rang. It had always been his rule to start sessions with a clear head, and right now his head was far from that. He stood, grabbed his journal and dashed toward the door, hoping by the time he saw Frank his focus would have shifted solely to his patient.

When he opened the door, his heart missed a beat. Standing before him was someone who looked like an imitation of Frank, a copy of the person he met a week ago but with extreme dissimilarities.

The man's hair, still medium brown, was slicked back with a gel or conditioner of some kind that made it appear wet. Black eyeliner ran along his top and bottom eyelids, plus a touch drawn in each corner. Justin could've sworn there was a light pink gloss on his lips, but pulled his stare away from them as the young man started to speak.

"Am I too early?" he asked.

Justin swallowed. The voice was Frank's, but higher and softer, a bit more feminine than the last time they'd met.

"No, not at all. Right on time."

"Good," the stranger said. "The Uber driver was late and the traffic was horrific. I won't even *discuss* the smell in that Uber. I swear, if I didn't dab the Estee Lauder on my wrists before I left, I don't know what I would've done. I kept sniffing my wrists the entire way here. If I didn't, I would've died from holding my breath!"

Justin forced a laugh. "Please, sit," he said, using his journal and pen to point toward the chair.

"I mean, the driver was kind of cute. But between the way his car smelled and the fact that he wouldn't even look at me, it was obvious he wasn't gay. Que será, será."

Shit, he thought, *another alter we're going to have to deal with.*

The man walked to the chair with an effeminate gait, his long wool cloak swaying behind him. It looked like a woman's opera coat. When he took it off, Justin had to force himself not to gawk at the man's pink-hued shirt, flowered scarf and tight denim jeans. Everything about his appearance had changed since their last session, except, oddly enough, his sneakers.

"There's a coat hook here for your... your coat. Right here on the wall," Justin said.

"No, this is fine," the man replied, folding the cloak over the back of the chair and sitting down. He crossed his legs, interlaced his fingers and held his knee with his hands. "I'm more comfortable having my coat with me, if you don't mind."

"Not at all," Justin responded. "Whatever makes you comfortable."

He sat across from the patient and opened his journal.

"So..." Justin didn't want to use a name without knowing how this identity referred to himself. "Has anything changed since the last time we met? Anything new you'd like to discuss, or should we begin where we left off?"

The man looked around the room as though someone was hiding behind the desk or closet door. When he turned back to Justin, he leaned forward in his chair so he could whisper.

"I think you should know that Nathan is pissed. And I mean *really* pissed."

"How do you know he's pissed? What did he say?"

The man waved his hand in the air. "He was yelling and screaming some shit the other night about how *he* shouldn't have come here to see you."

"Who? Who shouldn't have come to see me?" Justin asked, subtly working to find out the relationship between Frank and the identity sitting before him.

"You know *who*." He rolled his eyes. "Nathan calls him 'Loser.' But that's all bullshit. The point is, Nathan said whoever tries to get rid of him is gonna pay big time. Now, just so it's clear, I'm not here to try to get help from you or get rid of Nathan." He looked around the room again, as if Nathan was hiding behind the desk. "I just wanted you to know that if the 'Loser' does come back, you'd better tell him to watch his ass, because like Nathan said, if someone tries to take something from him, he's going to take something from them. And believe me, Nathan carries out his threats."

A wave of panic slithered through Justin's nervous system. Though an alter rarely threatened the "host," the consequences could be dire – self-mutilation and suicide very often among them.

"I hear what you're saying and I realize you're not here for therapy or to get rid of anyone. But since we do have some time, can I ask you just a few more questions?"

The patient rolled his eyes again and took a quick whiff of his wrists. "Yeah, okay. I'll just watch what I say."

"Thanks so much," Justin said ingratiatingly. "So the 'you know who' we're referring to is Frank, correct?"

Head nod.

"Does Nathan ever call Frank by his name?"

Shoulder shrug. "Like I said, usually calls him 'Loser' or 'Asshole.'"

Justin jotted a few notes in his journal. "Does Nathan call you by *your* name?"

"Nathan doesn't speak to me. He doesn't like me. It's like I don't exist to him." Another shrug of his shoulders. "Not up to his standards, I guess."

"If he did speak to you, what would he call you?"

"Probably by my name, what else?"

Shit. I need to know his name. I need to personalize this conversation. It's the only way to…

"Well, you say he calls Frank 'Asshole' and 'Loser.' So if Nathan were to meet you on the street and realize you *do* exist, how would you introduce yourself?"

"What is this, some kind of mind game? If I don't exist to him, he's not going to call me nasty names, or any name for that matter. And I wouldn't introduce myself with a nasty name anyway. I'd introduce myself as Matthew, though he probably wouldn't care *what* I called myself."

Hallelujah. Matthew! He wrote the name down in his journal and circled it.

"Why wouldn't he care?"

Matthew sat back, leaning against his coat. "Look at me, Doctor Wright. I'm an embarrassment. To both of them. I sleep with men. Some of them hang around for a while, some don't, some do things to me you can't even imagine. I think that's what bothers Nathan and you know who the most and why they pretend I don't exist. I just watch and listen to them both. Anything more and I'm sure the names they'd call me would hurt me more than the pain I endure from some of these sexual predators."

Journal note: *first mention of sexual predators.*

"I do have a question that might sound silly, but could help me. Why don't you call Frank by his name? Why do you call him 'you know who'?"

Matthew shrugged again.

"You're shrugging your shoulders, but I think you know the answer to the question," Justin pressed lightly.

"Then why are you asking it?"

"I want to hear you say it."

"Well, I won't."

Justin sighed softly enough that Matthew couldn't hear it. Then he tried another tactic.

"Can you just say the word 'frank'? Forget it's a name. Just say the word." He paused. "Like if someone said, 'I'd like to be frank with you and tell you how I feel.' Can you do that?"

"Doctor Wright, you're treating me like a five year old. I can say any word in the English language. If I don't want to say the 'F' word, you can't make me say it with your games."

The agitation in Matthew's voice was obvious and Justin had to calm him down before he completely clammed up or walked out.

"I hear you, Matthew, and I apologize. Now I don't want to sound presumptuous, but for some reason you don't strike me as someone who would like working in an accounting firm, like Frank does. Is there something you've always wanted to do or be?"

Matthew rolled his eyes.

Eye rolling, Justin jotted down, *'go to' expression.*

"Can't you tell? I'm really a clothes designer. I hope to have my own line of clothing one day with complex yet comfortable fabrics, you know, for today's generation."

Justin scribbled as quickly as he could, arriving in his own mind at a place where only his years of experience could lead him. His keen insight always occurred spontaneously, as if a spiritual energy seized his thought process and guided him in the right direction – the site in a patient's psyche that would give him exactly what he needed to help them live a happier, more fulfilling life.

"And when did you first realize this was your calling? That you wanted to be a clothing designer?"

"When I was about ten, I guess."

"Was there something you saw that made you say, 'aha, that's what I want to do'? Maybe something that happened or someone you met?"

Closing his eyes, Matthew leaned his chin in his open palm. His eyelids quivered and the corners of his mouth cringed.

"I remember standing inside Carl's closet," he said, his voice lower and louder than it had been since he arrived.

At this change in the young man's demeanor, Justin took care not to move or make a sound.

"It stunk like cigarettes with the slightest hint of mothballs. He was at work or something and I was off from school. The closet was dark 'cause it only had a lightbulb with one of those chains with a string attached. All I could see was flannel and polyester. Plaid and tartan, from left to right and top to bottom. Yeah, he'd wear these clothes all the time, so I should've been used to it. But seeing them all in one place, wrinkled, reeking of Marlboros and lined up sloppily from one end of this tiny shit closet to the other made me... made me want to puke."

Justin stayed quiet, sensing that for the first time, both Matthew and Frank were in the same room with him.

"He'd keep some of those clothes on when he'd sneak in my room and..."

The youth's voice was low and steady, his eyes still closed. It was now Frank who shifted forward in the chair.

"Sneak in your room and what?" Justin whispered.

"He didn't even sneak. He pretended to sneak. How can you 'sneak' when you have a lit cigarette in your hand?"

Justin leaned forward to replicate Frank's posture, even though he couldn't see him.

"He'd sit down on the bed and start stroking my hair," Frank muttered, a short groan ending his sentence. "And then I'd look outside before closing my eyes and going..."

The room was soundless except for the slight hum of a passing car. Justin waited for him to finish his thought. *C'mon, Frank, come on. You got this.*

Nothing. Frank's mouth was open but he didn't utter a sound.

"You'd close your eyes before going where?" Justin gently asked.

The young man's eyes jolted open and he shifted back in his seat. He crossed his legs and started to scratch his head as though bugs were crawling inside his scalp. When he stopped scratching, he licked his glossy lips and, with an odd twist of his head, looked directly into Justin's eyes.

"What is it? Why are you looking at me like that?" His voice had returned to a more high-pitched, feminine tone. He crossed his arms.

Justin sat back and tried as hard as he could to mask his disappointment. "No reason in particular. You were just telling me about when you decided to become a designer. Do you remember where you left off?"

"What do you mean, 'where I left off'?" He darted his head around the room. "Why does it smell like cigarettes in here?"

Justin shrugged. The memory the patient shared must have been so vivid that it triggered his olfactory senses, bringing him back to Carl's closet and the bed in which he was abused. *The trauma that led to his dissociative identity disorder.*

Matthew crinkled his nose. "Well, it smells in here. Maybe it's coming from the office next door."

"There is no office next door." Another push.

"Well, wherever it's coming from, it stinks. Now, let's get back to the real reason I came here, Doctor Wright."

"And what is that reason, Matthew?"

"I know you think you're doing something good for Frank… there, I said it. I said his name. But you need to know you're *not* making it better. You're actually making it worse for him."

"How is that?"

"Look, to be honest, I don't care if I stay or go. I don't really care what happens to me. But like I told you, Nathan is different. If Frank tries to… if he continues to… Let's just say Nathan will fight back. He'll cause big problems. And I mean *big*. He's done it before and he'll do it again."

"What has he done before?"

Matthew put his hand over his mouth. His words came out muffled. "That's all I can say. I've said enough."

"Okay. I just have one last question on that subject. Is that all right?"

Matthew looked away, shooting a glance outside. "What?"

"Will he hurt Frank?"

"I have nothing to say other than you have to tell Frank to stop."

Frustrated and not sure where to bring Matthew next, Justin took a deep breath. "Okay, well, I have an important question about *you* before we finish up tonight."

Matthew turned back toward Justin.

"Why don't you care what happens to you? Why don't you care if you stay or go? Don't you have a life? A career? Dreams of your own?"

Matthew's eyes filled with tears. He wiped them before any had the chance to fall.

He cleared his throat. "Doctor Wright, there are some people in this world who are or will be important. People who can make a difference. People who mean something to others." He forced a smile, which in the next instant became a scowl. "I am not one of those people. For as long as I can remember, I haven't been one of those people. Yes, I have a dream, but if I'm going to be honest, it means nothing. My days, and my nights, are pretty much meaningless, and realizing that has made life easier for me."

Justin had to hold back his own tears. A pang struck his chest. He wasn't certain if it was caused by sympathy, empathy or not knowing the right words with which to respond. All he knew for sure was this human being sitting in front of him needed help. Most importantly, he needed to be loved. That was one thing obviously missing from this boy's existence. It was something he might have never experienced throughout his entire life.

"How 'bout we do this, Matthew? You come back and we talk. No need to ever bring up Nathan again. Just you and me. We'll talk about things you *want* to talk about and *only* those things. You see, I don't like when people are unhappy and you, my dear boy, are unhappy. And I am here to help you change that, okay?"

A tear ran down Matthew's cheek. He brushed it away and sniffed. "And who's going to pay for that, doctor? I'm really not the one who has the money to…"

"No worries, Matthew. That's the last thing I want you to think about. Your thoughts should be on one thing: how one day soon you're going to see your great worth, how important you are to this world. Promise me you'll at least consider thinking that way?"

Matthew nodded as he stood, grabbed his cloak and threw it over his shoulders. "Frank is right, Doctor Wright. You *are* a nice guy."

He walked toward the office door, and once there, he turned around. "I'll check my schedule and call to make an appointment."

Justin closed his journal and rose from his chair. "I'll await your call and look forward to talking again."

Once Matthew left, Justin looked out the office window and watched him walk down the street until he disappeared into the darkness and throngs of people.

His heart hurt – for Matthew, for Frank, and even for Nathan. The question was, would he be able to help them all at once?

***

Wanting privacy so he could speak freely on the phone with Mandy, Justin had decided to take a car service home instead of the train. He realized he'd made the wrong decision when the driver sped off into traffic and appeared determined to hit every pothole in the road.

"What was that?" Mandy asked. "It sounded like a bomb just exploded."

Justin pushed on the plexiglass between the front and back seat of the car, testing its tension. The glass was supposed to provide some secrecy for a passenger's conversation, but Justin couldn't trust it. He'd just have to make sure he didn't use any names.

"It was one of those famous Manhattan potholes, and I'm sure there'll be more. But we should be on the Saw Mill Parkway any minute... unless we get a flat tire or the axles break in half.'

Mandy laughed. "Why didn't you get Jimmy to drive you home? You love the way he drives."

"It was a last minute decision and Jimmy wasn't available. I wanted to talk with you about something. I couldn't wait for Jimmy and I couldn't talk with you about this on the train. So here I am."

"So what's so important it couldn't wait until you got home?"

Justin looked out the window as they flew past the other cars. He held the phone close to his mouth and leaned up against the door.

"This new client I have, well, I have a dilemma and it could be legal in nature. So I figured I'd ask my favorite lawyer her opinion."

"Continue." Mandy sounded intrigued.

"As you know, I can't get into details, so let's talk hypotheticals. Let's say there's a man with dissociative identity disorder who decides to go to a psychiatrist. The patient has three split personalities, 'alters' as they're called. So the original patient seeking help, let's call him alter 'A,' tells the doctor that he finds himself experiencing loss of time, missing periods of the day. Another identity shows up for alter A's appointment, we'll call him alter 'B,' and tells the psychiatrist about a *third* identity. The third identity, we'll call him alter 'C,' is a very nasty and malicious personality who promises to make the person who tries to get rid of him suffer consequences. In this case, my sense is that alter C could in fact harm the host, alter A, if he continues trying to eliminate him. In essence, alter A is trying to cure himself by removing alter C, but alter C is going to retaliate because he feels he deserves to exist."

A few seconds of silence passed. Justin had begun to think he and Mandy had been disconnected when he heard a muted "hmmmm."

She then said, "Before I offer an opinion, I want to clear something up. If C is going to make A pay for what he's doing, he'll really be hurting himself, correct?"

"Yes," Justin responded. "And that's what concerns me. It's a very complex disorder where some alters are aware of others, but don't seem to comprehend they can coexist, that one doesn't have to be removed for the other to remain. In fact, I've had a patient or two who coexisted with their alters and did very well."

"Are you saying having multiple alters can be a *good* thing? As far as I'm concerned, having one personality is enough." Mandy said, half-jokingly.

"I hear you. But every case is different. Some fall into the complete integration category. That's when we work over a period of time to merge the alters because it works best for the patient. With others, I've used the functional multiplicity resolution. Those are the patients who live their best lives by retaining independently acting alters. It works well when one or all of the alters aren't sure how to navigate the world as one integrated person. They might fear they'll be unable to handle future trauma without relying on disassociation. Some of them actually need the other alters around for company, support and even entertainment. And now I have a patient with one personality who's afraid of being eliminated and another who's worried his two other alters will destroy one another. Either way, it could threaten a life. So it's not the psychiatric issue that's troublesome right now, it's the…"

"Legal issue," Mandy finished for him. "The 1976 court decision that stated psychotherapists must warn third parties of a potential threat to their safety if such a threat is verbalized."

"Exactly, Mandy. Exactly." Justin leaned back against the headrest. "In this case, we're really talking self-harm or potential suicide since the patient is verbalizing harm against himself, or a part of himself which is in a sense the third party, correct?"

"Yes."

More silence before Mandy broke it. "I know the answer to this question, but are you hesitant to report this to the authorities because of the Stephen Davis case?"

Justin closed his eyes and pinched his nose with his thumb and forefinger. Since Matthew had left his office, his thoughts kept returning to Stephen Davis no matter how hard he tried to push them away.

"You know how I feel, Mandy. It was the right thing to do at the time. Stephen was a reasonable threat to someone else, someone he actually named, so I *had* to follow the rules and get the authorities involved. Needless to say…"

"You had to, Justin. There was no other way – for your practice as well as to help save an innocent person's life."

"Well, the system did a great job, didn't they?" Two days into the 72-hour hold at the psychiatric hospital they found him hanging by a belt. "That call I made really paid off, didn't it?"

"Justin, honey, please. We've been through this. There was no other way."

Justin took a few breaths as his anxiety crept in, growing from a flutter in his chest into buffeting blows that tried to get the better of him. Mandy was right. They had been through this many times and he'd learned to forgive himself. It had taken months to realize he only had so much power when it came to helping someone who might take the life of another.

"You're right, Mandy. I'm sorry. Stephen Davis is not the issue right now. My new patient's problem is. I guess my question is, alter C is not saying he's going to hurt or kill anyone. He's just saying he's going to make alter A pay for what he's trying to do. That could mean anything. That could mean he's going to steal money from A and vacation in Aruba. It could mean he's going to paint the inside of A's entire house bright orange. It could even mean he's going to stick a knife in alter A's tires so he won't be able to use his car. I really don't want to get someone thrown into a mental institution when his threats could be insignificant. *Plus,* I've only heard these threats third hand, through alter B. That identity could be making the whole thing up."

"Oh, Justin. This is so complicated. I hear everything you're saying. I have to think and do some more investigating before I give you an informed opinion."

"One last thing, Mandy. I need to be sure I don't get him thrown into the system that will lock him up in a hospital with doctors who will let him out in a few days because he deceived them into believing he's fine. He'd never trust me again, and I don't think there's anyone else who could help him like I can."

"Okay, where are you now?"

Justin glanced out the windshield and saw the exit for 287. "Right off 9A. Should be home in about ten minutes. Can we talk more about it then?"

"Of course. I'll be waiting for you, Johnnie Walker in one hand and a spoonful of my white bean pork chili in the other. Sound good?"

He smiled. "Sounds perfect. See you in a few."

The smile lingered on his face until the car hit a bump that almost caused his head to hit the roof. He looked at the driver, who looked back at him in the rearview mirror and shrugged.

"Yeah, I know. Tough road. And there's a tougher road ahead," he said.

Justin thought about Frank, Matthew and Nathan.

"You have no idea…" he replied.

CHAPTER 5

D ylan sliced the lime in half, then into quarters and then again into eighths. He squeezed slim pieces into both Corona bottles before taking a slug from the one in his left hand. "Perfect."

He walked into the living room, handed the other bottle to Kyle and then plopped down on the sofa across from his best friend.

"Thanks, bud," Kyle mumbled, his eyes glued to the abnormal psychology book he was reading for his next exam.

"You sure you don't want a shot of tequila in that beer? There's a bottle of Patron Silver just waiting to be taken advantage of."

Kyle glanced at his bottle. "I'd better not. I have to remember this shit I'm reading. And you know tequila turns my brain to mush."

"I hear you. Mine, too. I guess that's why I like it so much," Dylan said, hoping to make Kyle smile. He watched his mouth. Nothing. "Can we talk for a second before Alex gets here? I want to make sure we're on the same page about him living here... that is, if we like him."

Kyle fished the grocery receipt he'd been using as a bookmark from the crevasse of his chair and placed it inside the book. He closed it, threw it on the table and took a swig of beer.

"Go for it," he said.

"Now you know I'm pissed as shit at Jim for screwing us over. But he was a great roommate and friend. It's gonna be weird meeting someone who might take his place. So we have to keep our minds open. His paperwork proves he's good for the rent and we need that. We just have to make sure he's a good guy, likes to have some fun and isn't a pig. Anything else you think we should look for?"

Kyle took another swallow of Corona and slid the rim of the bottle along his lips. "Other than him not being a psycho, I think you have it covered. I guess we'll have to go with our guts. As long as we both get the feeling he'll work out, we should go for it. Maybe we give him a three-month trial or something. We don't have to let him know it's a trial, though, we'll keep that between us."

Dylan nodded. "Great idea. Three months and he's either in or out."

They held up their bottles as though making a toast.

"Three months," they said simultaneously before each taking a swig of beer.

Dylan slouched back into the sofa and glanced at Kyle. He couldn't remember the last time he saw him smile, laugh or make a joke. Day by day his friend was changing, right before his eyes, and there was nothing Dylan could do to help. Or was there?

"Remember when I went to my parents' last week?" he asked, unsure how to broach the subject on his mind.

Kyle nodded.

"Well, before my dad and I started our typical arguing, he asked how you were doing. I'm not gonna lie…" Dylan's voice was fading, so he cleared his throat. "I told him you weren't doing so great."

"Why the hell would you tell him that?" Kyle placed his beer on the arm of the chair and wrapped his fingers tightly around it.

"Because you're not. C'mon, man. We've been through this already. You don't go out, you're depressed, all you do is schoolwork and watch TV. You have no life and it's just not good for you." Dylan paused, not sure if he should ask the question, but he was in so deep, at this point he had nothing to lose. "Is the Prozac even doing anything?"

Kyle closed his eyes for a few seconds, then slowly opened them. "Yes, the Prozac is helping. I feel better than I have in months, no matter what you might think."

"And what about the therapist assigned to you? What's his name, Robertson? Is he helping?"

"A little, I guess. We talk, I vent. Not sure I'm getting much out of it, but it does help me see how a therapist gets answers by asking the right questions without actually asking the questions. Like the prof said, going for therapy can help us personally *and* out in the field when the time comes. I think…"

He waited for Kyle to continue. When he didn't, Dylan said, "Well, just so you know, if Robertson doesn't really help you, my dad said you could see him any time. He *is* a great therapist and knows his shit when it comes to — "

Kyle leaned forward, his face turning red and his eyes looking bloodshot and glassy with tears. "Are you kidding me with that?" he yelled. "Go to your father for therapy? Holy shit, I can barely look at your parents after what I did. And now you think I can sit in a room with him and tell him the shit that's rolling around my head? You must be crazier than I am!"

Dylan set his bottle on the long wooden table between them and leaned forward. "Jesus, Kyle. How many times do we have to go over this? *You* didn't do anything! It happened. It just happened. Someone *took* Michael, you didn't *give* him to anyone. Why do you feel like it's your fault?"

"I've told you a million times," Kyle said quietly.

"Yeah, I know. You can tell me *two* million times and it's still bullshit. You're holding onto guilt that's not yours to own. *This* is the kind of shit you should be talking with the therapist about!"

"He was holding on to *my* coat going down those subway steps! He was counting on *me* to get him to the train! Someone grabbed him from *me* and I was in too much of a rush to even notice. That's not my guilt to own? Give me a fucking break, Dylan. Your responsibility was to get us to the right subway line. Mine was to keep an eye on your brother. As always, you succeeded and I failed."

Kyle used his sleeve to wipe away the tears streaming down his face, but more kept falling. Dylan walked over and sat down on the floor beside him.

"And I'll tell *you* a million times," he said softly, his hand now cupping Kyle's knee. "We were *both* with Michael at the time he disappeared. We were *both* there when it happened. And if you want to place blame, it's more *my* fault than yours because I'm his brother and *I* should've been watching every move he made in the middle of New York City."

Kyle rubbed his eyes. "If I just stayed home and didn't go into the city to meet you guys, it never would've happened. You were having a great time and then I showed up."

Dylan swallowed hard against the lump growing in his throat. He couldn't get emotional. It wouldn't help either of them. He'd been swept up by his own cyclone of guilt and had landed on solid ground just a few short months ago, thanks to his therapist, some self-help videos and the daily mantras he learned to help dissolve the guilt that had haunted him for nearly seven years. He was still wobbly at times but had recently been having more good days than bad.

Nighttime remained the worst, lying in bed, playing that horrific scene over and over again. Him and Kyle running up the subway steps, shouting Michael's name into a mass of empty-faced people who couldn't care less who they were or why they were screaming. Running in short-breathed desperation, their yelling barely audible over the piercing firetruck sirens and blaring automobile horns. Yes, nighttime was the worst, but it had been getting easier… at least he thought it was.

"Kyle, remember, it was *me* who called *you* and told you to meet us at the Empire State Building. And when we finished taking in the view from the 86th floor and met you at the entrance downstairs, do you remember how happy Michael was to see you? How he hugged you and wouldn't let go?"

Still wiping his cheeks dry, Kyle nodded.

— ALTERED —

"That's because he loved you. And he knew, and still knows, you would never do anything to hurt him. There's no blame here except for the piece of shit who grabbed him and took him from us. It's just… I don't know… circumstance. Something that there's no explanation for. And something that I believe will be made right. One day we'll see Michael again, safe and sound. And he'll hug you again just like he did that day in front of the Empire State Building."

As he rubbed Kyle's leg, Dylan held back his own tears. He tried as hard as he could to believe what he just told Kyle, but the fear in his heart that he'd never see Michael again was stronger than the words he spoke. His sudden lack of confidence made his stomach tighten – if he couldn't convince himself, how on earth was he going to convince Kyle? And what kind of therapist would he make if he couldn't help his patients feel better?

"You're right," Kyle said in a quivering voice. "I know you're right. I just have to learn to believe it."

Dylan forced a smile. *Maybe I'll be a better therapist than I thought.*

"And that's what takes time, believing it. Will you speak with your therapist about this?"

Kyle shrugged.

"Suggestion, bonehead, start talking to him about it. This is the kind of shit you need to work through. I don't know what else you talk with him about and I really don't care. But get to the real stuff so you can smile and party like you used to." Dylan grabbed his beer from the table and gestured for Kyle to grab his. Once he did, Dylan clinked the bottles together. "Will you do that?"

Kyle nodded.

"Promise?"

"Yes, I promise." Kyle took a sip of a beer. "You head shrinker!"

Dylan stood and tousled Kyle's hair. "You're the head shrinker!" He'd started walking back to the chair when there was a knock at the door.

"Shit!" Kyle patted his eyes with the palm of his hands. "That's Alex. Perfect timing. The last thing we need is for him to think his roommate is a crybaby."

Dylan took a slug of beer. "Well, better he knows the truth before he moves in."

"Asshole," Kyle responded, running his fingers through his hair as he stood and followed Dylan to the door.

"Takes one to know one." He laughed again, opening the door before Kyle had a chance to reply.

***

Alex sat on the sofa and straightened the brim of his Boston Red Sox baseball cap. Dylan and Kyle sat across from him, each in their own chair, staring at the red "B" on the cap that looked back at them.

"Thanks for the tour," Alex said. "This place is great."

"No problem," Dylan responded. "Glad you like it."

"Yeah, we like it too," added Kyle. He paused, looked at Dylan, then turned back to Alex. "But I do have one question."

"Shoot."

"Why the Red Sox? Why not the Yanks? That's a dangerous hat to be wearing in some parts of the city."

Alex smiled. "I grew up very close to Fenway Park. The place was like my second home. You can take the boy out of Boston, but you can't take Boston out of the boy. Same goes for the Sox. If I stay in New York after I finish school, I *might* consider wearing a Yankees cap." He patted the top of his cap. "Believe me, I get some pretty nasty looks sometimes, but I'm not going to stop wearing it just because I might get mugged or killed. It'll take more than that for me to turn my back on the Sox."

They all laughed, more of the ice breaking. Dylan leaned back, placed his hands behind his head and put his feet up on the ottoman. With him and Kyle on one side and Alex across from them, he wanted to loosen the bit of tension among them that wasn't fading as quickly as he'd hoped.

"So…" Dylan started. "Kyle told me that he explained our situation. How our wonderful, trustworthy friend left us high and dry and we need a third to help pay the rent. The info you gave us shows you definitely have the money to pay the rent. We just have to make sure you'll stick around and that the three of us will get along. Where are you living now?"

Alex glanced at them both, then rubbed his palms up and down the arms of the chair. "Okay, let me be totally honest," he said.

Dylan shot Kyle an "oh shit, here we go" look. Kyle crossed his arms and sat back.

"I already have a place on the Upper East Side. It's a co-op on Columbus Avenue and 106th Street. I'm looking to rent this room because it's closer to Fordham. So when I'm at the library real late or in a study group until midnight, I can have a place to crash without having to travel all the way uptown. You might not see me for a week, even two. I'll use it only when I need to." He stopped stroking the arms of the chair and let his hands fall to his sides. "Plus, it's a write-off."

Dylan and Kyle looked at one another, then back at Alex.

"That makes some sense," Dylan said, "but there's something missing here. I mean, obviously you have a lot of money. Why wouldn't you just buy a co-op down here? Why rent a room in an old brownstone with us?"

Alex bit his bottom lip.

"Friends," he said, a tinge of red flushing his cheeks. "I need to make friends. My study group is full of dullards. And it's tough to just walk up to someone in my giant classes and ask if they want to be friends. Plus, other than the elevator, you don't really meet people living in a co-op complex. When I saw your ad, I thought it might be a good way get a social life."

Dylan nodded, trying to figure out if this guy was being honest or slinging bullshit. Kyle wouldn't confront anyone to save his life; he let the awkward silence between them hang in the air for almost a minute.

"How much are you willing to put down as a deposit?" he asked.

"How much do you want?"

Without conferring with Kyle, Dylan blurted out, "Six months."

"Done," Alex agreed.

Dylan's insides trembled with excitement. In a few minutes, the pressure of missed rental payments was washed away like silt in a stream. He turned to Kyle, whose slim smile showed he was in complete agreement.

"I like that," Dylan said, "but now *I'll* be completely honest. I work a lot and go to school. This one over here" — he nodded toward Kyle — "goes to school and studies all the time. We don't have the most exciting social life. I can't remember the last time I closed a bar or went to a concert. And then there's girls. I haven't had a girlfriend in like three years."

"Yeah, but you've been on about a hundred dates," Kyle countered. "The girls love him. It's sickening. Every single girl he meets falls in love with him. It's like — "

"It's not my fault," Dylan interrupted. "It's just who I am."

"Sickening, I tell you."

Dylan wasn't sure if Kyle was serious or still kidding around. He didn't want to find out in front of a stranger, so he turned back to Alex and leaned forward.

"I just want you to know, if you're looking for party central, this isn't the place. We do go out once in a while and have some friends you might get along with. But we're pretty much about work and school. I'm not sure if that will work for you."

"That's okay. I have a feeling just being able to hang out in this neighborhood will be enough. There's a lot going on down here. Plus being able to crash so close to school if I need to is a big thing for me."

"And you're going to Fordham for economics or something like that?" asked Dylan.

"Yeah. Actually, a Master's of Business Analytics. I work at a big accounting firm and this will help me move up the ladder more quickly... I hope."

Dylan shook his head slowly. "Business Analytics, huh? That sounds like the most *boring* subject in the history of education – except for physics, which I failed twice."

Alex laughed. "Yeah, it's not up there with cinematography, marketing or psychology, but for some reason I'm really into it. I want to be able to identify and quantify a business's problems so I can figure out and implement solutions. For me it's like being a cancer researcher, trying to find a cure for a problem. Not as serious as a fatal disease, but as far as I'm concerned, the investigating is almost as exciting."

"Not judging," Dylan said. "Listen, some people can't believe I want to be a therapist. Lots of them ask me, 'You want to sit and listen to people's problems all day?' I try to explain that's just a small part of a process with a greater end. But they don't get it and I can't spend my time trying to convince them why I'm doing what I'm doing. Kind of like you shouldn't waste your time trying to convince me how statistics and mathematical models can be interesting."

"This is all very nice," Kyle interrupted with clear sarcasm, "but let's get to the core of things. If you decide you don't like it here, can we keep the deposit? Why do you work if you have so much money like your paperwork shows? Do you drink, smoke or take drugs? And are you an extreme liberal or conservative?"

"Kyle!" Dylan shouted. "Holy shit, that's a lot to ask. And political views? Really?"

"It's fine," Alex said. "I'd ask the same questions. No worries. Okay, if I remember the questions correctly, here goes… Yes, if I don't like it, you can keep the deposit. Yes, my parents left me a shitload of money but, like I said, I like this line of work. And what would I do if I didn't work? Travel and party all the time? That's not me. As far as drinking goes, I have a drink now and then, but I'm definitely not an alcoholic or anything like that. I don't smoke – the smell of cigarettes makes me ill. I don't take drugs – I don't even smoke pot. Regarding political views, I'm an Independent. I lean toward the person I feel will do the best for the people, myself included. Doesn't matter which party." He looked up to the ceiling as though trying to remember everything Kyle had asked. "I think that answers all the questions, right?"

Dylan nodded, though the only thought running through his mind was: *Sounds too good to be true.*

"Yeah, I think that answers the questions *I* asked. Dylan, you have any?"

He scratched the stubble on his chin, trying to come up with a question that might help to make a final decision. One hit him from out of the blue, and it fell out of his mouth before he had a chance to think it through.

"What are *your* thoughts about psychotherapy?"

The surprised looks on Alex and Kyle's faces made it seem as though he'd asked about his sexual fetishes.

"What?" Dylan turned to Kyle. "You can ask him about his political views and I can't ask about his view on psychotherapy?"

"That's different."

"No worries," Alex interjected. "Actually, I'm not a big fan of psychotherapy. That doesn't mean I'm invalidating your pursuit in any way whatsoever. It's just… from personal experience, I've never found it very helpful. I just think that sometimes it worsens the situation. Again, that's *my* experience. Who knows, maybe I just never found the right therapist." Smiling thinly, he looked straight into Dylan's eyes. "Maybe once you get your PhD, I can try therapy again. Who knows? You could be the therapist I've been searching for!"

Kyle chuckled. "It doesn't sound like you need a therapist, Alex. You seem to have your shit pretty much together."

Alex joined in the laughter. "I could say the same about you. But I've learned not to judge a book by its cover. We all have our issues. For instance, you're smiling and laughing and we seem to be having a good time. But your eyes are puffy and bloodshot. So you're either very high or you've been crying. You don't come off as a weedhead, so I'll go with crying."

Kyle turned to Dylan, his expression begging for him to run interference.

"Hmm," Dylan said. "Maybe *you* should be the psychotherapist. It's been a rough day and Kyle had to let out some frustration. But he's good now. Right?"

Kyle nodded, still looking embarrassed.

"Don't sweat it, man," Alex reassured him. "Like I said, we all have our issues. You should've seen me when I got dumped last year. Cried like a baby. Waterfalls. Talk about embarrassing."

Dylan stood and looked out the window. "It's getting late. Kyle has an exam tomorrow and I have to get some food in my gut. Can you give us the night to discuss and we'll let you know first thing in the AM?"

Alex stood and shook Dylan's hand, then Kyle's, before going to the door. They went with him. "Absolutely. I hope your decision is a positive one. I think it would work out great."

"I do, too," Kyle said, meeting Dylan's eyes with a skeptical expression.

Dylan opened the door for Alex.

"'Til tomorrow!" Alex called, walking down the steps and onto the sidewalk.

One second after Dylan closed the door, Kyle took his shoulder and turned him around.

"What the hell? Why didn't we just say 'yes' while he was here? He's like the perfect fit, Dylan. Seriously, what the hell?"

Dylan walked to the sofa and fell full-length on it, pushing out a blast of dust and lint. "You don't think he's just a little *too* perfect?" He watched Kyle sit in the chair across from him. "He doesn't really drink, doesn't smoke, doesn't take drugs, he works and spends most of his spare time in the library. He has a shitload of cash because his parents are dead — which, by the way, is a total mindfuck. You can't be 'normal' after losing both your parents at such a young age. I wasn't going to ask what happened to them, but we can be sure it was tragedy of some kind. It's just... Something just doesn't sit right and I can't put my finger on it."

"Well, let me put your finger on *this*: the guy is nice, smart and has money to pay the rent. Plus, he'll only be here when he needs to crash or get away from his boring co-op. It's the perfect scenario."

Dylan turned over on his side, resting his head on one arm. "You only like him because he's a crybaby like you."

"Oh yeah?" Kyle laughed, running to the couch and jumping on top of Dylan. He pulled him onto the floor and used his high school wrestling moves until he got him in a leg-trap camel clutch.

"Okay! Okay!" Dylan yelled. "Enough! He's in! I'll call him tomorrow and let him know! Now let me go!"

Kyle tightened his grip. Unable to see his expression and having trouble taking a breath, Dylan started to panic. *Is Kyle losing it? Is he taking his depression out on me?*

He was trying to grab the hand now around his neck when Kyle abruptly released his head, still laughing. He stood up and wiped his hands on his pants as though he'd just accomplished a long-awaited mission.

"What the hell was *that,* Kyle?" Dylan asked, panting on the carpet.

"What's the problem?"

"You went too far. You could've broken my freakin' windpipe."

Kyle chuckled. "Now who's the crybaby?"

Dylan shook his head and used the sofa to help himself stand. No matter how depressed or angry Kyle was, he wasn't going to let himself be used as a punching bag. "Don't ever do that again. I'm serious."

Kyle saluted. "Yes, sir."

"This isn't a joke."

"I know. I know. I'm sorry. I got carried away. Just having fun for a change. Never again, I promise."

"You'd better promise, asshole," Dylan said with a tight-lipped smile. "Now, I'll call Alex tomorrow and — "

"I'm going to call him now, Mr. Wright. With our luck, he'll find another place before morning and we'll be stuck paying the full rent for another month. I can't afford that."

Dylan tried to lighten things up. "Fine. Call him. But tell him to keep his baby tears at his co-op. Between the two of you, you'll flood this place and we'll have to pay for damages."

Kyle grabbed his phone from the end table and started tapping the keypad. "You little shit. Don't make me break my promise about that clutch hold."

Dylan headed to the kitchen. "You want some dinner?"

Kyle nodded as he waited for Alex to answer his call. "Yes, please."

"Then keep your paws to yourself or you'll have to cook your own."

By the time he reached the pantry, the irritation from the surprise wrestling match was dissipating and he felt a glimmer of hope for Kyle. He'd smiled and laughed in the same night for the first time in weeks. And now they would have a roommate whom Kyle appeared to like a lot. Dylan decided to leave his paranoia on the sidelines and accept Alex for what he seemed to be: just a nice guy, like the two of them, who needed a place to live. End of story.

For now, at least, that was what he'd allow himself to believe.

CHAPTER 6

The November wind whipped past the windows of Justin's office as streetlamps flickered in the descending darkness. Unsure which identity would show up for Frank's appointment, he dimmed the recessed lights to create a calming atmosphere. No matter which alter entered the office, he wanted them to feel welcomed, tranquil and at ease.

He and Mandy had quite a few in-depth discussions about the elements of this case, from patient-client confidentiality and patient-therapist trust to the possibility of an innocent person getting harmed and potential legal ramifications. She conferred with colleagues and then colleagues of colleagues so that Justin could make the best possible decision. Although he had plenty of information and conflicting opinions, he still hadn't made up his mind.

When Matthew implied, but didn't confirm, Nathan might "make someone pay big time," was he telling the truth? Making up a story? Creating drama for his own entertainment? Justin couldn't know the answer to those questions – he didn't know Matthew well enough –

and the phrase "make someone pay big" could mean a million different things.

The ruling in the 1976 case of *Tarasoff v. Regents of the University of California* held that mental health providers have an obligation to protect persons who could be harmed by a patient. In Frank's case, this wasn't the issue because there was no substantial evidence that harmful statements had ever been made. Plus, there was no specific perpetrator or victim, which is why Justin decided to gather even more information before making a determination. Since he didn't hear the threat from Nathan, the actual party who might harm another, it made the entire accusation hearsay. If all went as planned, Justin would have Nathan show himself so he'd be able to talk with him face-to-face.

The bell outside his office rang and Justin took a breath. When he opened the door, he immediately recognized Frank. Although he wore a heavy olive-green down parka with a faux-fur-lined hood covering half his face, Justin saw Frank in the young man's eyes.

"A little cold out there?" he asked, offering to take the coat.

"Yeah, just a little," Frank replied, sliding a book bag off his shoulder and onto the floor. He handed Justin his coat. "But it's nice and warm in here."

Justin hung Frank's coat on the wall hook and walked him over to the chairs. Frank sat down, rubbed his hands together and asked Justin how he was doing.

"I'm doing well," he said. "Very well. And how are you?"

"Good. Pretty good." Frank looked down at his sneakers and tapped his feet on the rug. "Sorry I missed last week. It was one of those times again. You know, when I start to do something and then it's four hours later and I'm at home wondering what happened. I was getting ready to come here and… I don't know. I just don't know." His voice grew shaky. "I was going to call to apologize, but I guess I was too embarrassed. I thought it best to apologize in person."

Justin opened his journal and clicked his pen. He took a quick glance at his notes and crossed his legs. "So, where were you and what were you doing when you realized you missed our appointment?"

Frank closed his eyes and pinched the corners. "I was sitting on my bed in a towel. My hair was wet. I had obviously just gotten out of the shower." When he opened his eyes, Justin saw them water. "I don't know how much more I can take, Doctor Wright. It seems to be happening more and more. I think I'm losing my mind and I don't know what to do."

The tears started rolling down his cheeks, and Justin knew it was time to talk blunt truth. He leaned forward, his knees only about a foot away from Frank's.

"Frank, we have a few things to talk about and I'd like you to listen carefully. The first thing you need to know is that we're going to get you better. I have the experience and you have the smarts to make that happen. Do you understand?"

Frank nodded.

"I really need you to understand that before I go any further. I also need you to understand you're a wonderful, intelligent person who can get through anything, especially this. Can you tell me you understand that?"

"Yes, I understand," Frank said.

"Great. Now, have you ever heard of dissociative identity disorder?"

Frank hung his head and let his arms fall by his side, his palms facing upward on the seat cushion. "Yeah, I looked it up."

Justin stopped his eyes from widening in surprise. *Don't let him see your reaction. Keep the tone of your voice even.*

"Oh, really. That's interesting. What made you look it up?"

"Let's see, I've been losing pieces of my day, I have texts on my phone from people I don't know, to someone with a different name, I get packages delivered for things I never ordered, I have clothes in my closet I'd never buy for myself. What was I supposed to do?"

"Well, first of all, I want you to know that you can call me if you ever feel like you're at your wit's end or need someone to talk to. That's what I'm here for. Secondly, before I ask you what you learned when you looked it up, I have to ask, do these packages you receive have *your* name on the label?"

Frank looked up, his eyes staring into Justin's.

"Of course they do! Who else's name would they…" Frank stopped talking and his expression softened. "Oh, I get it. You want to know if I ordered something using someone else's name. One of the other…"

Justin placed his fingertips on Frank's knees.

"Alters," he gently said. "They are called alters. Different parts of you that have been created for a reason. And I want you to know that this is a common problem. There have been millions of people with dissociative issues."

"I've read the facts, Doctor Wright. Two percent of those people have it the same way I do. Multiples. Alters. Whatever you want to call them. That brings the number down by millions. And I also read there's no cure. Most patients take drugs or learn how to make living with DID more manageable. That means I'm stuck like this forever, right? A one hundred percent psycho."

Justin leaned back into his chair and let out a big breath. "Do you remember what I asked you earlier? To understand you're smart, I'm smart and together we can work this out. We don't use the word 'psycho' in this office because there is no such thing. There are people who suffer from certain issues and it's my job to see them through those issues." He hesitated and decided to continue with complete honesty. "But you're right. There are great ways to manage DID rather than finding a complete or permanent cure. Some include medication, some behavioral therapy and some include both. We're going to go with the 'both' scenario to give us a greater chance of success. What do you think?"

"I don't have a choice, do I?"

"Yes, you do. You can keep going the way you've been going and wake up in places not knowing how you got there. Or you can learn to manage the situation so that you can lead a fuller, happier, more peaceful life. Those are your choices. Which do you choose?"

Frank sat back and clasped his hands. "I think you know my choice. I'm sitting here, aren't I?"

Justin smiled. "That makes me very happy, Frank." He opened his journal and began to write. "Before we get into the nitty gritty, I'm going to call in two prescriptions for you. One is Clonidine. Believe it or not, it's typically used to lower blood pressure, but has been proven helpful for the treatment of the symptoms you're experiencing. I'm also going to prescribe a very low dose of Xanax that you'll only take at night. Both of these can make you tired and cause coordination issues. I need you to call me if these or any other problems occur, okay? We can always stop or change medication as needed."

Frank nodded.

"Now," Justin started. *Take it slow. One step at a time.* "When you read about Dissociative Identity Disorder – let's call it 'DID' – did you read about how different the alters can be, to the point where they fabricate jobs they don't have or stories about lovers or family they never had?"

Frank nodded again and fidgeted in his chair. He scratched his head and then ran his fingers through his hair.

"Did you also read about the triggers behind alters? What might cause this kind of problem to occur?"

He wriggled in his chair.

"Are you okay, Frank? Do you need some time?"

"No," he snapped. His gaze fell back to the rug. "I don't need time. And yes, I know what causes this shit. Physical abuse, trauma, drugs, an unpredictable home environment." His breathing became rougher. "I told you! I read it all online! I know what I am and I know what causes it!"

Justin had never seen Frank act this agitated. It might mean he wasn't ready to face the demons, the memories he would have to confront in order to get better. At this moment, Justin's top priority was to calm him down.

"Frank, it's okay. You're safe here. I need you to know that. I'm here to listen to everything you have to say… everything you *want* to say… without any backlash or judgment. We'll talk about those things when you're ready. If you want to — "

A whimper came from deep within Frank's throat, a groan that quickly evolved into a growl. When Frank faced him again, Justin saw someone very different. Although he was still the man who walked through the door minutes before, his face had changed. His eyes were larger, his cheeks swollen, his lips thinner and their corners drooping like a sad face painted on by a clown. Except the face wasn't sad; the large eyes burned with absolute fury.

"Listen, shithead," the new Frank said, moving forward in his chair. "I'm in charge here. Not you and not that weasel running over here every week trying to get rid of me."

Justin tensed up. So, Nathan had finally made his appearance. He knew it was no coincidence that he'd shown up when the topics of trauma and abuse were raised. Although this was a good sign, a small but significant breakthrough, he had to keep his own safety in mind. *Don't make any sudden moves. Don't look afraid.*

"Who do you think this weasel came running to every time he cried himself to sleep as a kid," Nathan said, more of a statement than a question. "Who do you think he *still* runs to when he can't handle shit? Yeah, that's right — me!"

Since Nathan was still sitting, Justin felt safe for now. He didn't move, holding on to his journal as though it could be used as a shield.

He looked Justin up and down, then peered into his eyes. "Let me tell you something, Doctor Wright, or should I call you Doctor Wrong? That fag Matthew thinks I don't know about him, thinks he's hiding shit from me. But I know everything that homo does and I know everything he tells you, like how I won't let anyone try to get rid of me. I think that's the only thing that gay whore is right about."

Justin thought hard about when to speak and what he should say. He closed his eyes for a few moments and let his second nature take over.

"Nathan, I presume?" he asked, projecting confidence.

"Oh, you're a genius, doc. I see why Frank wastes so much time and money on you. What was it that gave it away? My good looks?"

Easy, Justin. Diffuse the tension and anger. Eliminate emotions.

"Actually, it's your honesty."

"What are you talking about?"

"You say what you feel, what's on your mind. You talk to me the way I'd like Frank and Matthew to talk to me. Straight and to the point."

"Oh really? So are you saying you like me better than them?"

"I don't have favorites, Nathan. It doesn't work that way in my line of business. I like all of my patients. And if I don't, I'd tell them we're not a good fit and it's best if they find themselves a new therapist."

"Well, I hate to be the one to break it to you, doc, but I'm not your patient." Nathan gripped the arms of his chair and squeezed them until his knuckles turned white.

Justin's muscles automatically tightened. Was Nathan getting ready to attack him? Should he be prepared for an assault? Should he stay seated and act calm to keep Nathan's rage in check? Before he could decide on a course of action, Nathan leaned back and loosened his grip on the chair.

"It's simple, Doc. I'm here to tell you head-on that nobody, not Frank, not Matthew, not anybody else is going to get rid of me. I'm here to stay."

No one else? Are there others?

"If they try to take something from me, I'll take something from them. An eye for an eye is the way I play the game." Nathan sneered and clutched the arms of the chair even tighter. "Listen to me, Doctor Wrong, and listen carefully. I'm not as dumb as you might think. I know how to do my own investigating. I know that if I say I'm gonna hurt someone, you can report me. That puts me in some insane asylum for a few days until I fake my way out or run out the clock. So I'm just gonna keep my mouth shut, 'cept to say that the weasel better stop coming here to ditch me or there's gonna be trouble. I wouldn't call that a direct threat of violence on anyone in particular, would *you*?"

Justin kept still. Nathan was intelligent. Unfortunately, he was downright conniving, and also clearly thrived on anger. The trick would be to reduce that anger to the point where the alters were willing to merge and allow Frank to always be the host *or* to exist together harmoniously so that Frank could live a more functional and tolerable existence.

"Absolutely not a threat," Justin said, the half-truth making his stomach churn. "I would like to say one thing, though."

Nathan rolled his eyes. "For Christ's sake. What?"

"I can understand you might feel like Frank wants to get rid of you, but the truth is, he wants to be *with* you. You're extremely important to him and he *needs* you. He needs your strength, your honesty and your — to be blunt — he also needs your anger. If he let out his anger like he *should*, it would probably lessen much of his pain."

"Thanks for saying that, doc," Nathan said as he stood and walked toward the office door. He grabbed the book bag and slid it over his shoulder. One look at the coat on the hook made him shake his head in disgust. He crammed it under his arm. "But I think you're full of shit. He wants me gone as much as I want this shitrag of a coat thrown in the trash. So if I were you, I'd tell him to stop coming here."

With that, he walked out the door and back into the frigid November wind. Justin slowly rose from his chair and stood by the window, watching Nathan as he dissolved into the swarm of bodies walking up Park Avenue. He shivered, unsure if the tingle crawling up the back of his neck was from the cold seeping through the glass or the chill Nathan had left inside his office.

***

Dylan jumped when the phone rang.

He'd been lying in bed, focused on highlighting a paragraph in his *Perception and Reality* textbook, when the sound jolted him out of his concentration. He looked at the display. *DAD*. He let it ring a few more times before deciding to pick up.

"Hey, Dad. How ya doin'?"

"Been better, son."

Dylan threw his highlighter in the seam of his textbook and smacked it shut. "What's wrong? You don't sound good. Where are you?"

"I just had a rough session with a client. I think I might have to get Van Sessler to help me on this one. It's a tough situation." After a short pause, Justin said, "Anyway, I didn't call to talk about that. I decided to take a car home instead of the train so I could talk to you without bothering the people around me. I wanted to apologize for what happened the last time you visited. I really don't like arguing with you. It upsets us both and I want to work on making things right. It also upsets your mom and I don't think either of us want that."

"No, we don't. I totally understand."

"Hmm. Do you really? Maybe she should live with you for a few days after our next argument. That will give you the *complete* picture of 'Life with Mandy Wright after her husband and son have a fight.'"

Dylan laughed hard. "No thanks. That's *your* specialty. Plus, I don't plan on having another argument with you. I apologize, too. Sometimes I think we're so much alike, we feel we *have* to fight in order to differentiate ourselves. I know that might sound a little strange, but it's something I've been thinking about."

Relief spread through him when he heard his father chuckle. "It's not strange at all, Dylan. It's probably closer to the truth than anything I could think of on my own."

He jumped off the bed and glanced out his bedroom window. A group of kids hung out in the alley below, passing around what looked like a joint. He pulled the shade's cord so it dropped and covered the view, but he could still hear them laughing through the glass.

"You were right about Kyle, too," Dylan said.

"What do you mean?"

"He's in bad shape and needs some intense help. We did have a good talk and I think I convinced him to discuss with his therapist what's *really* bothering him. He's actually been going to his therapy sessions but not talking about what's been making him feel so bad."

"Damn it. I hate hearing that. Did he tell you specifically what might be the source of his depression?"

Dylan heard the quiver in his father's voice, the hollow tone in his question. They both knew where this was going. The elephant had trampled through the bedroom door and now stood in the center of the room.

He walked down the hallway into the living room. Since he was the only one home, he was free to talk, but still kept his voice low from force of habit.

"I'm not sure if I should say," he admitted.

"It's your call, son."

"Okay. It's still about Michael. The feelings of being responsible. The grief. The guilt. He can't let any of it go. Not even a tiny bit." Dylan glanced toward the front door. "It's not like *I* don't think about it a thousand times a day or wish every night that we took a bus instead of the subway. But I had you and Mom and even Van Sessler to help me process what happened."

The silence on the other end of the phone wrapped itself around Dylan's stomach and squeezed. *Maybe I shouldn't have brought up Michael. Should I just shut up? Maybe I should say something.*

"To be honest," he continued, "I don't think I'll ever be a whole person again. But I know how to weather the storm and when the guilt starts to overwhelm me, I go back to the conversations we had and behavioral therapies we did for all those months. I just hope Kyle's guy can do for him what you and Van Sessler did for me."

His father cleared his throat and let out a breath. "I hope so, too. I really do. And from everything you've said, you understand it's something we'll never get over, just something we'll always be working to get through. If I'm being honest, there are things *I* can't let go of."

"What do you mean?"

"Have you ever looked in Michael's bedroom?"

"Yeah, I go in there just about every time I visit you guys."

"So you've noticed it hasn't changed? I didn't move a thing since the last time he was in there. Sure, we straightened it out a little, but the books he put on his desk are still there. The toothpaste tube sitting on his nightstand… Believe it or not, I log into his children-centric social network accounts each month to clean them up, to make sure there aren't any notification icons or things that shouldn't be there. He's even still a part of our cell phone family plan, because I can't bring myself to take him off. He'll always be a part of our family. There are just some things I just can't… don't want to let go of. But you know what?"

"What?" Dylan asked, the lump in his throat starting to ache.

"I'm allowed to do that. I'm allowed to hold on to what I want to hold on to. I'm allowed to feel the way I feel. As long as you, your mom and I continue with our lives, we're allowed to do what feels right to us." Dylan heard silence and then strained laughter. "There – Justin's justification in a nutshell. How'd I do? Did any of that make sense?"

Dylan nodded and then realized his father couldn't see him agreeing from the other end of the phone. "Yes," he said. "It all made total sense."

"So remember," Justin said, "if Kyle ever wants to talk with me, I have no qualms about it. I'm more than willing — "

"Yeah, I brought that up. He basically said he has a hard enough time just seeing you and Mom without the gnaw of guilt. There's no way he can sit and talk with you about it, at least right now. I'm sorry."

"Don't apologize, Dylan. It is what it is. If time goes on and you don't see him getting any better, let me know. Do you know the therapist he's seeing?"

"I think his last name is Robertson."

"Got it. Give me the go ahead if you want me to check him out. But I won't do it without your permission, okay?"

"Okay," Dylan replied.

"Speaking of an update, did you ever meet with that potential roommate?"

"Alex? Yeah, we did. He moved in almost two weeks ago. Well, if you want to call it 'moving in.' He actually has a co-op uptown and uses this as a place to crash when he studies late or wants to hang out in a different neighborhood. He has a job and spends a lot of time at school and the library getting his master's. I've only seen him here once over the last twelve days or so. He's clean, quiet and basically never here which gives him an A in my book."

"That's good to hear. I'm glad it's working out so far."

Dylan heard footsteps up the outdoor concrete stairs and the front door opened. When he turned, Alex walked in and gave him a nod.

"Speak of the devil. The man of the hour just walked in — a rare occurrence, let me tell you."

"Okay, I'll let you go," Justin said. "Tell him I hope to meet him soon."

"You bet. Thanks, Dad. And thanks for calling. Love you."

"Love you, too." Dylan threw his phone on the chair and walked over to Alex, who carried a bookbag in one hand and coat in the other. "Hey, dude. It's a little cold to be walking out there without your coat, isn't it?"

"A little," Alex said. "But sometimes freezing myself helps clear my head. I know it sounds crazy, but it works. Might want to try it sometime."

"I might. And I'll be sure to leave a note so if I freeze to death, everyone will know it was your idea."

Alex smiled and pulled the coat from beneath his arm to hang it in the closet. Dylan fought the temptation to say something about his ridiculous taste in outerwear. *If this was Kyle, I'd have a field day, but I'll give this guy a break... for now.*

As they grew closer, he'd be sure to tell Alex that if he didn't want to be mocked, he should know that the days of olive-green down parkas with faux hood fur were over decades ago.

CHAPTER 7

Mandy slammed her hand down on the desk and held herself back from knocking the pen container off the edge. It would only create a mess she'd have to clean once she got off the phone.

"Tom, it's been five months. I hired you to find out what happened to my son, not to roam around the streets of Manhattan testing the pretzel and souvlaki vendors."

"Not only is that unfair, Mandy, it's not the truth. You know how invested I've been in this investigation. I've worked my ass off to find something. Anything to help you — and, of course, Michael."

Mandy pulled her braid so it fell over her shoulder. She looked out her glass office door into the boardroom, where paralegals were choosing their sandwich wraps and sides. It was Friday, and that meant the practice had lunch brought in for all the employees. Mandy twirled her chair around so she could look out the window.

"I'm sorry. That was uncalled for. I'm just... well, as I said the day I hired you, I've never kept anything from my husband, and the longer it takes to find something, *anything,* the more possibility there is that Justin will find out I'm doing this. And he wouldn't be happy."

Tom's stubble rustled against the phone as he walked. "I understand. Although I'm still not sure why you don't want your husband to know about this. Are you sure, and I ask this again only because I'm an investigator, that I shouldn't be looking into Justin?"

Mandy jumped up. "Absolutely not! I told you what happened that day. Michael disappeared from the subway when my son and his friend were looking after him. Justin was and is just as devastated as I am. Don't you dare look into Justin!"

"Okay! Okay! I'm sorry. Damn it, Mandy. Help me out here. Any questions I ask or leads I follow, I do so with one goal in mind, to find out what happened to Michael. Period. Please understand that."

Leaning against the floor-to-ceiling window, Mandy looked out over the Stamford city landscape, the tiny pedestrians below. She was a little surprised that Tresser Boulevard was so busy on such a cold day, but it was lunchtime, and not everybody had free wraps in the boardroom. Feeding probably trumped freezing.

"Yes, I understand," she said. "And I'm only doing this because the police have given up. Sure, they're calling it an 'open case,' but that's bullshit. I don't think Detective Collins or any of his team have opened Michael's files in years. It's pathetic and extremely frustrating."

"I hear you. And — you never heard this from me — I've seen every one of those damn files. Nothing."

Unable to think of a reply, Mandy fell back into her chair.

"I have to be honest," Tom continued, "I have a few more leads I want to follow up on, but if those don't pan out, I'm not going to take any more of your money. I hate like hell to leave things where they are, but I just can't make any headway. It's like Michael literally disappeared without a trace."

She let her face fall into her empty hand, holding back the tears and screams that wanted so badly to escape. Once she'd swallowed them back down and gained a smidgeon on internal composure she lifted her head. Mandy almost slid off her chair when she saw Justin waving at her on the other side of the door. She feigned a smile and gestured with her index finger that she needed one minute.

"Shit. Justin is here. Please let me know if any of those leads work out. Again, I'm sorry for being so nasty."

"Please don't apologize. It's completely understandable. I'll buzz you when I know something. Bye for now."

"Bye," she replied before hanging up her phone and motioning for Justin to come in.

She met him in the middle of her office, kissed him gently on the mouth and pointed to the leather sofa in front of the windows of the other wall, overlooking Atlantic Street. He took a seat and watched Mandy lean on the front edge of her desk.

"You look beautiful," he said.

"You saw me this morning. Do I look more beautiful now?"

"You look more beautiful every time I see you." He smiled seductively.

"Okay." She closed a couple of manila folders on her desk. "To what do I owe this wonderful surprise?"

"Your beauty," he half-whispered.

"Enough!" She stood up straight, sauntered toward the sofa and sat down beside him. She tousled his hair, which had already been tossed into chaos by the wind. "No, really."

"No, really. You are absolutely exquisite today. 'Sexy' doesn't even come close to describing your elegance and charm."

"Well, remind me to thank you for those compliments later on. Now you'd better hurry up and tell me why you're here before my husband shows up unexpectedly."

"Beautiful *and* funny." Justin laughed. "I had a sit-down with Van Sessler up the block and just wanted to say 'hi' before heading back into the office."

Mandy pointed to the boardroom where there was still plenty of food on the trays set up on the large, oak conference table. "Would you like a wrap or something before heading back?"

"No, thanks. Jim's secretary brought in some sandwiches. He has a favorite place that uses 'real turkey, not that slimy stuff.' His words, not mine. He seems to like having an office in Stamford a lot more than being in Manhattan. Especially since he's slowly thinning out his practice."

"Was it worth your time seeing him? Did he help at all with your patient?"

"Actually, yes, he did. He's always got good advice. He agreed with me recommending sessions twice a week instead of once. He provided some new methods I haven't had a chance to catch up with yet. He also brought up some old ones I've used before but wasn't sure would work in this situation." He glanced out the windows behind her. "I hope I'm not losing my skills. It's not like me to need assistance like this."

Mandy slid closer to Justin and put her arm around him. She kissed his cheek and leaned her head on his shoulder.

"Don't you think James Van Sessler ever asked anyone for help?" she asked. "Do you think he made it through fifty-plus years of being a therapist without seeking guidance from a mentor or mentors of his own?"

Justin tilted his neck enough so his cheek rested against the top of her head. "Do you remember Mary Alice?

"I remember that's what you called her, at least when you spoke with me about it." She lifted his hand and kissed it. "You're kind of paranoid about giving real names."

"I'll seek therapy for that," Justin joked. "Do you remember I diagnosed her with DID and treated her based on that diagnosis?"

Mandy sighed. "Yes. And that was over ten years ago when —"

"When I thought I knew *everything*. I saw the symptoms and jumped to the DID diagnosis. If I gave it a little more time, did a little more research, I would have diagnosed correctly that she was borderline and imitating DID. If I did, things might've turned out differently."

"Correct me if I'm wrong, but this was the wife of a wealthy hedge-fund manager. A woman who secretly met men online and had sex with them for money. She came to you because she'd find herself in hotel rooms or men's apartments and claim not to know how she got there. Am I right?"

"Yes."

"She had her upper-class, submissive wife from Greenwich, Connecticut personality and a, well, prostitute-like personality, as well. You had about three sessions before your diagnosis. *That* I remember."

"Great memory, as always. But that was the problem. I didn't catch on that she was imitating DID. Her supposed second personality was her way of avoiding responsibility for negative behavior. It was also compensation for an overwhelming desire of not being seen, to be invisible. These dynamics are found mostly in patients with a borderline or antisocial personality disorders. I should've treated her for that, not for DID."

"So what does that have to do with your current case?"

"It's one of the main reasons I met with Van Sessler today. I'm ninety-nine percent sure I'm dealing with DID. I just needed that additional one-percent reassurance. I kept thinking how Mary Alice ended up. Divorced, losing custody of her children and leaving me a voicemail that almost had me calling the Feds to be put into protective custody. I just want to be sure that my new patient doesn't have the same unsuccessful outcome."

"I am no expert on this topic, by *any* means, but from everything you've told me so far, I think you're on the right track. That's for you to decide, of course, but trust your instincts. And Van Sessler's. You've had ten years more experience since Mary Alice. Trust yourself, please."

Justin kissed her cheek. "I do trust myself. I'm really just venting. And I'll trust you. And Van Sessler, of course, who agrees with my assessment. I want to do everything I can to get it right and make sure this man lives a long and happy life. I know I can do it. I just need a little more time. The last thing I want to do is have him committed. Like I've said before, he'd most likely get lost in the system or maneuver his way out and never trust me again."

"I know you'll do everything you can. You've been in this situation before. You'll say you're at a loss or can't do something and then, lo and behold, you find a way to make it come to pass. That's what'll happen this time. Trust me. I know you better than you do."

He smiled and kissed her on the lips. "Yeah, that scares me, too!" He laughed. "By the way, who were you talking to when I was standing outside your door? You looked very upset. Do I need to beat up one of your clients?"

Mandy offered up a fake giggle and sat upright. "First of all, if I wanted someone to beat up one of my clients, it wouldn't be you."

"And why not? Look at these arms," Justin said, posing like a body builder.

Mandy smiled. "Exactly. You're too pretty to fight. I know a guy…" she said, now walking behind her desk.

Justin followed her and faced her from the other side. "I'm sure you do," he said. "No, really, is everything okay?"

"Yes, everything is okay. Like you have problems with your patients, I have problems with my clients. It's part of being a lawyer."

"And a great one at that." He leaned over the desk and kissed her cheek. "Gotta get back. I'll see you tonight. Hopefully before seven."

Mandy brushed his salt-and-pepper hair off his forehead and looked into his eyes. *Such a beautiful blue. Just like Dylan's. Just like Michael's.* At the thought of the son she'd hired Tom to find, a pang of guilt hit her in the chest.

"I'll be waiting." She kissed him back.

Falling into her chair, she watched Justin walk out the door and down the hallway. When he disappeared around the corner, she placed her hand on her chest and patted it, trying to calm herself down. Her assistant Maria stood up and headed toward her office, holding about ten manila folders.

"Keep it together, Mandy," she whispered to herself. "You're a professional."

She thought about her call with Tom again.

Yeah, a professional liar, she thought.

***

Justin observed Frank's movement and expression as he walked across the office to the chair in front of him. It was easy to see the stress and sadness in the boy's face and, most noticeably, his posture.

"Tell me how the meds are treating you. Do you feel better? Worse? Are there any side effects?"

Frank ran his fingers through his hair and let out a big breath from his mouth. "Actually, I've been feeling a bit better. Less stressed and anxious. The lost time thing is still happening, mostly at night, but it only happens a few times a week, and it's not any worse than it was."

"How are you doing at work? And how are you getting your school assignments completed with everything that's going on?"

"I'm doing okay. I'm pretty much myself all day at work. Not sure why. There are times when I feel a little 'out of it,' but I get back into what I was working on and slowly return to normal. I do most of my schoolwork during lunch and on the nights I don't have class and… well… those nights I don't lose time. I'm keeping it together as best I can."

Justin leaned forward and tried to remember the words he'd been rehearsing all day.

"Okay. That's good to hear. Now I have two options I'd like you to consider. The first option, and honestly, it's not *my* first choice but it *is* my responsibility to make you aware of it. You can visit a state-of-the-art facility for a few months so they can work with you on a daily basis. In no way does that mean I'd be giving up on you. I'd be in constant contact with the staff and psychiatrists so that once you leave, I can continue treatment from exactly that point."

Frank leaned on the arm of the chair, squirming like a worm trapped in flooded soil. "No way. I'm not going to an insane asylum! First of all, I have a job. I go to school. I have a life. I'm not giving all that up for something *you* say you can fix, even though I'm not so sure about that right now. Anyway, no one's gonna put me in a straitjacket or electrocute my brain!"

Justin patted Frank's knee and fell back in his chair. He smiled, hoping it would be reassuring.

"Okay, first of all, Frank, this isn't the 1940s. Electroshock treatment is nothing like what you've probably seen in the movies.

And I really don't think you'd even be a candidate for that. There are new antipsychotics and other meds that can be taken instead. As far as straitjackets go, restraints are used only when the patient is a danger to himself or others, which I don't think you, Frank, are. I'm not talking about an ancient insane asylum here, I'm talking about a facility that feels more like an upscale hotel. Insurance would cover a lot, but some of the money left to you by your grandfather could also help fund this."

Frank shook his head vigorously. "I won't be put away. I need you to try everything you can first. You're the only one I trust. I can't... I just can't let anyone else in yet." His voice quivered and tears filled his eyes. "I can't even imagine going to... I can't... I just..." He covered his face with his hands and started to cry.

Justin walked to the side of Frank's chair and took one of his hands in his. "Frank, I said there were *two* options. And I also said it wouldn't be my first choice. I just felt it was my obligation to let you know about it. The second option is continuing with me here, in this office, but coming two to three times a week. More frequent visits help, especially at the beginning of treatment. We can continue sessions in this room and see how things advance. If we both feel like there's significant progress, we'll continue down that road, okay?"

Frank squeezed Justin's fingers and wiped his eyes with his free hand. He nodded and sniffed as Justin took the tissue box off the side table and handed it to him.

Justin had expected this reaction, so once everything had calmed down, he continued his rehearsed words.

"Okay, now that that's settled, this is how we're going to proceed. As we've discussed before, issues like the one you're having are often caused by trauma, typically childhood trauma. We're going to have to get to the bottom of those wounds and heal them from the inside out." He waited for Frank to blow his nose and nod in acknowledgement. "So far, whenever we're at a point in our sessions where we get *close* to a trauma, another one of your alters appears and you leave. That's why we have to change things up a bit."

Frank swept away the hair that hung in front of his eyes.

"Which alter shows up? Is it the mean one?"

Justin wondered if he should allow the conversation to continue in this direction. He heeded his instinct. "What do you mean by 'mean'?"

"Well, I haven't met him, obviously," Frank started. "I just know he's been around because it takes me some time to get rid of all the anger and hatred he leaves behind."

We're getting somewhere here. Keep going.

"So are you saying that you, *Frank,* never feel anger or hatred?"

"Not really," he said, looking around as if waiting for an unknown presence to agree with him. "No, I don't."

"Hmmm. Don't most people you know get angry or sometimes have bad feelings toward others?"

"Yeah, they do."

"Then why don't you?"

Frank scratched his head, then shrugged his shoulders.

"Could it be," Justin said, treading carefully, "that you found someone else to feel those feelings for you?"

"That sounds kinda stupid. Why wouldn't I just put up with them myself so I don't have to go through this whole 'alter' thing and ruin my life?"

"And *that*, my friend, is the question of the day... actually of the year. There's something holding you back. Something making you feel like you, Frank, are not allowed to have those negative feelings. We're going to find out what that something is."

Frank groaned. "God, I hope so."

"I know so. Now, as I started to say before, we're going to change things up a bit. You might think it's peculiar, but it'll help us get to where we need to go. I'm going to move my chair catty-corner to yours and you're going to keep your hand on your chair arm. If we get to a point where you, Frank, feel the need to hide, I will grab your hand. It helps to keep you here with me. I won't ever hit you or hurt you in any way. I will only take your hand and squeeze it so that you'll stay in the moment, with me. And hopefully stay as Frank."

He looked into Frank's eyes, and the unhappiness he saw hurt him. It wasn't because of what Justin just said, he realized, but it was because he had to say it in the first place. This young man just wanted to be enjoying his life the way other men his age were enjoying theirs, not sitting in a shrink's office trying to rid himself of multiple personalities.

For a brief moment, Justin pictured Dylan sitting before him. The thought of his son going through something like this caused a swelling in his throat that could easily make his eyes fill with tears.

He held them back by reminding himself that Dylan had parents to help him through it. Frank had no one. Not one soul. *I'm going to help this kid if it's the last thing I do.*

"Sound good?" he asked.

Frank nodded.

Justin moved his chair closer and at an angle to his. He took Frank's hand and placed it on the edge of the chair's arm. Frank gazed at his hand, lifted it once, apparently to ensure it still belonged to him, and then set it back down.

"I'd like to start with your father and what you remember about him," Justin said. "The first thing that comes to mind."

"Matches," Frank blurted out.

"Why matches?"

"You know those stem matchbooks, they're made of like, stiff paper, and you flip open the top and the matches are standing there like soldiers or something?"

"Yes, I know them."

"Larry would flick them at me. He loved his matches."

"Larry is your father, I presume?"

Frank blinked hard and nodded.

"And what do you mean he'd 'flick' matches at you?"

"I'd be watching television or doing homework and he would hold the matchbook in one hand and the match in the other. He'd hold the end that ignited against the book with his index finger and aim it at me. Then he'd slide it along the black part that lights the match and flick it so the lit match would hit me."

"Where would it hit you?"

"Anywhere. My head, my face, my back. One time I was watching TV and it landed on my shirt and burned a hole in it. I didn't even know it at first until I felt it burning my stomach. When I tried to get it off me, it fell on the couch and it burned a small hole in the cushion." Frank scratched his fingers along the edge of the chair arm. "He beat the shit out of me for that."

Justin tried his hardest to hold back his disgust. "How old were you at the time?"

"I don't know, seven... eight."

Holy shit. Justin had patients with troubled childhoods before, but this was something else.

"And did your mother know about this?"

"Evelyn? Ha! That's a good one. She'd be sitting right next to me, drinking some kind of booze out of a filthy glass. Fingerprints and dark red lipstick all over them. 'Larry! Cut the shit before you burn the house down!' That's what she'd yell at him, usually, while her eyes were glued to the television or some tabloid she stole from the grocery store."

"Was he drinking when he flicked these matches at you?"

"No. Flicking matches was his *fun*, I guess. He really only got drunk when he was out with his friends at a bar... which was pretty much every night. He'd be so wasted when he got home, he couldn't stand long enough to torture me."

Justin glanced at Frank's hand to make sure it was still close enough to grab hold of. "Do you have any idea why he would do that to a seven-year-old child?"

"I can only guess. See, we weren't poor. At least not until Larry got killed in a DWI... and guess whose fault *that* was? Anyway, I think he was pissed about my trust fund. His father had a lot of money and would only give Larry some when he asked for it. And then he tells my parents there's a trust fund for *me* which would probably be worth millions one day and they could never touch it. Larry should've taken his anger out on his father, but he took it out on me instead, I guess."

You probably guessed right. What shit parents. Growing up in that household was one huge trauma-fest.

But Justin knew there was more.

"One question, before we continue. Why do you call your parents by their first names, rather than —"

Frank flinched. "Rather than what? Dad and Mom? You mean like normal kids who have parents who give a shit about them? If I called them Shithead One and Shithead Two, you wouldn't know who I was talking about. So I use their first names instead to make it easier for you to understand. Does that answer your question?"

Justin pursed his lips and a offered quick nod of understanding.

"It certainly does," he said while jotting a few notes. " And I'm sure flicking matches wasn't all you had to put up with," he said sympathetically.

Frank bobbed his head in agreement, his expression glum, his eyes darting in all directions — an indication to Justin that he was done talking about his father.

"So you're ten years old and it's just you and your mother. Do things change much between the two of you?"

Frank's eyes seemed to get a tad darker and larger, his lips a slice thinner and his cheeks a tiny bit wider than they were just a few seconds before. Recognizing these transformations from the last time Nathan made his appearance, Justin took hold of his hand and squeezed it hard.

"Stay with me, Frank. Look at me. I need you to stay with me." He made his voice loud but not authoritative. He wanted Frank to trust him immediately, not fear him. Hopefully that would stop him from switching alters.

Frank stared at the hand on top of his.

"Look at me, Frank. Please, just look at me."

He obeyed, and although the merciless look in his eyes almost terrified Justin, he didn't let go of Frank's hand.

And then Frank yanked his hand away and puffed out his chest. Justin knew it was now Nathan who sat beside him.

"Are you kidding me with this?" Nathan's attitude of superiority was almost palpable in his smug tone, and even more so when he broke into laughter. "How many times do I have to say it? I'm not going away and even if he tries to make me, he'll be sorry he did."

Justin stood, slowly lifted his chair and moved it across from Nathan. He sat down and stared into Nathan's eyes without saying a word. The young man stared back like they were playing a game of chicken.

Justin wasn't up for games. "What do you mean, 'he'll be sorry he did,' Nathan?"

Nathan hung his head and shook it like a rag doll. When he looked back up, he was smiling from ear to ear. "Who did this coward turn to when Daddy slapped him silly 'til he cried like a girl? Where do you think he went when that pedophile Carl came into his room every night? Or those times that shitbag took him to his balding buddy's farmhouse out in Pennsylvania for a threesome?"

Justin didn't wince though this revelation made his stomach spiral to the point of nausea.

Nathan crept toward the edge of his chair. "He came to *me*." he hissed. "He ran to *me*! And he *still* runs to me! He's too much of a wuss to stand up for himself, so I do it for him. Get rid of me and this namby-pamby is toast. And if I were you, I'd leave the whole thing alone."

A chill crawled up the back of Justin's neck. This was the second time during this session Nathan had intimated revenge. Was this a true or veiled threat? Was he just trying to be intimidating? "Is that a threat, Nathan?"

"I already told you, Dr. Wrong, I'm too smart to make threats. I'm just sayin' that I need to protect myself. I got nothing against you personally. This wimp came to see you, not the other way around. So you're just doing your job… not very well, obviously. Just make sure it stays that way or he's in for a big surprise."

Nathan jumped up and sauntered toward the office door.

"By the way, doc," he said, grabbing his coat off the hook, "if he ever does come back for more of your pathetic help, make sure you ask him who it was who made that piece of shit uncle pay for what he did." He glanced around the room as if to be certain they were alone and continued, "I'll give you a hint: only one of us was man enough to watch that old bugger's eyeballs bulge out of his face while he swung from that rope." He headed toward the door, then abruptly stopped and turned around. "No one ever did take care of that Pennsylvania putz... yet. And I know he's still around. But trust me, he'll get what's coming to him. It's never too late when it comes to revenge."

Revenge reference number three.

Before walking out, he gave Justin a big smile, cupped his hand and moved it stiffly from side to side, like the Queen of England.

When the door closed, Justin fell back, his head tilting toward the ceiling.

"Holy shit," he whispered into the silence. "Just, holy shit."

CHAPTER 8

The train cab's lights were flickering and Justin's eyes burned. Fluorescent lighting always irritated them, but tonight they stung to the point of pain. Still, he tried keeping his focus on the laptop screen, forging ahead as best he could. Despite the lights, sharp turns and strong woody sage-scented cologne worn by the large man behind him, any one of which threatened to make him sick to his stomach, he had to get to the bottom of what he'd just witnessed in his office.

He started his Google search with "Larry Devlin," hoping that Frank hadn't lied and Larry was truly his father's name. Unfortunately, it seemed to be a common name. Scrolling down, he skimmed the results and didn't see anything that might somehow relate to Frank. When he hit the bottom of the page, he clicked "next," and at the top of page two was an obituary for a Larry Devlin in Hartsdale. He clicked on it, scanned quickly and stopped on a phrase that both delighted and made him queasy at the same time: '...leaves behind his devoted wife Evelyn and loving son, Frank.'

"Loving? You gotta be kidding me," Justin whispered.

Okay, so this was a good sign. Frank had been honest about his parents' names. Now he had to discover who this Uncle Carl was and what had actually happened to him. Had Nathan told a lie to rattle Justin so he'd stay away from Frank, or did he indeed make this pedophile pay for his behavior with his life?

A deeper search into Larry Devlin indicated he was an only child. Justin presumed this was the reason Frank inherited money from his grandfather – a man who, for whatever reason, didn't like his son enough to leave him his fortune.

That meant Uncle Carl was Evelyn's brother. Justin opened Frank's intake form and scrolled to the spot where his mother's maiden name was requested. And there it was: *Paige*.

"Bingo!" Justin said aloud. He didn't look around to see who might be staring at him. He didn't really care. He was getting closer to the finish line of a search he thought would take a lot longer than a train ride home.

He typed the words "Carl Paige death" and the third result reported that a man who lived in Queens, New York had died, as the headline read, an "unnatural death." Justin clicked to read more and saw a photo of Carl Paige in an article from *The Daily News*. The caption read, *Man found hanged*. Paige's appearance made it seem as though the photo was taken posthumously — emaciated cheeks exaggerated by dark, oversized eyes; long, uneven teeth, their yellowish tint evident through the heavily pixelated, black and white image on his screen. From the arms around both sides of his neck and a lone ear from someone standing on Paige's left side, Justin figured the picture must've been taken at a party or maybe even a family get together. Was Nathan hiding somewhere in the background of the gathering? Waiting? Scheming?

Revenge.

The article, five years old, presented the police as on the hunt for clues and denying any criminal activity until solid evidence surfaced. Authorities deemed Carl Paige's death a "probable suicide," yet they were not ruling out foul play.

Nathan's words clamored inside his head: "only one of us was man enough to watch that old bugger's eyeballs bulge out of his face while he swung from that rope." And now Justin was staring into those eyeballs, feeling seasick, unsure whether his nausea was from the man on the screen gawking at him or that Nathan was telling the truth about what he'd done.

Justin forced himself to continue reading. The article said the man had been found hanging from a beam in his living room. It appeared he — or someone else — had cut through the ceiling to expose a stud and wrapped one end of a rope around it. The other end was knotted into a noose. A bridge chair was found on its side below his body and a cigarette, with an ash about two inches long, dangled from his lips.

Justin kept searching for more information. Was there a formal investigation? Did they ever close the case? Did they decide if it was suicide or murder? He scrolled and clicked and scrolled some more only to find nothing. Not one single update on the death of Carl Paige.

That's pretty strange, he thought at first. Then, *Hmmm, maybe not.*

If the cops really gave a shit, they would have investigated this case a lot further. But after talking with neighbors and going through his possessions and website visits, they probably figured out who and what this guy was. They most likely decided his demise was best for himself and society in general.

How did someone die with a cigarette in his mouth, much less a two-inch ash hanging from its filter? If the cigarette was in Carl's mouth before he kicked the chair away, the snap of his neck when he dropped would have caused it to fall to the floor, even if he'd been holding it between his teeth.

Justin envisioned it, a movie in his mind that he couldn't pause. It started with Nathan breaking into Paige's apartment while he wasn't home. He used a jab saw to expose the stud, tied the rope around it and knotted the noose. He then sat in the dark, waiting for Paige to return home. When he did, he surprised the old man and threw him into the chair, the noose hanging above his head.

Hardly knowing Nathan, but having twice observed the hatred that filled his being, Justin couldn't believe for a moment that he killed Uncle Carl right away. No, he possibly held a knife or gun to the man's gut, forced him to stand on the chair and slip the noose around his own neck. "I'll let you live if you do what I say," he probably teased. Then he made Carl tighten the rope himself while Nathan tested the strength of the stud. He probably yelled a bit, called him names, made him beg for his life, and when Nathan felt fulfilled by scaring the living shit out of his abuser, he kicked the chair out from beneath the old man's feet.

Did he laugh as Uncle Carl's legs flailed in midair? Did he continue to call him names as his tormenter gasped for his last breath? Did he say "tick tock" as the man swayed back and forth like a pendulum? Justin didn't know. He couldn't know, but his insides were certain of one thing: when the man stopped moving, Nathan waited for a couple of hours for rigor mortis to set in. Then he lit a cigarette, took a long drag, turned the bridge chair upright again so he could stand on it and stuck the cancer stick between the man's stiffening lips. Kicking the chair back on its side, he crossed his arms and nodded, pleased at the skill with which he executed his plan.

Maybe he waved goodbye to Uncle Carl the way he'd waved goodbye to Justin about an hour ago. Maybe he sat down on the sofa and commended himself for a job well done. Maybe he brought Frank to the forefront of his mind so he could see how a real man gets revenge. Whatever he did, Justin had no doubt that Nathan had killed his uncle.

But did it matter? He wasn't going to call the authorities because he didn't have proof. And if they did reopen the case and arrested Nathan for murder, that meant Frank and Matthew would also go to jail for a crime neither of them committed. The images running through Justin's head of what might happen to this kid if sent to prison peaked his anxiety. He slammed his laptop closed and leaned his head against the train seat's headrest.

"I won't let that happen," he whispered. "Not on my watch."

***

It was rare for Mandy to have business in Manhattan and even more uncommon for proceedings to finish early. But it had happened, by 2:50 on a Monday afternoon, and that was typically around Dylan's downtime, so she decided to surprise him with a visit. She requested an Uber to pick her up at the courthouse. The walk from Centre Street to Dylan's apartment on West 11th would be less than two miles, but today's temperature was below freezing and Mandy simply despised the cold.

She worried he might feel this visit was an intrusion, but as she walked out of the courthouse, she fought to push those thoughts from her mind. All day, an undercurrent of anxiety coursed through her veins and she couldn't determine why. The only thing she did know was that she needed to see Dylan's face and hug him as tightly as she could. That thought was the only thing that seemed to take the edge off her agitation.

At first she thought her nervousness might be because she was in Manhattan, where she lost a piece of her life, where a psychopath stole her son and almost destroyed her family. But she'd become stronger over the years. *Strong enough,* she thought with pride, *to visit this city with only slight panic instead of a nervous breakdown.*

When the car reached the apartment, she got out, stood close to the sidewalk and observed the brownstone from a distance. Mandy had always admired the classic appearance of these buildings, the history they contained, generations of people who climbed the thick sandstone steps and held the wrought iron railings.

She still adored the classic Colonial in which she and Justin lived. It was close enough to downtown Westchester, but far enough from the city center to offer the privacy and suburban feel she'd always sought. The house had been the perfect size for the four of them. Dylan and Michael had their rooms on one side, allowed to do pretty much as they pleased. She and Justin were on the other, a secluded retreat of sorts. Yet once Michael was gone, Mandy felt like the house had grown. It became enormous, too big for just the three of them.

With the cold biting at the tip of her nose, she dashed toward the brownstone and up the steps, where she knocked twice on the door. "Be home, Dylan," she whispered and glanced at her watch. It read 2:35. "Please, be home."

After a few seconds without a response to her light tap, her heart dropped. She removed her glove and knocked again, harder this time. As she slipped her glove back on, she heard footsteps from inside and her heart beat quickly with excitement.

When the door opened, she saw to her surprise that the man who answered her knock wasn't Dylan. It wasn't even Kyle. He was about Dylan's age with big brown eyes, a full head of thick, razor-cut brown hair and a very inviting smile.

"Can I help you?" he asked.

It took a few moments, but as Mandy's mind cleared a bit more, things started to make sense.

"I'm sorry, you must be Alex," Mandy said, holding out her gloved hand.

He hesitantly reached out his own and shook hers. "Yeah, you got me. I'm Alex. And you are?"

Mandy pulled the leather messenger bag, heavy with file folders and papers, higher up her shoulder. "I'm sorry. My name is Mandy. Mandy Wright. I'm Dylan's mom."

Alex's face lit up. "Holy sh…! Oops, sorry. Come in! And let me take that bag."

He grabbed the messenger bag and placed it on the chair in the foyer. Mandy followed him into the living room, where they both stood, simply looking at one another. His eyes appeared even larger and rounder than they had in the doorway, and Mandy felt his facial expression was a bit *off*. It held a trace of "*Finally!*", as if they were supposed to have met many times before and she'd cancelled the plans.

Why is he looking at me that way?

She shoved her gloves in her coat pocket and rubbed her hands together. The apartment was warm, at least warmer than outside, and the air held a light scent of plug-in room deodorizer — Fresh Scent fragrance, Dylan's favorite.

"Please sit down," Alex said, pointing to one of the two chairs. "Can I get you some water or tea? Coffee or something else?"

Mandy sat down without taking off her coat. The chill from outside was stuck inside her bones and she wanted it gone before even considering removing her scarf. And despite the comforting fragrance, there was something in the room that made her uncomfortable. Was it Alex with his peculiar attitude of familiarity? The odd silence hanging between the two of them, the quiet for which she knew her anxiety was to blame? Was it all the dilapidated furniture that looked like it was bought at a garage sale? She'd seen a number of times before, but today it felt like a jagged thorn in her side. She couldn't put her finger on what was really bothering her, but whatever it was, it deepened the chill inside of her. For a quick second she considered leaving, but the thought of Dylan walking through the front door made her stay.

"No, thank you. I was really hoping to surprise Dylan. I was in the city and know that Thursdays are a light day for him, so I thought he might be home. But from the lack of noise, or should I say music, I'm assuming he's not here?"

"No," Alex replied. "It's just me. Which is kind of rare since I'm hardly ever here. I just stopped in to… to…" He glanced around the room and rested his gaze on a pile of books. "I came by to pick up some books."

He's lying. First he had to think up a reason why he was in his own home, and now his right foot was tapping against the rug like hummingbird wings.

He sat down, at first reclining against the back of the chair and then, as if an electric prod had jolted him from behind, sitting straight up.

"Are you okay?" Mandy asked.

"Fine," he replied and scooted further toward the edge of the chair. "Back problems. They get worse in the cold weather."

"I'm sorry to hear that," she responded, trying as hard as she could to sound like she believed his excuse.

She settled on her chair and looked him in his eyes. He looked directly back. The weird feeling she had since she arrived grew as she realized his expression wasn't that of a person seeking conversation, but more of someone observing a painting in an art gallery.

Through the vexing tapping of his foot, the silence stretched. There were moments when his expression appeared stern, as though he were about to accuse her of something, and then a second or two later he'd offer a timid smile.

"Do you also go to NYU?" she asked, already knowing the answer but wanting to say *something*.

"No, Fordham. Business Analytics." Alex's expression softened, but his foot tapped even faster. Mandy hadn't thought that was even possible. "I guess Dylan didn't tell you much about me."

She thought carefully about how to respond. Something was up with this kid and she didn't know what kind of fire she played with. His tapping foot, the way he acted so chummy one minute and then distant the next, his obvious lie as to why he was in the apartment. They all created a fleeting moment of fear and she wondered if she might be in danger.

"Yes, of course he did. He was very excited. He said you were the perfect roommate. I'm sorry. I just came from court and my mind is in too many places. Did you grow up in New York?"

Alex shuffled in his seat, shifting from his left side to his right and then back to his left. Not once did he lean against the back of the chair and at least pretend to relax.

Mandy decided to stop his obvious distress in its tracks. "I'm sorry," she said. "I didn't mean to pry."

Alex's grimace faded. She noticed how his lips seemed thinner, somehow, than she remembered when she first entered the apartment, and his cheeks wider, as if they'd expanded. He shook his head and blinked a few times.

Jesus. He's got strange things going on inside and *outside his head.*

"No worries," he blurted out almost unintelligibly. "That's not prying. It's a simple question. I come from out of town and a family I don't like… well, I'm not proud to talk about. I guess that's why I get a little weird when people ask me where I'm from." He let a big puff of air out his mouth and the swelling in his cheeks seemed to lessen. "I'm sorry."

"Oh, please. There's no need to apologize," she said. *Justin would have a field day with this one.* "We all have our pasts and things we'd rather not talk about — or even remember. Do you want to hear about how every kid in junior high called me Candy Mandy for years because I always had a piece of candy in my mouth? M&Ms, Milk Duds, Tootsie Rolls, you name it, I was eating it. And to make matters worse, I was overweight. They had names to call me for that, too."

Mandy laughed, but stopped when she realized Alex wasn't doing the same. He actually appeared confused, as if she'd just told a joke in a foreign language. Then his expression turned annoyed. *Yikes. Coming here was a mistake. I should make up an excuse and go.*

"That wasn't very nice of them. Although there are worse things to go through in life than being called Candy Mandy." His look of annoyance turned to a smile, and he laughed. "Although it is pretty funny, when you think about it. Can I ask what your middle name is?"

Is he just curious or is he leading up to something? A few more words with him and she'd leave.

"Patricia. Why?"

"Fatty Patty," he replied.

That was *exactly* the other name they used to call her in Junior High.

"Wow, you're good." Leaning back in her chair, Mandy tilted her head and looked him straight in the eye. "Why do I get the feeling you knew that already? I mean, the name they called me?"

Alex chuckled and stopped tapping his foot. "Deduction, Mrs. Wright."

"Mandy," she said. "Please, call me Mandy."

"Okay, Mandy. You said you were overweight. There's really just one overarching word that describes that situation, and it's the same word that's so easily rhymable with Pat or Patty."

"Very astute. So, how did you know it was Patty and not Pat?"

"Which sounds wittier? Which name would be more hurtful to a young girl already mad at herself for being overweight and sad that she's never been on a date or can't stop eating candy, or, I'm guessing, pizza and donuts? 'Fat Pat' is too short and curt. They had to drag it out just a little more to make you feel worse about yourself."

She felt the gut punch of someone calling her that name all over again, for the first time since high school. A lump worked its way into her throat and she had to swallow hard.

"Wow, you're good, Alex. Very perceptive. You sure you should be going to school for business and not psychology?"

Alex shook his head vehemently. "I have enough issues. The last thing I need is to know where my issues come from and how to, quote, 'work through them.' I'll leave the mind analysis to your psychiatrist husband."

"Oh, how did you know my husband was a psychiatrist?"

After a brief pause, Alex stood up. "Dylan told me. I think it was when we first met. We all pretty much gave our backgrounds and he told me about you and your husband."

Shit. He's lying again.

She heard footsteps coming up the stairs and a sense of relief swept over her like a refreshing ocean breeze. They both waited in silence as the front door creaked open, then closed with an even louder creak. Kyle turned the corner from the foyer into the living room. Though Mandy still felt relieved, disappointment flooded her entire body.

"Kyle!" she shouted, trying to hide the internal blow that he wasn't Dylan. She jumped up, darted toward him and gave him a hug so tight she was scared she'd crack a rib — either hers or his, she wasn't sure and didn't care. It felt like years since she'd seen him and his presence gave her a sense of comfort. It also gave her a break from Alex. One more second alone with him and she might've said something she'd regret.

She grabbed Kyle's arms and held him out in front of her like he was a dress she was deciding whether or not to buy. "It's been too long," she said. "Way too long. You look a little thin, but I don't want to sound too much like a meddlesome mom, so I'll leave it at that! How *are* you?"

Kyle kissed her cheek, slipped off his coat and threw it on the sofa. "I'm fine, Mandy. I'm fine. It's great to see you."

He turned to Alex and nodded. "I see you met Alex. Great guy, though I think I'm more surprised to see *him* here than *you*! He's like a ghost of a roommate." He laughed. "How are *you,* Mandy, and why are you here? Not that this isn't an amazing surprise."

She walked back to the chair, but still didn't take off her coat. "I was in the city for once — a deposition at the courthouse — and I wanted to surprise Dylan. For some reason I thought Thursday was a light day for him."

"It is. That's why he picked up a shift at Starbucks. He texted me this morning so I wouldn't wait for him to have dinner. I wish we knew you were in the city, we would've planned something." Kyle turned to Alex. "Did you offer Mrs. Wright here anything to eat or drink or did you grow up in a barn?"

Mandy spoke before he had a chance to respond. "Yes, Kyle. Alex is very polite and has very good manners." She hoped to leave this situation with a smile on Alex's face. "So don't tease him. Like I said, this was just a surprise visit. I'm not going to stay. But I did get lucky! I got to see you and I was also finally able to meet Alex."

She smiled at him. Alex returned the smile with what seemed more like a smirk. No surprise there. She stood and walked toward the front hallway to grab her bag. She pulled her phone from her pocket and ordered an Uber.

"Uber will be here in three," she said and kissed Kyle's cheek. "It was so great to see you, and I'm going to insist that Dylan bring you out to the house so you can have some real home-cooked food and we can catch up on *everything*."

"Well, I'm sorry you missed him," Kyle said, pulling the strap of the bag higher up her shoulder. "And I *know* he'll be sorry he missed you. I'll talk to Dylan about coming for a visit. I miss hanging out with you and your hubby."

"We miss it, too, Kyle," she said softly. "We really do."

She placed her palm on his cheek and felt the soft skin beneath his stubble. She'd known him since he was five years old and loved him almost as much as one of her own sons. They'd seen him at least once a day, if not more, until the day they lost Michael. After that, everything changed and...

A car horn sounded from the street.

"I'm off!" she said and kissed him on the cheek again. "Love you and see you soon."

"Same here, Mandy. Be safe."

She waved behind her as she ran down the steps, opened the car door and jumped into the back seat.

"Grand Central, please. But then, you already knew that." She was still getting the hang of ordering a ride on Uber rather than catching a taxi.

The driver was an older Asian man with a black scarf wound around his neck and vintage tweed newsboy cap tilted on his head. "Yes, ma'am. Times have changed."

"Yes, they have," she replied as she speed-dialed Justin.

Voicemail.

"Hey, babe. It's me. On my way back from the city. Couldn't see you because I wanted to surprise Dylan. Long story short, I met his new roommate. You have to meet this kid. I'll get into more later, but I'm not sure whether I like him or want to slap him. I'll leave you with that. Love you. Bye."

Mandy glanced into the rearview mirror and noticed the driver looking at her. She offered a smile and a subtle nod.

"Hope you don't mind I say you a very pretty woman. I, myself, a happy married man. But when I see beautiful woman, I think she should know. I hope not out of line or improper in any way. If yes, apologies."

"No apology necessary. Thank you very much."

She slipped on her Ray-Bans and looked out the window at the pedestrians walking up the avenue.

Fatty Patty, my ass.

CHAPTER 9

"Something's off with him, Justin," Mandy whispered into her cell phone.

Justin could hear the warning beeps of the closing train doors in the background. That answered the question he was about to ask as to why she was speaking so low. He waited for the beeps to stop.

"What do you mean, 'off'?"

"I can't say for sure what it is. There were times he seemed perfectly fine. He'd say normal things, with a normal expression on his face. Everything would be, like I said, normal. And then he'd... I don't know... change in some way. It was weird. Very unnerving. And I just don't like it."

Justin leaned back in his desk chair and looked at the clock on the wall. It was just past 4:30 and he wanted to get his folders sorted and put away before Frank, Matthew, Nathan or someone else he hadn't met yet arrived in a half hour.

"Mandy, slow down. You met him just once. Dylan and Kyle have been living with him for a while. I think if something was wrong, they'd know it by now. They're grownups. You have to have some faith that they can read a person well enough to make the right decision, don't you think?"

Silence.

"Mandy? Don't you think?"

"Yes," she agreed after more hesitation. "But I want you to meet him anyway. I want to know if you see what I see. Or at least feel what I felt when I was with him."

Justin glanced at the clock again. Time was slipping away.

"Absolutely, hon. I will meet him. Maybe we can have the three of them out to the house. Or meet up at a restaurant in the city. When I get home tonight, we'll discuss it. Right now, I have to get ready for a not-so-normal conversation of my own."

Mandy laughed. "I hear you. I'd supposed you don't have many normal conversations during the day, do you, my dear?"

"We won't go there, *my dear*. This is my job, my profession, and I love it… no matter how normal or abnormal it might get."

"Okay, I'll let you go. Good luck. Call me when you're on your way home."

"Love you," he said, files in hand as he headed toward the cabinet.

"You more," she replied.

Justin smiled, hung up and set his cellphone on the desk. As he placed the files alphabetically inside the cabinet, he rolled his eyes in amusement. *Mandy thinks* Alex *isn't normal? She thinks* Alex *changes in the midst of a conversation? If only she could experience one of Frank's sessions.*

He'd done a lot more in-depth research in the two days since his last session with Frank, including talking with a few colleagues he hadn't spoken with in years. What he learned felt counterintuitive and a bit disturbing.

Right now he had two alters who were being as helpful as they could, but couldn't seem to muster enough self-confidence and inner strength to overpower the third, more malevolent alter. The solution, some of his associates insisted, was not to keep Nathan out of the sessions, but to invite him in. They believed that since he was the most influential of the three, he was the alter who held the genuine and primary reason behind why Frank's alters existed in the first place.

Sure, Frank knew some of the experiences that had caused the trauma. And Matthew, well, he was a by-product of those events. But Nathan appeared to be the force that was developed to battle the aftermath. If Justin could get him to talk and free himself of the exhaustive protective behavior and constant defensiveness, he might be able to calm Nathan's rage just enough to make progress.

At a knock on the door, Justin looked at the clock again. *He's early. Odd for Frank. He's usually...*

Before Justin had the chance to say "Come in," the door opened. With a scarf wrapped around the young man's head and the same womanish cloak he'd worn to his last visit buttoned up to his neck, Justin immediately recognized Matthew.

"It's freezing out there," he said, hugging himself with gloved hands and rubbing his arms through the cloak.

"And I hear it's going to get colder," Justin replied.

"I heard the same thing."

Justin grabbed his journal and walked toward his chair. Just then, he decided to test Matthew's reaction to confrontation. It would show him if Matthew would challenge Nathan's aversion to staying in-session after he'd shown up so Justin could further the conversation and delve deeper into the trauma.

"By the way, Matthew, you never know if I might have another patient in here. So next time, please use the bell outside and allow me time to let you in, okay?"

Matthew hung his head as he placed his cloak on the hook and stuffed his gloves into its pockets. He shamefully crept over to the chair, humiliation covering his face.

Oh shit. If this is how he reacts to a benign request, what is he going to do if I push him?

"Okay, Matthew?"

Matthew shook his head. His eyes were tearing up as he sat and crossed his legs. He stared down and used his middle finger to pick at his knee through his tight jeans.

"Why are you so upset?" Justin pushed.

"I had a very difficult day and wanted to talk with you about it and now you're…"

"Now I'm what?"

"You're… you're being sort of mean."

Careful, Justin. Take it slowly.

"Mean? I'm sorry. In what way was I being mean?"

Matthew kept picking at his knee until a tiny thread appeared. He tried to grab it with his fingernails. "Just mean. Not nice."

"I still don't understand. I simply asked that you wait until I say it's okay to enter the office. You wouldn't want someone walking in on you while you were talking with me, would you?"

Matthew shook his head, still not looking up.

"Please look at me, Matthew."

He lifted his head and Justin's heart hurt when he saw a tear running down the boy's cheek. By the way he could barely look at someone who was the least bit harsh, it was obvious Matthew had nothing to offer when it came to handling Nathan. He was weak for a reason, and Justin had to discover why he existed in the first place.

"I apologize if I hurt your feelings. I like you and I respect you. I would never do anything to purposely make you feel bad, okay?"

Justin felt as if he were talking to a five-year-old. Perhaps he was.

"Okay," Matthew replied, using the arm of his oversized maroon sweater to wipe away the tear.

"Now tell me why today was so difficult. What happened?"

Matthew twisted in his chair so that Justin faced his back. He lifted his sweater and the loose tee-shirt beneath to expose deep scratches along both his sides.

What the hell is this? Justin struggled to not ask the question aloud.

Resembling railroad tracks, the scratches began at the shoulder blades and trailed down to just above his hips. By the scabbing and redness of the skin, they appeared deeper at the top and became more shallow and thinner as they reached the lower part of his back.

Justin stood and looked more closely at the marks to ensure there was no infection. The thought passed through his mind of touching them and inquiring about the pain level, but he decided not to. Matthew was too fragile, and simply placing a finger on him might cause damage to their already delicate relationship.

He backed up to his chair, sat again and crossed his legs.

"As you can imagine," Justin began, "my first question is 'how did that happen?'"

"I don't know," Matthew replied, lowering his sweater and turning toward him. "I mean, I really don't know. I woke up this morning and it hurt. It felt like my back was sticking to the sheets. When I turned on the lights, I saw blood on the pillow. I freaked out and ran into the bathroom. When I looked in the mirror and saw the scratches, I freaked out even more."

"Where were you last night?"

Matthew glanced around the office like he always did before bringing up Nathan's name.

"I can't remember. But I think Nathan was out somewhere, brought a girl back with him and things got rough." He crossed his arms and leaned forward. "I mean, I've done things I'm not proud of. And I've had things done to me that have caused pain. A *lot* of pain. But I never woke up with blood on the sheets. This *has* to be Nathan's fault."

A jolt of excitement shot through Justin. It was the first time Matthew appeared to be identifying himself with Nathan.

"So, are you saying Nathan was having sex with a woman and things got out of hand?"

Matthew shook his head. "That's all I can come up with." He snuck another darting look around the office. "And I think he was banging her so hard, she scratched his back and made him bleed. Not out of pleasure, but out of pain so he would stop."

Okay, now's the time. Push him just enough to get Nathan in here.

"So if Nathan was having rough sex, rough enough to have a woman claw his back hard enough to make it bleed, how come *you* have the scratches on your back?"

Matthew let out a cough that sounded like he was choking. Within seconds his jowls grew puffy and his eyes dark. His lips narrowed and the skin on his face turned beet red.

Nathan was back.

"What the fuck is wrong with you?" he shouted. "You're asking this girly fag what it's like to screw a woman? You think he knows how hard a girl likes it and whether she's crying with pleasure or pain? Trust me, this ain't the guy you should be asking. He's too busy taking it up the…"

"Nathan!" Justin shouted back, stopping the rant in its tracks.

His hope of confusing Matthew enough to bring Nathan to the forefront had been realized. Now it was time to take his colleague's advice.

"I was hoping you'd come here today. I really wanted to have a one-on-one with you."

Nathan twisted his head to the side and let out a huge sigh. "Jesus Christ, you just don't get it. I already told you I don't want *anyone* coming to see you. You think I want to be here right now? Well, I don't. But I *have* to. I can't leave anything up to those other idiots. I've told you once and I'll tell you again, anyone who tries to get rid of me is going to pay a price." He shook his head vigorously. "Why the fuck doesn't anyone understand that?"

So now he's not just threatening Frank, he's threatening Matthew, too. If I can't get to him now, I have no choice but to have him committed.

Shit.

"I *do* understand that, Nathan. And trust me, I'd rather none of you had to be here either. But there are things that happened in the past that brought Frank here... and in turn, brought *you* here. If we can get to the bottom of it, none of you will ever have to come back here again."

Nathan stared at him without saying a word.

"Imagine," Justin said, "you look at your texts and they refer to you as Frank. You wake up with blood on your sheets and you have no idea how it got there. Or you lose minutes, hours or days at a time. Wouldn't you want to find out what the hell was going on?"

Nathan snickered sarcastically, almost snorting. "You don't think I deal with that every day? It's part of life, doc. It's the way it's always been and the way it has to be. Change it up and we're screwed."

"Change what up?"

Nathan rolled his eyes. "Let me see if I can put it in a way you'll understand." He looked to the ceiling like a good idea might appear like an angel from heaven. "Okay, so today the sun rises in the east and sets in the west. Let's say some giant force of energy changes that and makes the sun rise in the west and set in the east. What would happen to the people on earth? The planet itself?"

Justin waited.

"Everything would go crazy! That's what would happen. Every living thing would go insane, if the planet didn't spin the wrong way and throw everyone off first. You see, the sun rising in the east and setting in the west is the way things are supposed to be. They're the way nature and the universe intended. This thing? This thing between me, Frank and those other shitheads? It's the way nature and the universe intended. Try to change it and we will all spin away into unknown parts of space. Sad to say, I'm the only one who can stop that from happening. Make sense now?"

"Actually, no, Nathan. It doesn't make sense. Would you like to know why I don't buy your reasoning?"

Nathan leaned back and grimaced. Justin guessed he'd rubbed the scratches against the chair. He laughed inside — it'd serve the jerk right to feel some of the pain he'd caused — as Nathan quickly, but as casually as possible, sat forward again.

"Oh, I'd *love* to know why! Go ahead, share your wisdom, Dr. Wrong."

The sarcasm hit Justin like a jackhammer, but he forced himself to continue. This might be his final opportunity to get through Nathan's formidable armor.

"Because it's so much work," he said softly. "I think you're scared that if I did help 'change things up', you wouldn't exist. It doesn't matter how many times I tell you that wouldn't be the case. You'll never believe me. So you keep working hard, pretending you're the ultimate warrior. When in reality, you're just a frightened soul trying to keep yourself relevant."

Nathan kept silent.

"If you can try, for just one minute, to put your disgust toward me, Frank, Matthew and everyone else in the world aside, I'd ask that you answer one question."

Nathan nodded.

"Would life be easier for you if you didn't always have to protect, defend and be on guard?"

Nothing.

"You're the one everyone runs to when things go bad... when someone hurts them... when they're wounded by everyday life. Wouldn't you want them to be able to take care of themselves?"

Nathan remained silent, though he ran his fingers through his hair in a way that seemed thoughtful to Justin.

Like in a chess game, Justin had made his move and now kept quiet, waiting for Nathan to make his. After almost a full minute, Nathan spoke.

"Yes," he mumbled.

"Yes, you'd like them to be able to take care of themselves?"

"Yes," Nathan repeated, louder this time.

For an instant, Justin saw a wave of fear move over Nathan's face. Though still grimacing, his shoulders were slumped and his eyes teared up. This was all the proof Justin needed to know that Nathan *was* tired. He was as exhausted as Frank and Matthew. Yet, he continued to be the protector for the same reason so many millions of people do things they dislike: he wanted to stay alive.

"Well, here's the thing." Justin paused, the next sentence possibly being the most important of his career so far. "And of course

I mean no disrespect to anyone, but they are not as strong as you. They don't have your courage and self-confidence. So much has happened to them that they constantly count on you to make them feel better and more powerful."

He waited for Nathan to say something, but got no words in response. He did, however, notice a softening of his scowl and thickening of his lips.

Progress, Justin thought. *Progress!*

"And that leads me to one last question, Nathan — aren't you tired?"

Nathan nodded his head and then let it hang down.

Justin wasn't sure what to do next. Should he continue talking? Touch Nathan on the knee? He could only see the top of his patient's head, so he wasn't even sure if he was still talking with Nathan. As he tried to make his decision, the man across from him made it for him.

"Can I go now?" It was still Nathan, but the voice was more tender and gentle than it had been only a minute before.

Justin looked at the wall clock. "We still have quite a bit of time left. Are you sure you want to leave? Especially right now?"

"Yeah," Nathan said as he rose from his chair.

Justin didn't want to push him, so he followed his lead and walked with him toward the office door. Nathan inspected the cloak hanging from the coat hook, closed his eyes and shook his head. Justin thought he heard him whisper, "What the fuck?" before he turned around and offered his hand.

"Thanks, doc. You made some sense tonight."

Justin shook his hand and smiled. "Thank *you* for working with me, Nathan. I hope I get to see you again very soon."

Nathan took a final glance at the cloak, grabbed it and wrapped it around his arm. He let out a sigh and walked out into the cold lobby with nothing on but his sweater and jeans. Justin held himself back from asking him to put the cloak on just to keep warm; Nathan could barely touch the piece of clothing, let alone wear it. So he stepped through the lobby doors into the frigid evening, shoulders up to his ears to shield himself from icy breeze.

He closed the office door and leaned his back against it. Nathan had initiated a handshake and offered him thanks. Justin put his hands in his pockets and closed his eyes. He'd either made a lot of progress tonight, or Nathan was one of the best actors he'd seen in a very long time.

***

A wave of exhaustion swept over Justin as he walked down the steps into the lobby of Grand Central Terminal and headed toward the Metro-North entrance to Rye. Mozart's *Eine kleine Nachtmusik* played in his earbuds — a serene contrast to the crush of people bustling through the giant atrium.

Despite the cold outside, the heat from the trains raised the temperature on the platform so much that he removed the scarf from around his neck and stuffed it into his coat pocket. He unbuttoned his coat as he strolled alongside the train looking for an open window seat. When he finally found one, he practically fell into the seat and leaned his head against the window, closing his eyes and hoping he'd be able to catch some shuteye before reaching his stop.

His mind swirled, thoughts of Frank, Matthew and Nathan riding its waves. Was he doing the right thing? Following the right procedure? What would his college professors say, the supposed "experts" whose words would fill the lecture halls every day with unwavering conviction?

These thoughts brought him back to the night before leaving for his undergraduate studies at Harvard. He'd been packing his bags when he turned to see his mother leaning against the doorjamb with her arms crossed and a slight smile on her face.

"What?" he asked, unsure of her expression's meaning. "What's going on?"

She walked over and hugged him tightly. He hugged her back, nestling his cheek in the curve of her neck and pushing down the lump in his throat.

"I am so proud of you," she said, her own voice quivering. "Just seventeen years old and on your way to an Ivy League school. You deserve every wonderful thing that's about to happen in your life. I can't even find the words to tell you how much I love you." A tear fell onto the nape of his neck and rolled down his back. "Your father would also be so proud. I know he would."

Justin broke down, collapsing onto his bed next to his suitcase. He'd been keeping his feelings hidden for so long, and with his mother's words he couldn't do it any longer.

"I don't want to leave you alone," he cried, trying to catch his breath like a weeping five-year-old. "I think about you getting up in the morning and having breakfast by yourself or just walking around the house alone and I get sick to my stomach." He grabbed a tissue off his nightstand to wipe his nose. "I swear. I can go to college around here. This way I can be here in case…"

His mother sat down beside him and stroked his head. "Shhh…" She kissed his cheek. "We discussed this, didn't we? I am fine. I will be fine. I have friends and family around in case of anything. Of course, no one could ever take your place, but there's no way you're giving up this chance just so you can keep me company."

He hugged her, still sobbing, unable to control himself. The guilt, sadness and homesickness he'd known he would feel was finally catching up to him.

"And think, Cambridge is only two and a half hours away. You can come back for a weekend now and then. And you'll be h-home for the holidays."

The tremble in her voice forced a stutter, which brought another river of tears from Justin's eyes. The holidays were already tough since his father's car accident three years earlier.

He had been on his way to Justin's baseball game when a tractor trailer carrying a full load of heavy machinery swerved to miss a deer running across I-95 in Greenwich. The trailer jackknifed and cars behind and to the side of it couldn't stop quickly enough to avoid a collision. More than a dozen drivers and passengers were killed, Ethan Wright being one of them.

It was the fifth inning and Justin was on third base when he looked in the bleachers and saw his mother standing motionless, holding her new flip phone to her ear. By the look on her face he could tell something was terribly wrong. He turned to the pitcher and then the batter at the plate, unsure what to do. Should he check on his mother or continue to play the game? As the uncertainty roared inside his head, he heard the crack of a baseball hitting a bat. He didn't move until somewhere in the background of his mind a voice yelled, *"Run, Justin! Run!"*

And he did. Straight onto home plate and then directly to the bleachers, where his mother was slowly coming down the wooden steps. She had a look of shock on her face and tears were falling down her cheeks.

"Mom, what is it?" he yelled over the screaming crowd. "What is it?"

She took his shoulder gently and walked him over to the team manager. She whispered something in his ear, words that drained the color from his face. He gave her a hug and bent down so he could be face-to-face with Justin.

"You be strong now. I'm here if you need me."

Justin's heart was pounding and his head felt ready to burst with confusion and frustration. *What's going on?*

He looked up to his mother. "Mom, what happened? Why are you crying? What did you tell the coach?"

Still holding his shoulder, she turned toward the parking lot and stared straight ahead. "We'll talk in the car," she mumbled. Justin could barely understand her.

"What?" he yelled, his heart beating faster and harder than it did after he ran from third base to home plate.

"I said we'll talk in the car!" she yelled back, her voice trembling. "Please, honey, wait until we get in the car."

Now, years later, her voice was trembling the same way as he prepared to leave for college. Justin wiped his face dry with his third tissue and looked into her sky-blue eyes.

"What if I don't like my roommate?" he asked.

"Hmmm…" she started. "Then you don't like your roommate."

"No, but what do I do if I don't like him?"

She tousled his hair and let out a delicate laugh. "First of all, Mr. Wright, I've never seen you not get along with anyone. Second of all, you'll know what to do if you don't like your roommate. And please stop the 'what ifs.' You know how much trouble they can cause. I'm sure your roommate… what's his name again?"

"Jon," Justin answered.

"Jon. I'm sure Jon is just as nervous as you are. So you both can be nervous together. You met him at the initial orientation and liked him then, right?"

"Yeah, but that's different. What if he — "

"There's that 'what if' again," his mother interrupted. "You know, it really stinks that you never got to meet your Grandma Ruth, my stepmom, but she was a wonderful, beautiful person. Just an angel. Whenever I think back, I get sad when I remember how she lived a 'what if' life. 'What if you ride your bike too far and get hurt? What if you can't get in touch with me? What if I go on a trip to Italy and the plane crashes? What if I go back to school but won't be able to take care of the family the way I should?'" She hugged Justin's shoulder. "It was the 'what ifs' that stopped Grandma Ruth from living life, and I don't want them to stop you from doing anything you want to do. You're too smart and talented and wonderful to let the fear of 'what if' stop you from reaching your potential. So do you promise not to 'what if'? Or when you do 'what if,' do you promise to recognize it and stop it in its tracks?"

Justin nodded.

"Not good enough," his mother said. "I need to hear you promise."

"I promise! I promise!" Justin laughed.

***

In a surreal state between consciousness and dreaming, Justin's eyes slowly opened when, through the Bach Symphony in G minor playing in his ears, the train conductor's muffled voice announced the next station stop, Rye. He forced them wider and tried to focus on the seat in front of him. The memories of his mother, and her passing from cancer two years earlier, made him homesick for his childhood. A dark cloud of grief now hovered above him and his grogginess wasn't helping his mood.

Justin held back tears as he struggled to get around the woman now seated beside him. She was so involved with her cellphone, she barely moved as he excused himself and slid past her. The back of his knees dragged against her giant pocketbook. It was only then she acknowledged him, fidgeting with annoyance and offering a scowl.

Nathan in drag, he said to himself, a thought that made him smile and help lift his spirits as remembered the progress he'd made earlier with Nathan. Or was he just kidding himself? Did he really make any progress or *was* Nathan acting to get "Dr. Wrong" off his back?

Justin sighed, his hesitance to completely trust himself tugging at his gut. Nathan was just too unreliable. Would he show up at their next session? Would there even be a next session? If he wasn't willing to get the help he needed, it was Justin's responsibility to ensure he didn't make Frank suffer the consequences. Nathan could hurt or even kill Frank for trying to "get rid" of him and it would be filed as a suicide. And because he had no friends or family to speak of, Frank Devlin would go to the grave a forgotten soul — just like his father and his uncle, the two men Frank hated most.

And Justin couldn't let that happen.

CHAPTER 10

If Frank wasn't so scared, he would've cried.

Sure, there were lots of times he'd find himself in a strange place, not knowing how or when he'd gotten there. But this time was different – and worse. This time he was in someone's home, someone's bedroom, alone and terrified of who might be on the other side of the door.

He slid off the bed and looked around the room. It reminded him of his bedroom at Uncle Carl's house — two windows, a few paint chips hanging from the ceiling, cracks running down from the molding into the corners, and old, seedy furniture that looked like it had been picked up on the side of the road. He jerked his head toward the closet door, where a shadow resembling his uncle slowly walked toward him.

He closed his eyes and then hesitantly opened them, hoping the figure would be gone. And it was. *Old memories die hard, I guess.* Now he had to figure out his next move. He went to the bureau and looked at himself in the mirror. The oversized maroon sweater he wore hung so low it almost looked like a dress. Worse than that, he didn't recognize the sweater or the jeans he was wearing.

What the hell is this pain on my back? It feels like a lion clawed my skin.

He lifted his sweater and turned his back toward the mirror. When he saw the giant scrapes, he almost fell over. Did he get them here, in this room? Did he get them before he got here? Who did this to him? Why?

The questions were piling up as they always did, but he didn't have time to search for answers. He had to escape this place and get back home, to somewhere familiar enough for him to have a breakdown and then, if he found the nerve, call Doctor Wright.

Frank opened the door to the closet. It was almost empty: two solid black short-sleeved Calvin Klein polo shirts suspended on wire hangers, a pair of Puma sneakers on a cracked shelf and a black bomber jacket crumpled on the floor. Hanging on a plastic hook on the back of the door was a wool cloak. It looked like the long capes he'd seen women on TV shows wear when attending the opera. He shook his head, this whole situation getting stranger by the second.

He picked up the bomber jacket and slipped into it, trying to avoid aggravating the spots on his back that hurt most when he moved. The jacket would not keep him warm from the November chill, he knew that, but it was all he had, so he zipped it up.

The bureau against the wall on the other side of the room looked oddly familiar. He crept toward it as though it would attack him if he moved too quickly. He slid his finger through the thin layer of dust on its surface, creating a circle that begged him to add the features of a smiley face. He placed two dots for eyes and held his hand mid-air, deciding whether to draw the mouth as a smile or frown. He couldn't make a decision and instead opened the bureau's top drawers. All he found was an open package of Lifesavers, a brass combination padlock and a jar of Vaseline.

Vaseline? A padlock? What the hell? Who lives like this?

He inched toward the bedroom door and placed his ear against it. Nothing. Silence. Maybe he was alone. Maybe he was lucky enough that no one was home, and once he found the front door, he could just dash out into the street and hail a cab.

Turning the knob as quietly as possible, he pulled the door inward to see a long, empty hallway with more doors on either side. Probably two other bedrooms, which meant two other people, or children, or roommates or…

No time to wonder about this shit. Get the hell out of here!

At the end of the hallway, a few steps led down to what was probably a living area, kitchen and the rest of the apartment. Since the windows in the bedroom behind him looked out at the back of other brownstones, not the street, the front door must be to the left of the stairs. A quick turn down a short foyer and he'd probably be ready to take some steps down to the street. This was all conjecture, but he had to make the best guess he could in case someone was home and he had to make a run for it.

He took a deep breath and held it as he sped down the hallway toward the steps. Glancing into the living room, he saw the back of a man's head. It looked like he was reading or writing, so Frank hoped he might go unnoticed, lightening his footfall as he went down the three steps into the room. On the final step, he turned to the left, where a short foyer led to the front door. He was right! And he was just about to step into the foyer when…

"Hey Alex! Finally leaving your room, I see. Going anywhere good?"

Alex? Who the hell is Alex?

The man in the living room, about his age, sat smiling at him as if he knew who he was. But why was he calling him 'Alex'? It took only a millisecond to realize that if he didn't play along, there'd be trouble. He didn't know what kind of trouble and he didn't want to find out.

He heard Dr. Wright's words playing in the back of his head: *They are called alters. Different parts of you that have been created for a reason.* Alex must be one of his "parts", someone already known to the man asking him questions and acting as if they were friends.

"Finally leaving your room"? The statement left Frank even more baffled. He had a co-op uptown. Why would this guy think that weird, mostly empty space was his room? He took a deep breath, wanting nothing more than to run from here out into the street.

"Hey!" he replied awkwardly. "Gotta pick up… gotta get some…" Frank couldn't think fast enough. He took another breath. "I left one of my books at the library. Just going to pick it up, then heading uptown to my place."

The man stood and walked toward him. *Oh shit. Does this guy even know I have a place uptown?* When Frank reached the landing, he held the railing, looked directly into the stranger's eyes and waited for the next part of the mystery to unfold.

"We really haven't gotten to know you," he said. "You're never here. Did Dylan or I do something to piss you off?"

Frank had no idea who Dylan was, but the combination of the man's sorrowful expression along with the underlying pain in his voice was so sincere, a wave of attraction coursed through the pit of his stomach. Staring into the stranger's eyes, he felt that peculiar, but frequently-appearing piece of himself emerge – a split in his character that would often try to make itself known, and at times came out full force when he wasn't strong enough to push it down. But the way this man looked at him, the tilt of his head, the way his tongue ran across his lips, a longing for intimacy so palpable Frank could feel his lungs breathing it in, made him stop from trying to suppress this part of himself.

A bit more comfortable, he smiled. "No. You and Dylan didn't do a thing. I'm just under a lot of pressure." He held out his hand. "Let's start again. I'm Alex."

The man took hold of his hand and shook it gently. "I'm Kyle. Nice to meet you."

"Nice to meet you, too," Frank replied, not wanting to release Kyle's hand. It felt good, their hands a perfect fit. The fact that Kyle also didn't let go helped make the moment complete. Frank didn't know what was happening inside of him and didn't really care. The part of himself still hiding in the background offered a wider smile and seductive glance – an action Frank didn't even bother to restrain.

Kyle offered a smile, another tilt of his head and looked to the floor. His reaction told Frank though the man was shy, he was definitely interested. Not sure what to do next, he spoke the first words that came to his mind.

"Would you like to come over tomorrow night?" he asked. "There's someone I'd like you to meet."

Kyle gently pulled his hand from their hold and slid it into his pocket. He looked into Frank's eyes as though searching for a long lost friend. Perhaps, Frank wondered, he was searching for the truth. He had no doubt Kyle was still in the closet and might be worried he was being played, set up to be outed in some way.

"Who— Who do you want me to meet?" Kyle asked.

"Please, Kyle. Trust me. There's no need to be worried or concerned. I have a feeling you'll be pleasantly surprised. It'll also give you a chance to see my place."

"What about Dylan? Do you want — "

"Just you, Kyle."

Kyle looked as nervous as Frank had looked in his reflection a few minutes earlier. He was amazed at his own calm.

"Okay," Kyle agreed. "Six thirty, seven?"

"Either one. I'll be waiting," he said, lightly gliding his fingertips down Kyle's cheek, leaving him open-mouthed and silent.

He stepped outside, where a wind gust hit him in the face, almost knocking him off his feet. The shock of cold immediately tossed his state of mind back to where it had been after finding himself inside a strange bedroom.

Confusion and fear pierced right through the thin bomber jacket and into his bones. He slammed the door shut, ran down the steps and darted his head in both directions. Though he had no idea where he was, he turned to the right and sprinted toward the street that had the most traffic. Once he was far enough away from this place, he'd figure out where he was and make his way back home.

If he didn't freeze to death first.

***

Hours later, Kyle heard the front door close and looked at his watch. It was close to midnight, but he had stayed up to make sure he caught Dylan before leaving for school the next morning. He had to let him know their Tuesday Tequila Pizza Night would have to wait until Wednesday because he had a date.

Of course he couldn't tell him it was with Alex since he hadn't yet come out of the closet to Dylan, or to anyone else for that matter. But if things worked out with Alex the way he wanted them to, he knew he'd have to have the conversation he'd spent most of his life avoiding.

Dylan looked into the living room and gave Kyle a big smile. "Wow. It's great to see a familiar face! What are you still doing up?"

Kyle stood and leaned against the arm of his chair. "Studying, of course. I also start class early tomorrow and wanted to let you know Pizza Night will have to be delayed for a day. Didn't want to leave you hanging."

"And why are we postponing?"

Kyle hesitated, still unsure how to answer. "A date," he blurted out.

"Wait! What?" Dylan hung his coat up in the closet. He rubbed his hands together as he walked into the living room. "A date? With who? Where did you meet her?"

Kyle held up his hand. "Hold up. Give me a break. Her name is Lisa and she's in one of my classes. Don't be asking me a million questions. If things work out, you'll meet her. For now, it's just one date."

His hunger for information sated — even if by false information — Dylan patted Kyle's head and tugged on his hair. "Okay, dude, okay. I'm just happy you're going on a date. It's been too long."

Kyle felt a surge of anger and closed his eyes to force it down. *I don't need Mr. Five Dates a Month telling me how long it's been since I've gone out with someone. Like I even wanted to go out with those girls in the first place. I did it to make everyone else happy... everyone but me.*

Dylan walked into the kitchen. "Beer?"

"Beer," Kyle called back.

Dylan returned and handed him a Corona. "I work all day and I can't come home to a kitchen with a lime?" he joked. "Seriously, how can I fully enjoy my Corona if I don't have a lime wedge?"

Kyle laughed. "Sorry, honey. I've been busy. I'll go shopping after my date."

They clinked bottles and sat on opposite ends of the sofa.

"They have you working til midnight now?" Kyle asked.

"Inventory. It's bullshit. I deal with customers for four hours and then they have me stocking, restocking and now taking inventory. But it's just for one more night. On Saturday, a nephew or some relative of a corporate bigwig is coming in to do the grunt work. He'll probably call it an internship and put it on his resume."

"Work him to the bone!" Kyle roared. "To the bone!"

"Oh, I am *so* ready for him." Dylan laughed. "I've been the gofer grunt worker for too long. It's someone else's turn to suffer. I heard he's a little weird, but that's fine. The weirder he is, the longer he stays in the back room doing the shit work."

"If you think about it," Kyle said, "we're all a little weird."

"You got that right." Dylan took a slug of beer. "Speaking of which, my mom texted me that she surprise-visited today and got to meet Alex. She actually used the word 'strange' when describing him."

"Yeah," Kyle said, deciding to ignore the 'strange' reference. "I got to see her. As usual, she looked great."

"That's my mom, always looking good. Especially when she goes to court. Anyway, you were here. Did you sense anything weird?"

"Not really," Kyle lied. "Everything seemed fine to me. I mean, you know, Alex isn't exactly Mister Congeniality."

"Yeah, but my mom is Miss Congeniality. For her to say she felt awkward just freaked me out a little. She gets along with *everyone*. I just wonder if there's something we missed and he's a nut case or something."

"Don't worry about it," Kyle urged, his sudden need to protect Alex surprising even himself.

Why did he feel this way toward someone he barely knew just hours before? Had Alex been such a mystery that he wanted to find out what made him tick? Or was he *so* desperate to have a relationship that he'd hook up with any attractive guy who showed him attention?

He shoved his thoughts aside worried Dylan might get suspicious. "I remember you telling me that you had talks with her about wanting your independence and shit, so she was probably feeling uncomfortable to begin with. Then she comes in, you're not here, but this stranger is. I bet it just took her by surprise and that's what made her feel awkward."

Dylan placed his bottle on the side table and crossed his arms. "I don't know. She can be an over-worrier at times, but she does have good instincts. What do you think? Did we make a mistake?" He yawned and rubbed his eyes. "Do we find another roommate before his three-month trial runs out?" He paused for another few seconds. "Have you ever checked out his room?"

Kyle shook his head. "Thought about it, but no. I felt kind of funny just going in without him being here." He paused, hoping Dylan wouldn't pursue the idea. "It's like an invasion of privacy."

Dylan smirked and jumped up.

"Screw that. Let's go!" he yelled, running up the steps to the bedroom hallway.

Kyle followed reluctantly. But it was true, he felt curious about the guy he now had plans to date. The questions piled up inside his head almost as quickly as the guilt and shame invaded the rest of his body. The cliche "curiosity killed the cat" kept running through his mind. He silently hoped this time it wouldn't kill his chances at a potential relationship. He'd have to make sure Alex never got wind of what they were about to do.

When they reached Alex's door, they looked at one another and simultaneously shrugged their shoulders.

"If we're gonna do it, let's do it," Dylan whispered.

He opened the door and they walked into the middle of the room. It looked exactly as it did during the time they were looking for a roommate. Nothing had changed. No pictures on the walls, the bureau and dresser tops bare. The bedspread had some wrinkles, as though it had been sat on but never removed for sleeping.

Dylan cautiously opened the closet door, peeked in and turned to Kyle. "What the hell is this?" he asked, grabbing a cloak hanging on the back.

Kyle hesitantly walked to the closet and after a quick glance, looked at Dylan. "I have no idea. It looks like something those fancy women wear to the opera."

"Yeah, so what the hell is it doing in Alex's closet?"

Fear shot through Kyle like a bolt of lightning: *Is this my first warning? Why is there a woman's coat in his closet?*

"How would *I* know?" Kyle said, looking around more closely. "Hmmm. Look!" he said excitedly, pointing to two men's shirts and a pair of sneakers. Had he just redeemed Alex's reputation with the simple discovery of men's clothing?

"You say that like it's a normal thing," Dylan replied. "Two shirts and a pair of sneakers? That's all? Doesn't he have any other clothes? I'm sorry, but this is freakin' weird."

Dylan was right. This was definitely strange, and Kyle made a mental note to ask Alex about it. Right now he wanted to leave the room before they found something else that made him feel uneasy about meeting Alex tomorrow night. Someone had finally showed interest in him and he didn't want to spoil a potential relationship with fabricated fears based on clothing and bed sheets. "Can we just get out of here, please? I mean, shit, Dylan, we wouldn't want him going through *our* rooms."

As if Kyle hadn't spoken, Dylan walked to the bureau against the far wall. He opened each drawer and slammed them shut, empty handed and without expression. He moved to the other bureau with the mirror and pulled open the top left drawer.

"Found something," Dylan said.

Kyle made his way to where Dylan stood and peered over his shoulder to look into the drawer. "An open package of Lifesavers, a padlock and Vaseline," Kyle said, his voice a bit shaky. "Holy shit. Why... what does he...?" His insides shuddered. He had a date with a guy who kept candy, a lock and Vaseline in an almost empty bedroom. Why? What did they mean? He closed his eyes in an effort to straighten out his thoughts when he remembered Alex saying, *"There's someone I'd like you to meet."* What the hell was he getting himself into? The word "cancel" flashed in his mind's eye like a bright red neon sign.

"Something's not right," Dylan said. "There's no toothbrush, shampoo, barely any clothing in the closet except a woman's coat. Nothing in the dresser drawers. I don't get it. Why would he pay a shitload of money every month and not even live here? We've really only seen him a handful of times since he moved in." He ran his fingers through his hair. "I'm pretty beat from work, so maybe I'm not thinking straight, but this whole thing just doesn't make sense to me."

"Or maybe," Kyle said, "maybe we thought it would be like it was when Jim was here. The three of us would hang out together, have some fun and be… like… friends. Maybe that's just not the way it is with Alex." He turned to look at the bed and empty walls. "Maybe the guy is a workaholic and studyholic. Spends his time at work, school and mostly his own place uptown. This apartment is like an emergency stop for him. If he wants to get away or needs to crash somewhere, he has this place just in case. It could be…"

"Wait a second, Kyle," Dylan interrupted. "Are you actually trying to give me good reasons why he's barely been here and his bedroom is like a vacant hotel room, without the art reprints and flowery drapes? Which is it? Is he a kook or not? Let me know now, please, because I have to get some sleep before my nine o'clock class."

"I don't know, man. I just don't know." He closed all the dresser drawers and the closet door and headed into the hallway. "Let's talk about it on Wednesday. Maybe you're making more out of something than there is."

"Me? *I'm* make more out of something? *You're* the one who makes mountains out of a molehills. That's your job." Dylan's playful sarcasm sliced the severity of the moment into pieces. "Like when you called the cops because you thought the woman next door was getting murdered and the screams were coming from her TV. Hmmm... I think she was watching *Scream 2*. Wasn't that the movie — "

He went to slap Dylan in the head, but Dylan put up his arm to block his hand. "Slapping you in the head is my job!" Kyle yelled, following Dylan as he ran down the hallway back into the living room.

Dylan took a final slug of Corona from the bottle and brought it into the kitchen. "I'm done. Gotta get some rest. Remember, *we* decide who lives here and who doesn't. We'll talk about it more in the morning or on Wednesday... *after* you tell me about your date."

Kyle rolled his eyes and took one last gulp of beer from the almost empty bottle. "I'll be gone by the time you get up, so we'll talk on Wednesday."

Dylan held his fist up and Kyle banged it with his own.

"Have fun, be safe and do everything I wouldn't do," Dylan said.

"Definitely," Kyle said, now uncertain if he was even going to meet Alex. What he saw in the man's bedroom, and mostly what he didn't see, gave him goose bumps.

"Cool. See you then."

Kyle watched Dylan walk up the three steps to the bedroom hallway, turn left, and disappear behind the wall.

"See you then," he whispered back to no one.

He shivered, a sharp tingle crawling up the back of his neck – the same strange sensation he had that fateful day when he turned around and Michael was no longer behind him.

CHAPTER 11

"Is it possible to love and hate someone at the same time?" Kyle asked the man seated across from him, then stared at him, waiting for the answer. If anyone had the answer to this question, he hoped it would be Dr. Robertson.

"Anything's possible. Especially when it comes to feelings and emotions. The more important question is, why did you ask me that? What's going on?"

Kyle turned to the window as dusk's shadow settled over the buildings on Washington Place. People walked by, winding through construction scaffolding like rats in a maze. Could he tell Robertson everything he was feeling? He'd already told him so many things no one else knew. Why go to a therapist if you're not going to spill your guts?

"Dylan," he said.

"What about Dylan?"

"You know he's been my best friend since we're like six years old. We're pretty much inseparable." He looked back at the doctor. "Maybe that's the problem."

"What problem, Kyle?" Robertson asked. He crossed his legs and rested his chin on his hand.

"Basically… well… I guess… he always wins. I'm the second place guy. The runner up. No matter what we do or where we go or who we meet, I'm like, I don't know, behind the scenes."

"Can you give me an example?"

Kyle closed his eyes. When he opened them, Robertson hadn't moved. It was time for more spilling of guts.

Kyle picked the edge of the fabric on the chair arm with the nail of his index finger. "Okay, for instance, every so often when our heads are out of the textbooks, we'll go to a party. Everyone pays attention to Dylan and he pretty much has to introduce me. Like he has to make sure people realize I'm there." He quickly stopped picking when the suede started to fray. "Even in high school, he was the best at everything. The pitcher on our varsity team. I was the useless right fielder. Believe it or not, he was number 12 and I was number 6. Half. Always half of what he was… and is." Kyle shook his head. "I know, it sounds petty. Numbers on a baseball shirt. Pretty ridiculous, huh?"

"Kyle, if something bothers you, it's not ridiculous." Robertson uncrossed his legs. He placed his elbows on his thighs and leaned forward. "You mentioned the word 'hate.' Is it 'hate' you feel or do you think it might be 'envy'?"

Kyle looked to the floor and followed the geometric pattern of the hand-tufted area rug. Unsure how to respond, he wished he could crawl into fibers of the carpet and get lost in the labyrinth of lines – never reaching an end or finding an answer to the doctor's question.

How could he hate his best friend? Someone who had been there for him no matter what. Someone who has always stood up for him. Someone whose brother he'd lost.

"Kyle?" the doctor said delicately.

Kyle didn't respond. His thoughts of childhood with Dylan, junior high basketball practices, undergrad classes, all night discussions about the meaning of life – they flew through his head like a team of wild horses escaping an unlocked stable.

"Kyle?"

He sighed and bit down on the left side of his bottom lip. "Both, I guess. Hate and envy. I just don't know which one is stronger."

"Did something happen recently that made these feelings more intense?"

"I didn't tell you this, but a little over a month ago, we interviewed this guy Alex to be our roommate. Of course, Dylan took charge of the whole thing and I could tell right away that Alex liked him better. I even thought he might be attracted to him, even though he didn't say anything about… you know… about…"

"His sexuality?" Robertson asked.

"Yes," Kyle answered quietly.

"And Dylan still doesn't know about *your* sexuality?"

Kyle shook his head. "No one knows. Except *you*. It's not the right time yet. I really think Dylan might have a problem with it, mostly because I never told him. And my parents? We already discussed that. It's just not gonna happen. At least not now."

"We'll get back to that in a few minutes. You said you felt like Alex might be attracted to Dylan. Did that make you jealous?"

Kyle nodded. "I guess. But I always think everyone is attracted to Dylan, so I was probably imagining it. Dylan's pretty perceptive. I think he would've gotten a vibe if it were true."

"But Dylan's not gay. So there really isn't any competition, is there?"

"Doesn't matter. Just like every woman loves Dylan, so do the guys. Dylan gets the high grades. Dylan gets offered the management position at work when he's there for less than two months. Dylan gets parents who actually give a shit about him. Dylan gets the girls. And Dylan gets the guys. Even if he doesn't want them."

Dr. Robertson spun his chair around and grabbed the tablet off his desk.

"Are you late for an online Scrabble game?" Kyle asked as he flipped open the cover and tapped the screen with his stylus. "Candy Crush tournament? I mean, is my life *that* boring?"

Robertson laughed. "Hold on, Kyle. I'm going to read you something." After a few more seconds, the therapist held the screen in front of him and started to read. "The definition of *envy* is… a feeling of discontented or resentful longing aroused by someone else's possessions, qualities or luck." He placed the tablet on his lap. "Does that sound like what you're feeling?"

Kyle nodded again, now biting his entire bottom lip.

Robertson picked up the tablet and typed something else. "As verbs, the *difference* between envy and hate is that envy is to feel displeasure towards someone for their good fortune or possessions, while *hate* is to dislike intensely or greatly." He set the tablet back on his lap and looked Kyle in the eyes. "So what do you think you're feeling toward Dylan, envy or hate?"

Kyle didn't have an answer. Can envy turn into hate? Did you have to feel one or the other or could you feel both?

He couldn't hate his best friend. Especially after what happened with Michael.

"Envy. It *has* to be envy."

"So, before you asked me if you could love and hate someone at the same time. What is it that you *love* about Dylan?"

Kyle grinned. "He's fun and he's funny. He cares about me. He helps me. He's understanding and he's just an all-around good guy. Which is probably why everyone else likes him so much."

"And just so I know for sure, you *love* him because of these qualities. You're not *in* love with him because of them."

Kyle laughed. "No. Those days are long gone. I think I used to be. I mean, I had feelings for him way back in high school. But he's always been straighter than an arrow and when I finally realized there was no way anything could happen, I let it go. Just another thing I couldn't have, I guess."

"Kyle," Robertson said, his hands moving in a circular motion like a psychic trying to sense an aura. "I'm detecting a sense of defeat from you today. As though you're a victim. A victim of Dylan, as a matter of fact. I'll ask again, has something happened to make this feeling more intense? Are you still taking your Prozac?"

"Yes, still taking Prozac."

"Well, you know as a psychologist I can't prescribe. But maybe you should see a psychiatrist or psychopharmacologist who can make sure you're on the right medication path. We will, of course, continue our sessions. I just think a psychiatrist is better able to help in this than I am and better suited to evaluate your medication needs than a general practitioner. Didn't you once say that Dylan's father had offered his services?"

Kyle squirmed in his seat. *Is this guy serious? Is he telling me that I should see the father of the kid I lost, to help* me *get through my shit?*

"You know, half the reason I'm here is because the Psych Department professors think it's a good idea to go to therapy. It's supposed to show us how the process works — you know, handling people's problems — from a patient's perspective. And you're telling me I should see someone else? Gee, that's a really good lesson to learn."

Robertson took a deep breath and leaned back. "Kyle, did you listen to what I said? I *said* we would continue our sessions. I just want to be sure you're taking the medication that's best for you. In my opinion a psychiatrist is a better judge of that than your internist, and I *can't* do it. That's why I suggested Dr. Wright. He would make sure you're on the correct medication and I would still be your therapist."

"Yeah, that would be great. Me talking to Justin Wright about my envy, hatred, jealousy, or whatever you want to call it, toward his son. Me being gay and the rest of the shit you and I discuss. Then maybe we add on that I got his son kidnapped."

He ran his fingers through his hair and gripped the arm of the chair right above the suede he'd damaged. "Then, after the session with my best friend's father, I can swallow all my pills and jump off the George Washington Bridge." He paused and rubbed his eyes with his palms. "I recommend we stick with the way we're doing things. It's just a bad day."

"I hear you. I just — "

"But," Kyle interrupted, "things might be getting better. I have some news."

The doctor's expression brightened. "Good news? Okay, we'll get off the path of that other topic for a minute."

"Yes. Alex actually asked me yesterday if I wanted to come over to his apartment and hang out. So after I leave here, I'm going there."

Robertson's eyes squinted and he tipped his head slightly. "Wait. I thought you said he interviewed to be your new roommate. Did you and Dylan accept him?"

Kyle nodded.

"So he's your roommate and he has another apartment?"

"I know." Kyle laughed. "It's actually a co-op. Sounds weird, but he goes to Fordham and wanted a place closer to the campus so when he finishes up late, he has a place to crash. Beats having to get up to Park and 106th in the middle of the night. Plus, he says it's hard to make friends up there and there's a lot more going on by where we live."

Robertson turned toward the window.

"Wait. You *never* look out the window," Kyle said. "Why are you looking outside? *I'm* the one who always does that. What are you so interested in out there?"

"I'm just thinking, Kyle. Am I not allowed to look out the window while I think? Do I have to stare at the wall? At you? Please tell me what I can and can't do while I'm thinking."

Kyle covered his face with his hands. He was egging Robertson on and if he didn't stop, he'd have no one on his side. *Be nice. Just be nice.*

"Sorry. I just got carried away. I guess I just wanted to know what you were thinking. I'm sorry."

Robertson pursed his lips. "It's okay, Kyle. I get it. There's no doubt you're extra stressed tonight and I apologize for being sarcastic. That was inconsiderate of me. What I was thinking was why wouldn't Alex just get rid of the co-op and move downtown? It just hit me as strange. That's all. Is he that well off?"

"He does have a lot of money. That's the main reason we told him he could move in. He gave us six months' deposit. So at least we're set for half the year. Plus, I might *like* him, like him, if you know what I mean. I guess we'll find out tonight if he'll give me a chance."

Robertson raised his eyebrows and patted the cover of the tablet sitting on his lap. "You're a big boy. I'm not going to tell you to 'be careful,' 'watch out' or 'keep an eye on this guy,' because I think you're smart enough to know when something isn't right."

"You do realize that you just told me the things you said you weren't going to tell me."

Robertson smiled and stayed quiet.

"Yes, I'm a big boy and I can take care of myself. But thanks for your unsolicited advice, or should I say 'warnings'?"

"So here's a question." Robertson tapped the stylus pen against his mouth. "Let's say things do work out between you and Alex. Will you tell Dylan about it? I mean, you'll all be living together. How would you keep something like that from him?"

"You know the story, Doc. I've had sex three times in my life with three different men. I have no idea what I'm doing, what I'm supposed to do or how to turn these one-night stands into relationships. I'm constantly making up stories about being with women to keep Dylan and my family happy. This way I don't have to deal with the consequences."

"We really need to discuss your thoughts behind 'consequences,' Kyle. I have a feeling — "

"Not now. There's too much shit going on. If something more than just one night *does* happen with Alex, maybe he'll be able to help me figure out how to deal with the whole sexuality thing. It's one day at a time right now. It's the best I can do."

His face was flushed. What if, as Robertson said, things worked out and something *did* happen with Alex? They'd only be able to have sex at Alex's until he decided to tell Dylan. Would Alex put up with that or would he want to flaunt their relationship in front of Dylan?

Holy shit. What are you doing? You don't even know if Alex will like you enough to even consider *having sex with you.*

"What is it?" Robertson said.

"What's what?"

"By the look on your face, your mind is going in a thousand different directions."

"Well it wasn't until *you* got ahold of it!" A thick tension spread throughout his entire body. "What are you, maybe ten years older than me? Thirty four? Thirty five? Do you really have enough experience to deal with someone like me? A depressed, closeted gay kid who lives with resentment, anger and guilt that hangs on like a blood-sucking leech? Do you really think you have what it takes to make me happy? To live the life I want to live? Do you?"

"Where is this coming from, Kyle? Your anger is now pointed at me and I need to know why. For *your* sake, not mine."

Kyle shook his head. "Forget about it. I'm sorry. I just have a lot to think about and I'm trying to make sense out of it."

"I understand. But you make it sound like you're a lost cause and you are *so* far from that. Listen, I'm sorry if I offended you in any way, Kyle. But if you're going to 'learn,' as you say, what goes on in a therapist's office from a patient's perspective, you also need to know what goes on from a therapist's position. Our number one job is to have our patients trust us so they will tell us the truth about what's bothering them. This allows us to get down to the bare-bones facts."

He took the tablet off his lap and gently placed it on his desk blotter. While Robertson's back was turned, Kyle rolled his eyes. The doc was thinking up his next load of therapist crap.

"Forensic psychology, your field of study, also relies on facts. Doesn't matter if you end up being a jury consultant, a criminal profiler or a forensic social worker, you'll need the truth to reach your final goal. But I'm not interrogating you in court, Kyle; I want to earn your trust. Because if I'm going to help you, I need the truth. For example, no avoidance of topics that bother you. Those are actually the most important topics to discuss. I give you as much leeway as I can, but you have to help *me*. It's the only way I can help *you*."

The guy was right, but Kyle didn't care. He had a 'date' to get to and talking about his problems would only get him in a worse frame of mind, one of those moods that made seeing or speaking with *anyone* impossible. He couldn't let that happen, especially tonight. Keeping this shrink appointment had been a bad idea.

"I gotta go," Kyle said. He stood, walked toward the door and grabbed his coat off the hook on the wall. "I don't want to be late."

Robertson got up and crossed his arms. "Kyle, we have about half an hour left to our session. Why are you leaving?"

Kyle zipped up his jacket and opened the door as if escaping prison.

"I need to be in the right state of mind when I see Alex. Going through this shit with you is only bringing me down." He pointed toward the ceiling. "I feel like there's a giant cloud floating above me just waiting to pour its shit all over my head. I'm getting out before that happens."

He walked out of the office and dashed down the hallway. Robertson's muffled words bounced off the walls, but Kyle couldn't understand any of them.

It didn't really matter anyway. He'd never return to this office or most likely, this building. He had enough downers in his life and didn't need a thirty-something know-it-all bringing him further down once a week. This date with Alex was the one positive thing he had going for him and Robertson had tried to pick it apart at every turn. He didn't need that crap. He'd take care of things on his own until he found a person who really knew how to help him.

Could that person be Alex?

He looked at his watch. 6:30. He had half an hour to buy a bottle of wine and make his way uptown.

You'll find out soon enough, he thought as he ran three flights down the stairwell to street level. *Soon enough.*

***

Kyle pressed the 4C button. After a few seconds, static and a strange voice reverberated from the panel's speaker.

"Kyle?"

"Yup!"

There was a long buzz and a click as the door unlocked. Once inside, Kyle did a 360 as he took in the décor and its opulent minimalism.

A floor inlaid with black rainbow, honey onyx, cappuccino and gold marble segments in a bold pattern. *Wow this is freakin' beautiful. Wish I had enough money to live like this.* The walls were just as intriguing with paintings and sketches by artists with names he wouldn't recognize if spelled out for him phonetically. Three black-speckled marble steps led him up to the elevators. He pressed the button and waited, his heart beating twice as fast as the second hand on his watch.

He looked at the label of the wine bottle he held and tightened his grip on its neck. Since he knew nothing about wine, he had to ask the owner of the store about the best wines under fifty dollars.

"I would normally go with a Cabernet," the man said with a thick but intelligible Italian accent. "But, by the way you a' dressed and the way your hair is slicked back, I think this date calls for a Mala-back."

Kyle had no idea what a Malaback was, but followed the man to the back of the store, where a narrow black sign with white lettering read, *Malbec.*

"Oh," Kyle said. "Malbec. I've heard of that."

The man grabbed the Catena Alta 2018 and held it up like a World Series trophy. "This is the one. You will love it. She will love it. You will have a wonderful night. Perfetto, dico. Perfetto."

The man's words echoed inside Kyle's head as the elevator doors opened and he stepped in. Little did Signore Malaback know this wine was for a date with a man, not a woman. But why ruin it with the truth? He simply smiled at the owner and paid, saying "Grazie" as he walked out the door.

And now he stood in an elevator designed as lavishly as the lobby. Looking around the posh surroundings, he was relieved he spent the extra money on the Malbec. One wall was black, marble he supposed, and shiny enough to see his reflection. He unzipped his coat and used the impromptu mirror to straighten the collar of his white polo shirt. Once comfortable with the way he looked, he pressed the "4" button. He was about to iron out the wrinkles in his pants with his palms when his thoughts abruptly stopped him.

You're getting ahead of yourself. This could just be a night of bullshitting, hanging out and getting to know each other as friends. Nothing more. Plus, Alex had said he wanted Kyle to meet someone, so they weren't going be alone anyway. Or were they? Was Alex lying about there being someone to meet so he could get him to his apartment? Or was Alex straight and Kyle making himself anxious with fantasies of something that would never be?

Shit, he thought as the elevator door opened. Should he have brought a six-pack of beer? If Alex was straight, would the wine make it obvious that Kyle had other plans in mind?

Kyle stepped out. Following Alex's directions, he made a left and walked down the hallway with his wine.

Too late now.

***

When Alex opened the door, it took a few seconds for Kyle to recognize him.

It was Alex, but a *different* Alex. His eyes looked brighter than he'd ever seen them before. And for a quick second Kyle thought he saw a thread of eyeliner along the man's lids. Was he imagining things?

His lips were pinkish and shiny, almost as if he had gloss on them, and his cheeks had a reddish hue. He wore a solid sheer mesh top, a tight pair of ripped black skinny jeans and white Reeboks.

Did Alex have a twin? A gay cousin? Who the hell was this guy?

Unsure what to do, Kyle held up the Malbec.

"Catena Alta! My favorite," said the Alex impersonator. He took the bottle from Kyle and opened the door wider. "You sure know how to pick your wines. Come in."

Though still unsure who now stood in front of him, Kyle was taken in by the soft light of the apartment — mostly light ochre, with a few accent walls as dark as ground coffee — and the chill music that played in the background. Something about the place helped calm his nerves enough not to turn around and walk out.

The furnishings were contemporary and elegant, but also appeared comfortable and inviting. A shelf filled with books, both old and new, covered one side of the living room. As he tried to read some of their titles, he was able to relax and breathe more deeply. His nostrils filled with the smell of food. Not takeout or microwaved pizza, but real food cooking on a stove or in an oven. It had been a long time since he smelled such an appealing aroma coming from an apartment kitchen.

He turned slightly as the man slid off Kyle's coat. When he returned from hanging it in the closet, he planted himself directly in front of Kyle and presented him a slight smile.

"I see confusion all over your face. No worries. I'll explain everything in a few minutes. First things first. Do you want a glass of wine or a beer?"

"Wi-wine," he said, trying to hide his stutter by clearing his throat. "Wine is fine."

Oh shit, now you're rhyming. Stop talking until you get your shit together.

The man opened the bottle of wine and poured it through an aerator into two goblets. He was as good-looking as Alex, with the same sincerity and unintentional charisma as when they first met. But this person was much more feminine, more like a queer, effeminate version of Alex.

What the hell is going on? This isn't the guy I was talking to yesterday. Maybe I should get out of here while I still can.

"Here you go," he said, handing him a glass and gesturing toward the plush sofa. Kyle sat at one end, and before the man sat down, he clinked their glasses and said, "To new friends."

Kyle took a sip. It *was* good wine. Signore Malaback was spot on. He yearned to be back in the liquor store, so he could cancel his plans to meet Alex and buy some Corona to drink by himself in his apartment instead. He took a second sip. Then a third.

Alex's doppelganger sat down at the other end of the sofa and traced his index finger along the rim of his glass. Maybe the gesture was meant to be seductive. He looked up at Kyle.

"Okay," he said. "Now, I don't want you to freak out — "

"Too late," Kyle interrupted, taking another swig of wine.

"I know. I know. I've tried to figure out how to explain it, how to start, but there really is no good way. So I'll just try to clarify things the best I can."

Kyle kept quiet, now trailing *his* finger along the rim of the glass. *Lunatic or not, this guy is hot. But he's* SO *effeminate. I never liked that before. Why is this different? Why am I not out the door?*

"Do you know what an 'alter' is?"

Kyle shook his head. "No."

"Do you know what multiple personalities are?"

Holy mother shit. "Yes."

Kyle slugged rather than sipped his wine. He wriggled on the sofa, crossing and then uncrossing his legs, glancing at the front door, still wondering if he should make a run for it.

The man took a sip of wine and was silent for a few seconds.

"My name is Matthew," he said. "Alex is another, well, *part* of me. The part of me that rents a room in your apartment."

Kyle's body, and mind, went numb. He heard this "Matthew" guy talking, but his words were like speeding cars on a busy highway. Whirring, buzzing, whizzing by without making a bit of sense. How could they? The man was talking about his other personalities, "alters" living inside his head.

Why me, Kyle wondered, the only words that reached his weary mind. *Why me?*

"Kyle?" Matthew said as he leaned forward. "Are you still with me?"

Kyle shook his head and tried to regain focus.

"Yeah — yeah, I'm with you. Just trying to process," he mumbled. *Also trying to figure out why I'm still here. Am I* that *curious?* That *desperate?*

"I know," Matthew said, sitting back. "It must sound very strange. I'm sure you've seen all the movies about people who have alters, multiple personalities, and they're portrayed as crazy. But I can assure you I'm not them. That's pretty much a lot of bullshit. In a nutshell, I depend on my other 'parts' to help me live my life, depending on the situation I'm in. It's my way of coping, for now at least. Well, that's the way Dr. Wright puts it."

Kyle managed to place the wine glass on the side table and sat up straight. "Dr. Wright? What the fuck? You're seeing Dr. Wright?"

Matthew nodded.

"So wait, hold on. You have multiple personalities. One is gay, that would be you, Matthew. Then you have another personality, Alex, who at least *acts* straight and moves into the apartment of his therapist's son."

Kyle leaned his elbows on his knees and let his face fall into his hands. How did he let himself get into this situation? This guy was playing me — and Dylan — from day one and neither one of them saw it. Even worse, he was still sitting here listening to him try to explain his way around it.

"Before I get my coat, run out of here and tell Dylan we let a lunatic into our home, tell me why you chose us. What the fuck are you up to? Did you lie about being closer to school? Or wait, do you even *go* to school?"

Matthew set his wine glass on the coffee table and twisted his body so he faced Kyle. "First of all, if you do some research on alters, you'll find out I'm not a *lunatic*. Listen, I chose to live with you and Dylan for a few reasons. To answer your question, *yes,* I *do* go to school. Being closer to where I study is half the reason I moved in. Another reason is *you*. I was doing research on Dr. Wright to see if he could help me and I saw he had a son. When I checked Dylan out on Facebook, I saw you. I don't know. I can't explain it, but I felt an attraction. And not just physical."

Kyle fell back against the sofa's soft pillows. Why hadn't he left yet? What the hell was keeping him there? *Am I as crazy as he is?*

"I'm great at talking to strangers and making friends. But when it comes to starting a conversation with someone I'm attracted to, shyness takes over and I clam up. Fear of rejection? Maybe. I don't know." Matthew continued. "Alex helps me make that move when I can't do it myself."

"So why couldn't this 'Alex' come up to me on the street or in one of my classes or even when I get my coffee in the morning? Why did you — I mean *he* — have to move in with us?"

Matthew picked up his wine glass, took a sip and placed it back on the table. "Do you promise not to freak out?"

Kyle pretended to chuckle. "You're kidding me, right? Do you think I'm not already freaked out? I'm not sure what else you can say to unfreak me out."

Matthew smiled. "Okay… well… there's Nathan."

"No way." Kyle scratched his head and shook it back and forth. "You're not going to tell me there's *another* one, are you?" His thoughts were fighting each other. *Leave. Stay. Leave. Stay.* His curiosity conquered his fear and he stayed put... for now.

"Yes." Matthew hung his head. "He's the part of me that shows anger and rage. He doesn't hide his feelings, so he helps me get out my frustrations. And that's another reason I wanted to have you over tonight." He held the bowl of the wine glass in both hands and clasped his other fingers around its stem. "Nathan, well, he made a threat and Alex needs to keep things under control."

"What threat? What did he say? And who is he threatening? Me? Dylan? Dr. Wright?"

"I know this is a lot, so I'm going to try to explain it as clearly as possible. Dr. Wright says it's possible for alters to have a full, rich life by learning to exist with each other in a functional way. The problem is that Nathan falsely believes that Dr. Wright wants to merge all the personalities into one. If that happens, then Nathan, Alex and I will be gone forever."

"Then who would be left?" Kyle asked, finding it difficult to take a breath. He was already dealing with his own shit and now he was learning that the one person he thought he might have a relationship with was literally out of his mind.

Matthew didn't respond.

"Who's left, Matthew? Please don't tell me there's a fourth one. Please. Don't."

"I promise," Matthew said, "it's the last one."

Oh my God.

"I usually don't call him by name, but because I want you to understand, or at least *try* to understand, what is going on, I'll use his name. Frank, who Dr. Wright considers the 'host,' is our main 'part.' He's the one who first sought out therapy. He's the one who has the money and pays for everything. He's the one who got us all here in the first place."

"So let me get this straight," Kyle cleared his throat. "Frank is the main guy. You, Alex and Nathan are the, I'll use the word 'consequences', of trauma," he held up his hand. "Before you ask me how I know that, remember, I'm a psych major. Nathan is the troublemaker and Alex is the only one who can keep him under control. Do I have it right so far?"

Matthew nodded.

"Now Nathan is making threats because he thinks Dr. Wright wants to get rid of him. Still correct?"

Another nod.

"So who is he threatening? Right now, that's my number one priority."

"Nathan said whoever tries to get rid of him is going to pay. And going to pay big. I think Dr. Wright is concerned that since Frank is the one trying to fix things, Nathan is going to do something to Frank."

"But wouldn't he be hurting himself? And Alex? And *you*?"

"Yes, but he doesn't get that. Don't ask me why. When he takes control, he doesn't care who else exists. It's like sometimes he wants to protect us and does or says things that none of us would ever do. And other times it's as though he couldn't give a shit about us. This is so impossible to explain."

"Obviously," Kyle said. He was exhausted. First he had the disastrous therapy session with Robertson. Then there was the anticipation of what was going to happen tonight. And now this bombshell. Every word Matthew spoke made him weary.

"This is all just way too much," Kyle said. "It's like watching a movie where you say, 'there's no way this shit could happen.' You get that, right? You understand how this all sounds like the plot to a crappy B-movie?"

"Yeah, I do."

The look on Matthew's face and the tear crawling down his cheek made Kyle's heart ache. Should he really feel bad for this guy? Was his own life not screwed up enough without dealing with someone who had four personalities?

Matthew snatched a tissue from the copper tissue holder on the side table and blotted his tears.

"Alex knows that Dylan is a psychology grad student and is hoping Dr. Wright will talk with him about our case. Something that will give him an idea of the doctor's next step with all of us and if he's telling the truth that he wants all of us to exist and live together. He's also trying to keep Nathan under control so that he doesn't do anything stupid."

"Like what?"

"I don't know. He's just… well… just untrustworthy."

Kyle stood up and slid his hands into his pocket. He glanced around the room. Should he say what he was thinking? Would he totally blow a possible relationship? Did he even *want* a relationship with this person… these people?

"So since I can't trust Nathan it means I can't trust *you*." He turned to the bookcase and then to the huge piece of art hanging in the dining room. He'd seen this painting before in his Art History class. Was it Van Gogh? DaVinci? Botticelli? Picasso? He rolled his eyes. *Who cares who painted it? You're in the middle of a shitstorm!*

"Holy crap," Kyle continued out loud. "I can't believe how confusing this is. If I let Alex stay in our apartment, we're letting Nathan stay. If Nathan somehow gets in control, then you, Dylan and I are at risk — of what, we don't know. But just the thought of a possible threat makes me nervous." Kyle looked down at the oak floor and tapped it with his toe. "And if we tell Nathan to leave, that means you would have to leave, too."

Matthew got up from the couch. Slowly, he made his way toward Kyle. When he reached him, he combed his fingers through the hair on the side of Kyle's head. Kyle didn't pull away. Matthew gently slid his hand downward until it cupped the back of his neck. A tingling sensation ran down Kyle's spine and into his groin.

"I totally get it," Matthew said, his voice soothing and seductive. "But Alex has Nathan under control and, well, I really don't want to have to leave. Mostly, I don't want to have to leave *you*."

"So are *you* the person Alex wanted me to meet?"

Matthew nodded. "Yes," he whispered.

Kyle stared into Matthew's eyes, a shade of dark chocolate with a depth he hadn't noticed until this very second. That depth held secrets, and even suffering. But right now he couldn't focus on that. The man staring back at him liked what he saw, and Kyle liked him back. Just a week ago the idea of that would seem impossible, a fantasy. And now, along with so many other unbelievable things, it was happening.

"How did you know?" Kyle wasn't sure how to ask the question. "How did you know that I was, well, you know…"

"Gay?" Matthew finished his sentence with a slight smirk.

"Yeah, gay."

"Alex knew it from the first moment he saw your eyes, all tear-filled and bloodshot. And I knew it from the moment I opened the door and you handed me a bottle of wine instead of a six pack."

Kyle smiled. "I figured that might give something away. What about the others? I mean, do they like… well, are they also…"

"Go ahead, Kyle. You can say it. C'mon."

"Okay. Gay. Are they also gay?"

Matthew leaned over and placed his lips over Kyle's right ear. "Does it matter?" he whispered, tracing his tongue along the lobe.

Kyle's entire body shuddered with chills. His heart raced with anticipation and his insides ached for what was to come.

No, it doesn't matter, he thought. *It doesn't matter at all.*

CHAPTER 12

"I can't tell you how sorry I am, Mandy, but I've hit a dead end. I literally have no next steps. I've followed every lead, covered every possible area, found video footage I never even knew existed. I don't know what to say at this point other than I'm terribly, terribly sorry."

Mandy held her phone in one hand and her head in the other. She had a feeling this day would come. That she'd get a call from Tom telling her the investigation was a bust. That there was no way to find out what happened to Michael or if he was even still alive. The pain shredding her stomach climbed through her entire torso until she could barely take a breath.

"Mandy? Are you still there?"

She cleared her throat and brought the phone closer to her mouth. "Yes, Tom. I'm here."

"If there's anything I can do in the future, please, please let me know. If anyone contacts you or you read or see something that might help in any way, please call me. Will you do that?"

"Yes. I will. Thank you for all of your hard work and help in trying to find my boy. I know you did your best."

Silence, and then, "I did do my best because you and your family are good people. I'm here if you need me. Please take care."

Mandy nodded her head to no one. "You also take care, Tom. Goodbye."

She hung up and set the phone down on the kitchen island. It was a good thing she decided to take half this Friday off. For a second she thought she might vomit. As she hurried toward the bathroom, a sharp pain, something close to an electric shock, crept up her spine to the base of her skull. She stopped walking and leaned against the wall.

These symptoms were all too familiar, exactly how things started with her breakdown after Michael was taken. They had to be nipped in the bud before she wound up like she did seven years ago, depressed and bedridden.

She straightened and forced herself the rest of the way to the bathroom, where she opened the medicine cabinet. Like a stalwart soldier, a bottle of Xanax stood behind the aspirin, moisturizer, toothpaste and tubes of mascara. She stared at it for a minute before realizing it had been more than a year since she'd taken one of those pills and they were probably way past their expiration date.

Mandy closed the cabinet and looked in the mirror. She stared directly into her own eyes and watched the tears fill her lower lids. It was time to have a talk with herself, set herself straight. What she felt was disappointment, the loss of any hope.

But she should've known how naïve she was being. Did she really believe someone would be able to find her son after all these years? Find a boy who'd been taken in a crowd of thousands, surrounded by strangers who protected themselves from the blustery wind by hiding in hoods and covering their faces with scarves? They didn't care about anyone or anything else. Certainly not a boy they didn't know. If she wasn't so angry about giving in to false hopes, she'd probably pity herself.

***

She'd had peculiar thoughts after Michael was taken. There was a time she felt that Justin and Dylan were too much a reminder of her loss. She had convinced herself that in order to get past the tragedy of what had happened, she had to live by herself, perhaps start a new life, alone. This was the only solution she could come up with to help her forget about what she'd been living through and what had been taken from her.

She secretly started searching for homes in different towns and then thought, *why not move across the country?* Far away from the East Coast, a place as cold and bare as her heart was without her son. She'd be able to look out over the Pacific Ocean and stare to the horizon, the opposite edge of the earth from where a psychopath had destroyed her life. Michael would always be inside her, but it was too much to sit at the kitchen table without him there to watch as he ate his cereal, smiling when he caught her look. Or to pass the closed door to the bedroom where she'd sweep aside the wisps of hair dangling across his forehead.

She and Justin were in the kitchen, Mandy washing the dishes and him drying them, when she couldn't hold back any longer.

"I can't stay here anymore. I need to get away. From everything..." She paused and let out a deep breath. "And everyone that reminds me of Michael. If I stay here much longer, I'm going to break. I need a fresh start."

Justin placed the dishtowel on the island and took a few steps back. He leaned against the counter without saying a word. She turned her head to see his expression. He stared at her like he was trying to assess how serious she was.

He rubbed his temples for a few seconds and then slid his hands into his pant pockets. "Did I hear you right?"

She nodded, embarrassed but still convinced she was making the right decision.

"I actually found a place online. To rent, at first, but then in time, I'll find a house to —"

"And by getting away from 'everyone', you're including me and your other son, Dylan?"

She nodded again.

"Just so I know," he said, the tone of his voice still calm and controlled, "can you please explain the logic behind this decision? I just want to be sure I understand how leaving the two people in this world who love you the most, who would do anything for you, is *good* for you."

"I've thought about this — " she tried to speak, but Justin raised his hand with a gesture that told her stop. So he didn't want to hear about her logic after all.

"There's a boy in the other room who needs his mother more than he's ever needed her before. And a man standing in front of you who would literally die for you. Someone who would walk to the ends of the earth just to see you smile again." His voice was shaky, but the anger and disbelief wafted in the air between them. "And yet you'd leave these two people behind because you need a fresh start? Please, Mandy — why?"

She searched for an answer, digging for the reasoning she'd come up with earlier that day. But when she thought about saying it aloud, it didn't make as much sense. Yes, she had to find a way to escape the reminders, but at the cost of the two people who meant everything to her? What was she thinking?

"I'm waiting for an answer, honey. One that makes sense. I'll wait forever if I have to."

She dropped the dish. Shards of glass slid across the bottom of the farmhouse sink. Mandy held onto its ceramic edge as she went to her knees, trying to keep from utterly collapsing and curling up into a fetal position on the cold kitchen tile.

Before she had a chance to take another breath, Justin had picked her up and was carrying her to the family room sofa. He gently laid her down, sat on the floor beside her and placed a pillow beneath her head.

Kissing the tears rolling down the side of her face, he took her hand and held it to his cheek. "Don't you think I've wanted to run away? Get away from everything that reminds me of Michael? His room? The scent of his clothes hanging in the closet? The morning routine that feels like a puzzle with missing pieces? I think about it every day, but as I've said so many times before, we can't run from this, Mandy. This pain will be with us forever, no matter what we do or where we live. It's about getting through every day, one minute at a time if we have to, until we've learned how to live with those missing pieces."

What an idiot she'd been for believing she'd be able to live without Justin and Dylan. How could she have even thought, for one second...

"I... I just need help," she stuttered as she wept. "I... I... don't know how to do it. What to think when the pain... when it's too hard to even breathe, thinking about what went through his mind as he was being dragged away. Where is he?" Her voice box was tense, the words struggling to escape. "Is he alive? Is he dead? Is someone doing some unimaginable things to him? I think about it all the time and can't stop. The thoughts won't stop, Justin. They just won't stop!"

She twisted her body so she was face down in the pillow. It was hard to breathe, but she didn't care. If Michael wasn't breathing, then she shouldn't be breathing. If Michael was being tortured, then she should also be tortured. If Michael was dead, then she should be dead, too.

Justin's hand slid under her face and turned it toward him. "The thoughts will never stop, Mandy. Never. But they will slow down and get easier to deal with. I promise." He kissed her forehead and gently rubbed her cheek. "I promise you that with all my heart."

It was those words that helped her find the strength to sit up and grab both of Justin's hands.

"I'm sorry. I'm so sorry for even thinking of leaving the two of you. I guess I lost my mind for a little while and let the bad thoughts take over. I'm trying. I really am."

"I know, hon. I know. And never apologize to me about this. You need to let out your thoughts. You need to tell me your fears and your feelings. If you knew how many times I apologized to Van Sessler during our sessions and he told me to just 'shut up and let it out,' well, there are too many to count. We're entitled to let out our anguish. We shouldn't have to apologize for it."

She wrapped her arms around him and pulled him toward her. Her tears soaked his shirt collar. When she could finally take a breath, she gently kissed both his cheeks and then his lips.

"I could never live without you," she said, trying to wipe her smeared mascara off his face. "Never."

He pulled her close and kissed her neck. "And you never will," he whispered.

The ringing of the phone in the kitchen pulled her from her thoughts of seven years ago. She ran to get it and saw Justin's picture on the display.

"I was just thinking about you," she said, leaning against the pantry door.

"And me, you," he replied. "My 'alter' patient didn't show and the rest of the day was just calls and paperwork. So I'm going to come home early and spend half of your half-day off with you. I called Michele at Le Provencal Bistro and made a reservation for tonight so you can enjoy your favorite French food. And then you can have anything you'd like for dessert… if you know what I mean."

She laughed and fiddled with her braid. "You mean crème brulee?"

"No, I meant *Justin* brulee!"

"I know what you meant, silly. I'd have Justin brulee every night of the week."

"Be careful what you wish for," he quipped.

"I'm a lawyer," she teased affectionately back. "I'm very careful with the words I use."

"Wait! You're a lawyer? Who is this? Who did I call? Is this Mandy? I meant to call Candy."

"Do you hear me laughing?" she half-joked. She heard *his* laughter to himself over papers rustling in the background.

"No."

"Then finish your paper pushing and get home to me. I'm feeling moody and need professional help."

"Well, we can't have that," he said. "I'm on my way. See you in about an hour. Two the most."

"Love you."

"You more," he said.

She was glad he was coming home early. They'd both been so busy over the past two days, they hadn't even eaten dinner together — Justin having pizza delivered to his office, Mandy forgetting to eat altogether until Maria placed Mandarin takeout on the pile of court filings she'd been glued to all day. And they were so tired the night before, they didn't get to talk about anything significant before

Justin's head hit the pillow and he was out like a light. At least now she'd have time to discuss her surprise visit to Dylan's apartment and her encounter with Alex.

As Justin drank his Bordeaux, she'd make him promise to meet Alex and see if he felt the same as she did. She got goosebumps on her arms just thinking about this kid. She could only hope that when Justin met him, his skin would crawl as much as hers and she'd have someone on her side when she brought it up again to Dylan. No matter how mad Dylan got, she was determined to let him know her feelings — there was something up with this kid, something disturbing going on behind those chilling, menacing eyes.

***

Justin smiled as his wife savored her lobster bisque. The glow of the candle flame made her complexion look like silk. Charmeuse. He couldn't help but reach over and gently glide his forefinger down her cheek.

Mandy swallowed her soup and dabbed her lips with the black cloth napkin. "What was that for?" she asked.

"Well it was a silent way of saying how beautiful you are, but now I'm saying it aloud, so it's not so silent anymore."

She smiled back, dipped her spoon in the bisque, and softly blew on it before placing it in her mouth. Then she took another mouthful.

"It's easy to see *your* priorities," he joked.

Mandy filled her spoon again. "I'm sorry. Thank you for the lovely compliment, but you know how I feel about this bisque."

"Yes, it's pretty obvious," Justin said. He laughed and took a bite of his avocado toast. "I guess I'll be fighting food for your attention tonight."

"Pretty much," she said, making her way to the bottom of the bowl.

Once she finished the soup, Mandy placed her spoon on the rim of the bowl and clasped her hands beneath her chin.

"You were saying?" she asked, patting a drop of dried bisque from her lips with the napkin.

Justin wiped the crumbs off his hands onto his empty plate.

"I said you're beautiful," he answered.

Mandy looked out the window at the passing cars on Mamaroneck Avenue. "It's the candle," she said, speaking into the glass. Her breath fogged up the pane in front of her, blurring the view of the street. She turned to Justin and reached for his hand. "If you saw me during the day, you might think differently."

"I won't even dignify that with a response, other than you're always beautiful – morning, day and night."

"You're really looking for that dessert tonight, aren't you?"

Justin laughed. About to respond, he stopped when he noticed Michele making her way over to the table.

"How were your appetizers?" she asked, her heavy accent adding that extra bit of French ambience to the occasion.

"Perfect, as always," Mandy said.

"Yes." Justin added, "It seems Mandy is taking more of an interest in your cuisine tonight than her own husband."

Michele grinned as she removed the bowl, plate and utensils from the table. "I doubt that, Doctor Wright. I doubt that very much."

"Justin, Michele. Please, call me Justin."

Michele shook her head while keeping her steady smile. "Je m'excuse. I keep forgetting."

"No need to apologize," he insisted. "You were nice enough to get us in last minute and we appreciate it very much."

"I second that, Michele," Mandy added. "We needed this marvelous ambiance tonight. It's quiet and, well, just very pleasant."

Michele nodded. "Mon plaisir," she replied. "Your duck confit will be out in just a moment." She then looked at Justin. "And your coq au vin will come right along with it... Justin."

"Merci," Justin and Mandy said in unison.

Mandy took her hand from Justin's and placed the napkin on her lap. She flattened it out before bringing her hands back to the table.

"Can we talk about this Alex character for a few minutes?"

Justin imitated her actions, down to positioning his hands on the table in a mirror image of Mandy's. "Of course. Go!"

"Justin, this isn't a joke."

He took his hands off the table and placed them on his lap. "I'm sorry. You're right. Tell me what's on your mind."

Mandy leaned forward. "You've always said I had good instincts, right? Especially when it comes to people. You said that's probably why I win over ninety percent of my cases."

Justin nodded.

"Well, my instinct tells me something is off with this kid, Alex. And please don't ask me exactly what it is, because I've been trying to identify it and whatever *it* is escapes me. There's something in his eyes, his voice, the way he handles himself, the things he says. All of it combined gives me the creeps and I don't think he should be living with Dylan and Kyle."

Justin took a deep breath and slowly exhaled. When Mandy had her mind set like a stone wall, it was often impossible to penetrate. She did have good instincts, but he needed to make sure she wasn't being overly protective — or unduly suspicious.

"Can you give me some examples? One or two that might shed some light on why you're feeling this way?"

Mandy scratched her head and looked out the window again. After a few moments of silence, she leaned forward.

"His eyes are empty. It's like there's no soul behind them." She waved her hand as though swatting a fly. "Okay, I know. I know. That's not an example. Let's see... he shuffles back and forth when he talks, taps his feet on the floor like he's nervous, like he's getting ready to run somewhere. His facial features change in the middle of a conversation. One minute he looks like he's evaluating me, the next he's acting as though we've been friends for years. And then, oh you're gonna love this one..."

Mandy jumped when Michele appeared next to them holding two plates.

"I'm so sorry if I scared you," she said.

"No worries," Mandy replied.

Michele set the plates of food in front of them.

"Is there anything else I can get you for right now?" she asked.

Justin checked their wine glasses, which were both half full with Chateau Canon Bordeaux. He glanced at Mandy.

"No, thank you," Mandy said. "We might need some wine in a little bit, but we're okay for now. Thanks so much."

Michele bowed slightly and walked away.

Mandy lifted her fork, but before starting on her duck, she continued where she left off. "I don't know how Alex and I got on the subject, but I'm telling him about how kids used to tease me by calling me Candy Mandy. And you know what he does?"

The aroma of the cooked pancetta on his plate brought a burst of saliva to Justin's mouth. He swallowed and took another deep breath. "No. What does he do?"

"He asks me my middle name," she said and sat back in her chair. The expression on her face begged for agreement with her outrage.

"I'm sorry. Is there a new law I'm not aware of? We're not allowed to ask people their middle names anymore? I'd better create a Post-It for that one."

"Justin. This is serious."

He cleared his throat in an attempt to convey a sense of seriousness. "Sorry, continue."

"Long story short, I told him my middle name was Patricia and out of *nowhere* he blurts out 'Fatty Patty.' Like he was using it to tease me, not only as a nasty name, but to show me how smart he was that he could figure it out."

Justin took a sip of wine. There was no way he'd be able to get a sense of who Alex was without actually meeting him. Mandy's story didn't strike him as something to worry about. Sure, guessing her high school nickname was a little odd. A good guess maybe? A smart aleck trying to show his intellect? This was definitely not the typical conversation one would have with a roommate's mother and he'd be sure to bring it up at some point with Dylan. There was no doubt he'd have to meet this guy in person. And by the look on Mandy's face, he figured it better be sooner rather than later.

"Okay, I hear you. But since I haven't met him, I really can't say one way or the other where he might be coming from or if he's any real threat to Dylan or Kyle." He scooped up a few pieces of diced pancetta with his fork and ate them, savoring each bite. "We'll be spending next Saturday with Dylan. I can mention that I'd like to meet Alex, or he might even be there when we're at the apartment. One way or the other I'll figure out a way to meet him and see if I get the same sense that there's something up. Can we please eat before the food gets cold?"

Mandy nodded, but paused in cutting her duck to hold the knife up like a conductor's baton.

"And just so you know, even if you don't get to meet him, I'm going to tell Dylan how I feel. I gave him an inkling the last time we texted, but I'm going to be completely honest when we speak. I'll be as pleasant as I can. I'm sure he'll think I'm being paranoid or making things up. He never did believe in woman's intuition, let alone a mother's intuition. Which is why I need *you* to meet him."

"Oh, because Dylan listens so astutely to every word *I* have to say." Justin swallowed a piece of chicken and took a sip of water. "Let's just wait and see how things go. One annoying parent at a time, my dear. One at a time."

She picked up her wine and raised it to Justin.

"A toast," she said. "To one paranoid parent at a time."

They clinked glasses, then each drank a generous portion. Justin placed his wine down, surprisingly disappointed — for some reason, the wine didn't taste as good as it had only minutes before.

CHAPTER 13

K yle stared at the face of the man lying beside him in bed and, in fear of waking him, forced himself not to touch his smooth, perfectly-shaped lips.

He glanced at the bedside clock: 6:00. They'd only gotten home three hours earlier from Uncle Charlies, Matthew's favorite piano bar where he would walk around the venue like he owned it. It was the third gay bar they'd been to since they started seeing each other over four weeks ago. Kyle was constantly amazed how easily Matthew got along with people; sociable, approachable and extroverted to such a degree, he was not only the life of the party, but also its creator.

And it was the same wherever they went — art galleries, bookstores, restaurants. Matthew would somehow end up talking with strangers and making new friends. There was one night, at Pisticci's Restaurant on LaSalle, when Matthew heard the table of four behind them talking about furniture and decorating. Within ten minutes, they had all moved to a table for six where Matthew offered his creative ideas and innate design expertise. The original foursome ended up paying for his and Matthew's dinner and promised an invite once their places were furnished and ready for company.

Matthew's openness and casualness with others was helping Kyle see there was more to life than living inside his head. He was still far from having his new boyfriend's social skills, but just being with someone who appeared to enjoy life the way this man did helped him feel more a part of the human race than he had in years.

Although it had been a little over a month since their first night together, Kyle still couldn't understand what Matthew saw in him. Why would this smart, vivacious, "full of life" guy want to be with an average Joe who ran the spectrum of mood swings? A guy who was so often depressed and sometimes wasn't sure how he'd get through the day?

He watched Matthew's eyeballs move back and forth behind his eyelids. And that's when it hit him: *talk about unstable. This guy has multiple personalities!* Of all the men he could possibly have had a relationship with, *this* is the person he ended up with? Why? How?

But did it really matter? Alex came into his life, introduced him to Matthew, and there was something about his personality that grabbed Kyle somewhere deep inside — holding him without saying a word when something was upsetting him, cooking special dinners for their "weekly anniversary" as he called it, texting him "Good Morning, Babe" at the exact moment Kyle would be typing the same words. Maybe they were so much alike that if he let Matthew go he'd be losing a piece of himself.

When Matthew's eyes fluttered open, Kyle gave him a smile and touched his lips as he'd wanted to for the past hour.

"What time is it?" Matthew asked, stretching and yawning.

"Six thirtyish."

"Can't sleep?"

"No. Getting off this Prozac is killing my sleep. Plus I was waiting to see if I'd get to meet anyone else this morning."

Matthew rolled onto his back and said to the ceiling, "Don't be a smart ass. I already told you, when I'm with you, there's only me."

"Is that why I can't sleep over on weekdays? Are you afraid I might meet the guy who goes to work every day?"

"Why are we talking about this now?" he asked, half yawning. "I just woke up and definitely didn't get enough sleep." He turned on his side and ran his index finger across Kyle's forehead. "Plus, I don't want you meeting Frank because he's a bore. And Nathan, well, he's just mean and nasty. Trust me, you don't want to meet them."

"It's gotta be weird knowing these, I don't know, these people, personalities exist inside you. Do all people with alters know there are others or are you just special?"

Matthew sighed. "I don't know, Kyle. And I don't want to know. When you find a new psychologist, you can ask him, or her, any questions you have about psychological disorders or alters or whatever you want to call it. I really don't have any answers, so let's let it go, okay?"

"Okay. I'll stop," Kyle said, trying to hold back a smile. He lifted the blanket. "I just thought maybe I'd find one down here."

Laughing, he lifted the lamp from the top of the nightstand. "Or maybe I'd find one under here."

"Kyle!" Matthew snapped, his irritation apparently growing with each tease.

"Or maybe — " Kyle said, opening the night table drawer. He fell silent when he saw a pistol and box of bullets inside. He turned to Matthew, a chill running like cold ice through his veins. "What the hell is *this* shit?"

Matthew leaned over Kyle, peered into the drawer, then fell back onto his pillow. "It's not mine," he said.

"Well, it's not *mine*. So whose is it?"

"Jesus, Kyle," Matthew said, getting out of bed and walking toward the bathroom. "I really don't know. But since Nathan is the troublemaker, I have to assume it's his."

Kyle looked back into the drawer, unable to take his eyes off the gun. "Are you saying you've never seen this before? A gun, for God's sake?"

"I probably have," Matthew yelled from the bathroom. "But I can't say for sure."

He can't say for sure? Is this alter thing that *fucked up?* He waited for Matthew to return and sit on the edge of the bed before asking aloud, "Do you realize there's a box of bullets in there, too? A gun and what looks like a pretty full box of bullets? That's pretty scary shit to have in your bedroom and not know about it."

Matthew slipped on a pair of gray woolen sweat socks, grabbed the white Turkish cotton robe off the hook on the back of the bedroom door and stood in front of the bed. Kyle looked him up and down, unsure whether he was upset about the gun in the drawer beside him or the pangs of lust he felt for the man standing before him who didn't realize there was a gun in his bedroom.

"Babe, I've told you again and again, all of us are always here, it's just that only one of us is up front, taking the lead. It's so hard to explain. There are times when I'm sort of in the background, listening and watching. Most of the time it depends on the situation I'm in or what's going on around me. When I'm with you, I'm the one who's up front. And that's all I really want in this life. For me to always be in the lead and live with you happily ever after."

He walked to the side of the bed and gently kissed Kyle on the lips. Kyle inched back, trying to ignore Matthew's attempt to get him off the subject.

"But you know that's not possible until Dr. Wright, well… until he — "

"Fixes me? Is that what you're trying to say? I need fixing?"

"No," Kyle said, rubbing Matthew's shoulder. "You're perfect the way you are. I mean that. It's just that we need to live a life where I know *all* of you… *all* the parts of you. It's the only way I'm going to be able to… to be a part of your *entire* life, not just a piece of it."

Matthew hung his head. His hair covered the side of his face, but through it Kyle saw a tear fall. He drew Matthew toward him and hugged him tightly. He kissed the back of his head.

"The others aren't gay, you know," Matthew said, his voice trembling. "I know one of them thinks what we do together is disgusting. I think he might try to put an end to it."

Kyle held Matthew tighter. "We won't let that happen. We can't. There's got to be a way that you and I can live — "

"Live what? Normal lives? I don't think that could ever happen. To be honest, I think I know why that gun is here."

Kyle moved backward so Matthew could lie on his back. He leaned on his elbow and placed his palm on his lover's chest. "What are you talking about? Tell me what you know."

"I can't say for sure because I only get pieces, fragments of what goes on with the others, but I think the last session with Dr. Wright was a turning point."

"What do you mean? Who was the lead at the last session? What did they say?"

Kyle was scared to hear the answer, but he couldn't let this go. He'd been hanging on to his own sanity by a thread before he and Matthew started seeing each other. That thread was now a braided stretch of rope that was helping hold his life together. He wasn't going to allow anyone to fray it, no matter what.

"Frank was in the lead most of the time. There were times when I thought I would be able to speak, but just wasn't strong enough. I heard something about 'merging' again and that's when Nathan took over. I heard him yell and curse. He called me and the others 'losers', like he always does. Other than that, I don't really remember anything else."

Kyle closed his eyes. There were so many missing pieces. "So what does that have to do with the gun? What does Nathan plan on doing?"

Matthew took a deep breath and exhaled slowly. He turned to Kyle. "He's always said that whoever tries to take something from him will pay for it and have something taken from them. So I think he's either going to use that gun on Frank, because he started therapy so he could get rid of Nathan, or…"

"Or what?" Silence. "Or what, Matthew?"

"Or take something away from Dr. Wright because he *thinks* he's the one trying to merge us all together and get rid of Nathan."

Kyle's heart pounded so hard he could feel his ribs vibrate. "Do you hear what you're saying? If Nathan kills Frank, he kills you *and* himself. How can you talk about it so casually? This is your *life* we're talking about!"

"Oh honey, don't you get it? Whatever Nathan ends up doing, I'm screwed. I'll either end up dead or in jail. And honestly, I'd rather be dead. Look at me. Do you think I'd make it a day in prison?"

Kyle could feel his heart pounding as he buried his head into Matthew's neck. He had to figure out a way to stop this Nathan asshole from taking Matthew away from him and possibly hurting Justin. His mind rotated like a fidget spinner.

Not the best time to stop the Prozac, he thought.

"You have to let me talk to Nathan," he told Matthew. "I think if I could just get a few minutes with him, I can make him understand that — "

"I told you, Kyle, it doesn't work that way. It's not like I can close the Matthew door and open up the Nathan door. If it was that easy, I'd lock all the doors except for this one. I can't just order Nathan to 'show up' so you can have a conversation with him." Kyle sighed and wiped the tears from his face. He slammed the nightstand drawer shut, stood and headed toward the hallway. "I don't want to talk about this anymore. Can we just have some breakfast please?"

Kyle stared at the ceiling. The panic in his gut turned from a tightness to a searing burn. He had to do something, he just had to figure out what. He thought about going back to Robertson and getting his opinion. But the guy was an idiot and would never understand. He'd probably tell Kyle to let Matthew go and call the cops. He'd tell him he had enough of his own problems and he shouldn't take on Matthew's as well. *Screw you,* his thoughts screamed. *Screw you! I'll take care of this on my own.*

"By the way," Matthew yelled from the kitchen, "do you want to go to the MOMA with me tomorrow night? There's a Matisse exhibition I've been dying to see."

Kyle leaned over the side of the bed to pick up his sweatpants. He slid them on and glanced around the room, looking for his shirt.

"Can't," he yelled back. "My brother wants me in Philly to help him with some engagement party stuff. I'm taking the four o'clock train tonight and getting back Sunday afternoon. That's almost three full days with my brother. Hopefully I'll be able to last that long."

Though he wanted to spend as much time as he could with Matthew, he was a bit relieved for the schedule conflict. Staring at nonsensical paintings not only bored him but had always made him agitated. People saying things like 'the artist must be conveying this' or 'this man is a genius' made him want to scream.

His few moments of relief were quickly replaced with worry. How could Matthew be so indifferent about the situation? If Nathan held the gun up to his own head to kill Frank, would Matthew even *try* to stop him? Or if he tried killing Dr. Wright, what would Matthew do? He was going to have to somehow warn Dr. Wright without betraying Matthew or disclosing their relationship.

He found his shirt on the other side of the bed. When he stood, he saw Matthew standing by the door.

"You have a brother? How could I not know you had a brother?"

Kyle shrugged. "I guess I never mentioned him because he's pretty much a dick. His name is Scott and for reasons unknown — maybe just because I'm his brother — he wants me as his best man. So I have to help out with some things. The train ride's a little over an hour. Like I said, I'll be back by Sunday night if you're still free."

"Scott, huh? You want to know all pieces of me and I never even knew you had a brother." Matthew walked in the bedroom and slapped Kyle's butt with the spatula. "Think about *that* before you start asking so many questions."

Kyle ran away from the spanking and into the bathroom. He slammed the door and yelled, "Okay! Okay! I will! I promise!"

He looked in the mirror and ran his fingers through his hair. Shaking his head, he took a deep breath, the fidget spinner now out of control.

"I told you *weeks* ago about Scott and his engagement," he whispered aloud. An iciness ran through him, his arms now twitching from its chill. As he rubbed his shivering muscles, he wondered if Matthew had simply forgotten or if he was actually talking to someone else when he announced the news.

***

Kyle watched the buildings whizz by as the high-speed train made its way through Trenton on its route to Philadelphia. The locomotive seemed to accelerate as it passed the cars along Trenton Freeway. From past trips, he knew within minutes he'd be traveling over the Delaware River and crossing from New Jersey into Pennsylvania.

He was more than halfway to his final stop at 30th Street in Philly and Dr. Wright hadn't yet returned his call. He'd left a message at three thirty when he got on the train at Penn Station. No details, just a request for a call back. Now that more than an hour and a half had passed, Kyle's anxiety started to kick into third gear.

When Dr. Wright did call back, Kyle had decided to tell him that someone in one of his psych classes had mentioned him by name. The girl, he'd say, had spoken with a friend who had coincidentally been a patient of Wright's. This patient was so unhappy with the outcome of his sessions, he hinted at some sort of retribution. Financial? Physical? Kyle didn't know, since that was all he could get out of her and he hadn't seen her since. "I just want you to be aware," he'd say, "in case you see or hear anything weird near your home or office."

He pulled his cellphone from his coat pocket. Nothing. Not even a spam call. He checked the bars on his phone to make sure there was cell service available. All were black and standing tall. His battery was only half charged, though. That's when he realized he'd left his charger on the kitchen counter, where he'd been using it before leaving for the station.

"Idiot!" he whispered to himself, slapping his forehead with an open palm.

He gazed out the window, up the length of the Delaware River. The banks looked motionless, the river's reflection so bright he had to put on his sunglasses. As he sat up in his seat to get a better view of the water below, the phone in his hand vibrated. He looked at the display: Matthew.

"Hey," he whispered, taking off his sunglasses.

"Hey," Matthew said, his voice sounding shaky. "Problem."

Kyle watched the river disappear behind him, then closed his eyes, not wanting to ask the question he was about to ask.

"What's the problem?"

Matthew sighed into the phone and didn't say anything. He waited a few seconds longer. Nothing.

"Matthew, what's the problem?"

"There's a message from Dr. Wright on my phone for Frank. He said he'll stay late at the office to help him through his emergency. Kyle, I have a bad feeling about this. I don't know how to stop Nathan from doing anything or even from leaving the house. I'm scared because I can literally feel myself slipping away. I'm not strong enough to — "

Kyle leaned forward, the top of his head coming against the seat in front of him. "Wait, what's the emergency? What's going on?"

"That's why I'm so concerned. There *is* no emergency. He's having Dr. Wright change his schedule so he'll see him *tonight*."

"Where are you right now?"

"I'm sitting on my bed," Matthew said. "And that's what's making me even more scared."

"What do you mean?"

"The nightstand drawer is open," he said.

Oh shit, no.

"Please, don't tell me — "

"And I have no idea where the gun is."

Kyle leaned back in his seat and tried to breathe. "Seriously, Matthew? How could you have no idea? *You* took it out of the drawer!"

"Kyle, how many times do I have to explain this to you? Was I the one who called Dr. Wright and said I had an emergency? Was I the one who went out one night and got my back clawed up? Was I the one who — "

"Okay, okay. I get it. We just have to figure out what he's up to. Who's he going to hurt?" The blur of the passing trees out the window made him nauseous. He looked straight ahead at the headrest on the seat in front of him. "If there's any way for you to keep yourself from leaving, for you to — "

Kyle heard a cough and then a grunt. Then another cough. A sniffle. The person on the other end of the phone cleared his throat.

"It's time to say goodbye, Matthew," a voice said.

"Matthew!" Kyle yelled, without a care in the world who heard him. "Matthew! Matthew!"

"Goodbye, Kyle," the voice replied before hanging up.

Kyle banged the window with the side of his fist and dropped the phone into his lap. He ran his hands through his hair and slapped his bouncing legs, unsure of his next move. The couple across the aisle stared at him like he'd just committed murder.

"What?!" he yelled at them.

They looked at one another, shook their heads, then continued gawking at their cellphones.

Before he had a chance to respond to their scowls, his phone vibrated. It was Dylan.

Holy shit! Why didn't I think of Dylan?

He tapped the green phone icon and placed the phone to his ear. "Dylan!"

"Yeah, dude. Where are you?"

"I'm sorry. I forgot to tell you that Scott needed my help with some engagement party stuff and I'm on the Acela to Philly. I was supposed to stay 'til Sunday, but I'm actually going to be — "

"Shit, Kyle. You just take off for the weekend without even telling me? Don't get pissed off, but I have to say that since you've been seeing this Lisa girl, things have gotten weird. I don't see you, you don't tell me anything, we don't talk anymore. It's like you're hiding something. And now you go to Philly and don't even let me know? What if I — "

"Dylan, stop! Listen, I'm sorry and we'll talk about it when I get back. Which should be tonight because as soon as I get to Philly, I have to turn around and take the next train home."

"What? Why?"

Kyle closed his eyes to think more clearly. It didn't help. What was he going to say? *There's going to be trouble because the woman I'm seeing is actually a man with multiple personalities who is trying to save his own ass by killing either your father or himself"?* That wasn't exactly the best conversation to have over the phone.

"We'll talk about it when I get home. I promise. In the meantime, I need you to do me a favor."

Dylan sighed. "What? What do you need?"

Okay, here goes. "I need you to get in touch with your dad. I need you to tell him to lock his office door and not let anyone in. I mean *anyone.*"

"You're kidding me with this, right?" Kyle didn't respond. "You won't tell me anything but now you're basically telling me someone is going after my father? What the hell is going on, Kyle?"

Kyle closed his eyes tighter. His head felt like it was splitting right down its center. It hurt so bad he thought he'd throw up. How did he end up here? Like his life wasn't already fucked up enough? He swallowed hard to keep down the puke.

"Dylan, I told you we'll talk about it when I get back. Right now all I can say is that someone told me a past client of your father's never got better after seeing him for therapy. And now he might try to get back at him somehow. I left a voicemail for your dad, but he hasn't returned my call. He'll pick up the phone for you. I'm sure of it. I need you to do this, Dylan. Now!"

"Kyle, you *do* know how crazy this sounds, right? Let's say I do get in touch with him and tell him not to let anyone in. He's going to ask me why. What am I supposed to tell him, for God's sake? And by the way, is this person a man or a woman?"

"A man," Kyle replied. "A bad man who apparently has lost his grip on reality. Just tell your dad the same thing I told you. Tell him I heard that a past client might be coming to take out his dissatisfaction in a dangerous way. Tell him I heard it from someone in class or something. Just get off the phone with me and call him. Please. We're running out of time!"

"Okay. I'll do it. But as soon as you get off the train, you'd better get your ass back here so you can explain this to me. *And* to my father."

"Call him now, Dylan. And please let me know that you got in touch with him."

"Okay. I'll call him now. Bye."

When he heard the dead silence on the phone, Kyle hung up and took a deep breath. A small sense of relief ran through him, but it wasn't enough to settle the creeping feeling of doom. The only thing that would put him completely at ease was a phone call from Dylan saying he'd gotten in touch with his father, the office door was locked and he agreed not to let anyone inside.

Until then, he'd hold his phone in his hand and pray he didn't run out of power before the call came in.

CHAPTER 14

The snow flurries looked like glowing duck feathers. From his office window Justin watched them fall, floating and swaying, struggling against the breeze to reach the ground and slowly melt.

He should've been on his way home by now, but Frank had called with some kind of "emergency" that couldn't wait. Even though he'd been looking forward all day to sitting in front of the fire with Mandy and sipping his favorite Cabernet, he couldn't break his promise to Frank that he'd always be there for him.

Peering into the street, he saw movement near the front entrance. It was Frank, hood up, hands in pockets. Justin was about to open the office door when his cellphone vibrated. He opened the drawer his desk that held it. The display read DYLAN. As he picked up the phone, the bell outside his office door chimed. Though a soft sound, it filled the room. He looked at the phone, then the door. The phone, then the door. Finally, he placed the phone on the desk.

"Later, Dyl."

He opened the door to see Nathan looking directly in his eyes. His hands were in the pockets of a short black leather coat worn over a black hoodie, and his expression in the shadows of the hood was emotionless. A fleeting fear surged through Justin, but he'd been with an agitated Nathan before and he would handle it exactly as he had in the past. He stepped aside and gestured for his patient to enter the office.

"I'm sure you've heard of them before, but I like to use those things called gloves," Justin joked. "They help keep your hands a lot warmer than your coat pockets."

Nathan didn't respond. He marched over to the chair in the middle of the room and seated himself on its front edge. Justin grabbed his pad from his desk and sat in the chair facing him.

"I'm a little surprised to see you, Nathan, since it was Frank who called and said there was an emergency he needed help with."

Nathan slid the hood back, exposing his entire face and head. He put his hand back in his pocket, as the other one had remained, and kept the same blank look he wore when Justin first opened the door.

"Would you like to take off your coat?" Justin asked.

Nathan shook his head, his stare not leaving Justin's eyes.

"Okay. So tell me what's going on. Do you know what Frank's emergency was? And, not that I don't enjoy talking with you, but why are you here instead of him?"

Nathan didn't move or react until a few more seconds passed. Then he shifted his gaze from Justin to his lap.

"I figured you'd see Frank before you'd see me," he said in a notably softer tone than usual. "I know he's your favorite, so if he had an emergency, you'd make time for him."

Favorite? This was the second time Nathan raised the idea of Justin liking another alter better, but tonight it sounded like it was coming from a place of true insecurity. When he spoke of the others, he called them names and mocked them: out of jealousy? *This might be an opening, a new way in,* Justin thought. His insides felt warmed by the light at the end of this long tunnel.

"Nathan, as I've told you before, I do *not* have favorites. Not you, Frank, Matthew or any of my other clients. You are all people I respect, honor and hope to help to the best of my ability. I hope you understand and believe that."

Nathan looked up and offered a slight smile. There was something about it Justin wasn't buying, and he shifted in his chair. He glanced at the closet by the office door and did a quick inventory in his mind. Was there anything in there he could use if he needed to protect himself?

Don't even think about it. Everything is fine.

"Yeah, I understand it," he said, his voice stronger and sounding more like the Nathan that Justin was used to. "But here's the problem. Unlike the other weaklings, I know and hear everything that goes on. I'm sure you won't believe that, and maybe your Abnormal Psychology books say something different, but I'm aware. Very aware. And the way I see it, you and Frank are leaning toward us 'merging' more than letting us co-exist, as you put it. The both of you want us all to become one. And do you know what that means? It means you're both trying to get rid of me."

The venom in Nathan's tone was unmistakable, and Justin's stomach clenched. He looked again at the front door closet.

No, you can talk him through this. Keep calm.

"Nathan, you can *think* whatever you want, but you are mistaken. No one is trying to get rid of you. There were quite a number of times Frank and I talked about resolving the situation with the functional multiplicity method. And to be honest, this morning I made the final decision to go in that direction. It means we'll find a way for *all* of you to live your lives by retaining independently acting alters. At the same time, we'll work through issues with each alter to help one another —"

"You are so full of shit, Justin Wright. What the fuck is with this 'functional multiplicity' and 'retaining independently acting alters' crap? You're just saying that you made the decision today because you don't want to piss me off. I know you better than that. You want to bring us all together into one. It makes it easier for you and for that loser, Frank. I get it. And now you're bullshitting about multiplication or multicity or whatever you're calling it because I'm sitting here in front of you bitching about it."

A chill ran through Justin like a jolt of cold electricity. He stood and walked behind his own chair. The fury in Nathan's eyes made Justin want to run for the door, but before he could, Nathan stood and pulled his right hand from his coat pocket.

When Justin saw the pistol, the hairs on the back of his neck prickled. The skin below them felt clammy, almost wet.. Fear had taken over and like a deer staring into the headlights of an oncoming tractor trailer, he was paralyzed, his feet glued to the rug. He knew if he tried to move in any way, Nathan would shoot him. What Nathan had said showed there were no words that would soothe him or settle him down. Unable to speak or move, Justin couldn't do anything but wait for Nathan to make his next move.

"So here's the thing, Dr. Wrong," Nathan said, pointing the gun directly at Justin. "I've been saying it since day one, whoever tries to get rid of me is going to pay big. Do you know what that means?"

Justin didn't respond. He held onto the back of the chair to stop himself from falling over.

"What that means is *you're* gonna pay...." He took a step closer to Justin, lifting his arm.. "Or *Frank's* gonna pay!" He planted the tip of the gun's barrel under his chin.

Justin raised his hand. "No!"

"No? Did you say, no, Dr. Wright?" Nathan pointed the gun back toward Justin. "What are you saying? Is it going to be you?" He shook the gun in Justin's face.

"Or Frank?" he asked in a softer tone, placing the barrel tip flat on his temple.

"You?" He flicked the gun toward Justin.

"Or Frank?" he asked again, louder than before, gun pointing to the center of his forehead. "C'mon, genius doctor. Make up your mind! Who's it gonna be? Who's gonna pay for trying to get rid of me? You or — "

Before Nathan could finish his question, the office door was flung open. Justin yelled and tried to grab the gun, but couldn't before Nathan turned around and pulled the trigger twice.

Understanding dawned on his face. He opened his hand and let the gun drop to the floor.

"I was only trying to scare you!" Nathan yelled, falling to his knees. "I swear, Dr. Wright. I just wanted you to stop! It was an accident... I didn't mean to... I would never..."

Nathan's words faded as Justin held Dylan's head in his hands, kissing his cheeks, begging his son to stay with him. At the moment he realized his pleading was futile, he placed his head on Dylan's chest and wept – his heart sinking into a shadow of grief he never before imagined could exist.

***

Dylan had felt a sense of dread since the moment he woke up.

From his morning shower to each class he sat through and every walk across campus, his anxiety swelled. There was nothing specific he could attribute it to and he knew better than to waste his time trying to pinpoint the reason. It was his generalized anxiety, ebbing and flowing as it did every day, like the tide of an infinite ocean.

But something about the way he felt today was different from his past uneasiness. It was like the air was thick with fear and each breath he took filled his lungs with soot and ashes. He called in sick to work so he could get home early, drink a few beers and relax with some music. Maybe he'd even sneak in some extra study time. He hoped Kyle would be home so they could shoot the shit and do some catching up.

And it turned out Kyle was on a train to Philadelphia, giving orders to tell his father to lock his office doors because he was in danger. *What the hell's going on?* What did Kyle know that he didn't? Although he didn't know the answers, the panic in Kyle's voice, along with his own growing anxiety, drove him to take action.

He had tried calling his father as soon as he hung up with Kyle, but got voicemail. So he grabbed his coat, requested an Uber and ran down the brownstone steps so he'd be waiting when his ride showed up.

Standing in the freezing cold with snow flurries melting on his nose, he wondered if Kyle's warning was the reason behind the dread he'd been suffering with all day. Was he having some sort of premonition? A foreboding of tragedy, a sign of terrible things to come?

Cut the shit, he said to himself. *You're thinking like a mystical putz. Stop it.*

Within a few minutes, a blue Honda Civic pulled up and the male driver waved, gesturing for him to enter the car. He jumped in and slammed the door.

"Sorry. I'm not sure if I input the right address. I need to get to Park and 51st."

"I'm on it," the driver replied.

His attitude was more friendly than most taxi or Uber drivers he'd encountered. *Maybe that's a good sign.* He rolled his eyes, irritated at himself for straying from his education in psychology to a supernatural, almost occult way of thinking. *Reality, Dylan, deal in reality.*

He tried calling his father again. Voicemail.

Shit.

He thought about calling his mother but knew she'd ask questions he couldn't answer. She'd also get alarmed and probably start pacing the floors the way she did when she was rattled. She'd done it for weeks after Michael was taken. But if he didn't call her, and something happened, she'd be furious.

At that moment his phone started to vibrate. It was Kyle.

"Hey," he answered.

"Hey, did you get to talk to your dad ?"

"No. Just voicemail."

"Shit," Kyle whispered.

"But I'm on my way to his office. So this better be worth it or I'm gonna kick your ass when I see you."

"Better safe than sorry. I'll get on the next train back and meet you at your father's office. There's stuff the three of us need to talk about."

From the back seat, Dylan looked out the dashboard window. As the snow was getting heavier, the windshield wiper blades worked hard to push the thick flurries aside. The headlight beams looked like shattered glass on the wet pavement, the cars in front of them crawling to avoid skidding. Dylan's stomach trembled from both fear and frustration.

"Can you speed it up? I'm in a rush!" he said to the driver, trying to keep from yelling.

"Going as fast as I can. Do you see it out there? I don't have snow tires. If we get in an accident, you'll never get where you want to go."

Dylan rolled his eyes.

"Shit. Perfect timing for snow," he grumbled to Kyle. "And what do you mean 'the three of us have to talk about'? What could you possibly have to talk with my dad about?"

Kyle sighed and cleared his throat. "Listen, Dyl, I have almost no power left on this phone and I forgot my charger. I don't have time to get into it right now. Just get to your dad's and wait for me to get there. I'm hoping I can catch another Acela and be in New York in about an hour and a half. You should bring in some food and have dinner with him anyway." He paused, and Dylan heard a stuttered laugh. "Make sure to get me some of whatever you're eating."

"Of course, it's always about food with you. Okay, whatever. We're at 45th Street now. Traffic is brutal. I'm going to get out here and run the rest of the way. I'll see you in a few hours. Gotta go."

He didn't wait for Kyle to say goodbye, nor did he say anything to the driver as he stepped into the street and slammed the door shut behind him.

The frigid breeze whipped across his face. He ran up the city blocks, wiping the melted snowflakes from his eyelids so he could see where he was going. By the time he reached 49th Street, he was out of breath and had to stop. He leaned against the steel pole that held both the street signs and traffic lights. After a few deep breaths, he wiped the liquified flurries off his cheeks and walked as quickly as he could until he reached 50th.

He made a right off Park and because the office was so close to the corner, he could see a glow of light coming from the window. Breathing a sigh of relief, he pulled open the building's front glass door and made a quick left. He didn't stop long enough to ring the bell to let his father know he was about to enter. Trying to catch his breath, he opened the office door.

The first thing he saw was Alex holding a gun up to his own temple.

"Alex!" he yelled.

Before he could say a coherent word, Alex turned toward him. He heard a loud bang. And then another.

His legs wobbled, and then his head banged on the wooden floor. He brought his hand up to his throat and felt warm liquid oozing from a hole in his neck. He was surprised at the lack of pain and how rapidly numbness was spreading throughout his body. His throat felt like it was swelling up, closing his airway. He fought out a gasp and heard a soft gurgle. Did he just make that noise? Was blood filling his throat? He tried taking another breath and heard the same sloshing liquid. His mind went void of thought, his body, frozen.

Suddenly there was muffled yelling, unintelligible screams. Something that felt like a hand cupped the back of his head and soft skin brushed his cheeks. As time passed, seconds… minutes... hours… he couldn't be sure, everything faded except a weightlessness enshrouding him, a gentle sense of calm. He closed his eyes and listened to the blood pump, with each heartbeat, through the opening in his neck.

From some obscure corner of his mind, reality edged its way back in and he struggled to open his eyes one last time.

Through the haze of his dissolving vision, he saw his father's face hovering over him. Anguish twisted it, and as if from a long distance away Dylan heard the cries and moans falling from his mouth.

Dylan wanted to cry, grieve for them both, but once again his heavy eyelids fell down. The weeping and mumbling became a fading hum and then ultimately silence.

His final thought was not about his father, his killer or the "why" behind what just happened. It was the hope that he'd see Michael again — a hope that made him smile inside as a comforting warmth enveloped his body like the most snug of blankets warmed by the sun itself.

CHAPTER 15

Detective Parsons placed her hand on Justin's shoulder as he stared out the window. There was commotion outside the office door, and it wasn't good to have this disturbance — for her investigation or Dr. Wright's frame of mind.

"Let me see what's going on out there," she said, her tone soft and calming. "I'll be right back."

Walking to the door, she scraped her fingernails through her weave until they reached the barrette that twisted and held her ponytail. *What a tragedy.* In the hall just outside the office, a young man stood a few feet back from Officer Williams, the cop positioned to keep possible intruders away. The man was yelling something about being friends with Dylan and how he should be allowed in to see Dr. Wright.

Parsons slid her notepad into her blazer pocket and walked toward him. She reached her hand out to both introduce herself and try to quell the conflict. "I'm Detective Parsons, NYPD Homicide. And you are?"

The color vanished from the young man's face, a stunned expression wiping away his scowl. Ignoring her hand, he took a step back and looked to the floor. When he looked up again, there were tears welling up in his eyes. He used his palms to wipe them before they fell.

"Homicide? What happened? Is Dr. Wright… is he… did someone do something that — "

"What's your name?" she asked. "And what is your relationship with Dr. Wright?"

"I'm Kyle. Kyle Harper. I'm his son's best friend. I've known the Wrights since I was five years old." His voice was quivering. "Please tell me what happened."

"Why are you here, Kyle? It's an odd time to be visiting Dr. Wright at his office."

Kyle slid his hands into his jean pockets, letting the tears fall. "I came to make sure Dr. Wright was okay. The train had to stop. Some kind of mechanical issue. It was two hours late. My phone went dead. Dylan said he was coming here to — "

Parsons glanced at Williams and motioned with her hand for Kyle to stop talking.

"Come here," she said, leading him to the office door. "Dr. Wright, do you know this man?"

Justin turned from the window and rushed to the door. "Kyle!"

When he reached him, Justin hugged him tightly and started to sob. Kyle hugged him back and laid his head on Justin's shoulder.

"Thank God you're okay," Kyle said. He looked around the office and then down to the bloody carpet beneath his feet. He took a step back. "What's that?" he asked, pointing to the red stains on the rug. "Where's Dylan? He was on his way here. Did he make it?"

"Kyle," Parsons said, closing the office door. "Can you please sit down?" She pointed to the chairs in the center of the room.

"Where's Dylan? Is that blood? Can someone please tell me — "

"Kyle," Parsons said in a louder, firmer tone. "Please sit down and we'll get this all straightened out."

Kyle complied, not taking his eyes off Justin. "Justin, what happened? Where's Dylan?"

Justin sat in the chair opposite Kyle and reached out his hand. Kyle took hold of it and grasped tightly.

"He's gone, Kyle." Justin took a splintered breath. "He was killed. Shot by one of my clients."

Parsons watched Kyle fall back in his chair and hang his head. His uneasiness and awkward expression told her he knew something, information that would either widen this investigation or wrap it up faster than she imagined.

"Kyle," she said, wheeling Justin's desk chair over so she could sit beside him. "Tell us what you know. Why are you here, and how did you know Dylan was coming?"

The pained look on his face suggested that he fought to hold something back. The grief in his eyes made her hurt for him, but this was no time for sympathy. Whatever it was forcing his mouth closed had to be brought to light. She felt it in her gut: this boy had the missing pieces. She slid her notepad from her pocket and clicked her pen.

"Kyle, I know this is difficult. Imagine how Dr. Wright feels." She gave him a few seconds to look at the doctor, hoping the grief he saw there would encourage him to speak.

"Who shot him?" Kyle asked. "Who shot Dylan?"

Justin sat back in his chair and shook his head. "That's a complicated question, Kyle." Restlessly, he stood and walked to the window. "I have a patient who has alters, multiple personalities. They're each unique. The one who showed up tonight is a rotten son-of-a-bitch." He rubbed his eyes. "I'm not at liberty to go into detail. I'm sorry."

Parsons jotted down on her pad: *Kyle - twitched/closed eyes when Dr. mentions multiple personalities.*

"The strange thing is, when Dylan came in and saw my patient pointing the gun at me, he yelled 'Alex.' That's the name of your roommate, isn't it?" Justin's voice had trembled as he said his son's final word, and now he put a hand over his weeping eyes. "I don't understand any of it. And I don't know how I'm going to break this to Mandy. She's called twice and I haven't picked up. I just can't. I have to think this through."

Kyle opened his eyes and moved forward in the chair. "Is Matthew one of the personalities?"

Justin looked up, his eyes widening. "How did you know that?"

Kyle didn't answer.

"Kyle, how do you know Matthew?"

Kyle looked at Parsons and then at the ceiling. He took a deep breath, exhaled slowly and grabbed the arms of the chair. "Before I answer, tell me where Matthew is," he quietly demanded.

"Kyle," Parsons said, "how do you know about Matthew?"

"Where is he?" His tone turned angry. "Tell me where he is."

"Right now he's at the police station. Soon he'll be taken to a mental health facility for a psych evaluation," Parsons said, holding back her impatience. "Any other questions before you tell us what you know about this?"

Kyle shook his head, but did ask one more: "Is he okay?"

"Kyle!" Justin yelled. He rushed over and grabbed Kyle's chin, lifting his head so he could look in his eyes. "Kyle, my son is dead. Your best friend has been shot to death. Why do you give a shit about Matthew?"

He twisted his head from Justin's grip and said, almost in a whisper, "He's my boyfriend."

Justin very slowly sat back down.

"Kyle, I didn't even know you were gay," he murmured. "Dylan never mentioned that — "

"Dylan didn't know. No one knew. Except my psychologist, but he's history."

Parsons rose, stood behind Justin's desk and leaned on it with both hands. "How long have you and Matthew been seeing each other?" she asked.

"A little over a month."

"Did you know he had multiple personalities?"

"Yes."

"Did you ever meet any of them? Besides Matthew, of course."

Kyle thought for a few seconds. "No. Not really. I mean, I knew Alex because he was our roommate. That's how I met Matthew." His eyes moved between Justin and Parsons. "I might have spoken to Nathan for a few seconds today. I'm not sure. It's just so confusing."

You're telling me.

"Kyle, you're right," Parsons said aloud. "It *is* confusing. And it's complicated. That's why I need you to start at the beginning. From what I've heard so far, it sounds like Alex is the first *alter* you met. Is that correct?"

"Yeah. He answered our ad when we were looking for a roommate. We needed someone to help pay the rent. He told us he already had a place way uptown but wanted to be closer to school and in a neighborhood with more action. When Matthew finally, well, showed up, he told me that while he or Alex or Frank or *whoever* was researching Justin's credentials, they found Dylan's Facebook page. That's where he saw the post that we were looking for a roommate and also saw *me*. Matthew said *I* was the main reason for him moving in with us."

Parsons looked at Justin, whose head was tilted, his brow furrowed. Although she could tell he was listening to some of what Kyle was saying, his mind was understandably somewhere else. She wasn't going to be getting much help from him. Carefully she considered her next few questions.

"So, up until about a month ago, you only knew Alex. Then you met Matthew and things started up between the two of you. Is *that* correct?"

"Yes."

"So why would you say you 'might have' spoken with Nathan today? Why would you use the words 'might have'?"

Kyle grasped the arms of the chair tighter. Parsons detected a surrender of tension in his eyes and his face. His body loosened up, the telltale sign he was about to spill what he knew.

"One morning I was at Matthew's, opened the nightstand drawer and saw a gun. Matthew said it must be Nathan's because *he* had no idea how it got there and Nathan was the only personality he knew with bad intentions. Anyway, while I was on the train to Philly today, Matthew called in a panic. He said the gun was missing and he didn't know where it was. Also, there was a message on his phone from Dr. Wright saying that he'd stay late at the office to help Frank with an emergency. Matthew knew nothing of an emergency and said he could feel himself slipping away and had no idea how to stop Nathan from doing anything. While I was talking to him, a strange voice got on the phone and said, 'say goodbye, Kyle.' And that was it. The line went silent and Matthew was gone. I have a feeling Nathan took over and forced Matthew out of the conversation."

Parsons slowly walked around to the front of the desk, where she crossed her arms and moved the pen and pencil holder so she could half-sit on the edge. "Go on, Kyle," she said, hoping Dr. Wright was absorbing some of his words.

"Here's where it gets even more complicated." He turned to look at Justin. Sadness overwhelmed his face, an apology trembling on his lips. Once he started to say how sorry he was, he might never be able to stop. But she couldn't let him go off-course now. She'd physically squeeze an explanation out of him if she had to.

"Kyle, please, continue."

"Okay. Okay. Matthew told me that Nathan said whoever tries to get rid of him is going to pay for it. It sounded to me like he was going to get back at Frank, since he was the one going to therapy to get better. I asked Matthew if that was what he meant. Or did it mean he could be angry at Justin? He didn't know for sure, which means I didn't either. But I couldn't take any chances. When he told me about the so-called 'emergency' meeting at Dr. Wright's office, I had to warn Justin. So I called and got his voicemail. I was going to try again halfway through the train ride, but Dylan called me and I told him he had to get in touch with his father. He started asking a shitload of questions and I promised I'd tell him everything when I got home. I just needed him to tell Justin to lock the door and not let anyone in the office, no matter who."

"And then?"

"I hardly had any power left on my phone, but after a few minutes I called Dylan back to see if he got in touch with his dad. He said he was stuck in traffic but was close to the office, I think. Then he hung up. When I got to Philly, I looked for the next train back. But my shitty luck showed up and the hour and ten minutes it should've taken took three hours instead. That's when I got off the train and ran here as fast as I could."

Parsons was about to sit again in the rolling chair when Justin stood and went back to the window. After about a minute, he turned and looked at Kyle.

"That's what he said to me. 'Whoever tries to get rid of me is gonna pay big.' And since he always blasted Frank for trying to get help, I was convinced he was talking about getting back at *him*. I spent hours trying to get Nathan to understand he'd always be around, that he had nothing to fear. I was so concerned he'd hurt Frank, which meant he'd hurt himself." He closed his eyes and held his head in his hands. "What a fool I am. What a stupid fool."

Detective Parsons joined him at the window and took hold of Justin's arm. As she was about to say a few of the words she'd learned over her years of homicide, words that didn't really console the bereaved families but at least let them know she cared, the cellphone on his desk vibrated. She went over to read the display. "It says Mandy is calling. Would you like to speak with her?"

Justin shook his head and waited for the phone to stop vibrating. When it did, he picked it up and started scrolling through his contacts.

"Where is Dylan now?" he asked Parsons.

She looked down. "The Medical Examiner has probably completed his evaluation. Since you identified your son on premises, there's no reason for you to go to the ME's office." She turned to Kyle. "I need *you* to stay in the city over the next few days, in case we have other questions or inconsistencies. Do you have family here?"

"My parents," he replied.

"Can you stay with them?"

Kyle shrugged then nodded. "I guess so," he mumbled.

"Then I suggest you do that. At least for tonight. Best to be with people you trust after something like this." She turned to Justin. "Dr. Wright, I'll probably need you to come in tomorrow so we can discuss next steps regarding charges against your client. In the meantime, is there anything I can do for you?"

"I can't keep Mandy hanging much longer. She's probably climbing the walls wondering where I am. I'm going to call her sister Marj and have her go to the house because I know Mandy. When I call to tell her I'm coming home, she's going to ask a million questions. I need someone there for her in case I have to tell her the news over the phone."

"Would you like me to call your wife's sister for you, Dr. Wright?" Kyle asked. "I've met her a few times. At least she'll know who I am."

"No, thank you, Kyle," he said heavily. "This is on me. I screwed up and now I have to take full responsibility. For Dylan, Mandy and even you."

He took a deep breath and held out his arms. Kyle ran to him and hugged him close.

"This is not your fault, Justin. Not at all. There's only one person to blame for this. Just one."

Holding Kyle, Justin glanced at Detective Parsons. By the expression on his face, she knew they both were wondering the same thing: when it came to alters, was there really only one person to blame?

***

At 11:15 PM, the Henry Hudson Parkway looked deserted.

Fortunately, Justin had decided to drive into Manhattan that morning rather than take the train. It allowed him to drive home on his own schedule, alone with his thoughts rather than with people who had no idea, nor cared, what he'd just been through.

Driving slowly through the dark night on a road still wet from the earlier snowfall, he felt completely isolated. The only sign of life were the brake lights of three cars cruising slowly over a hundred yards in front of him.

Marj was probably getting to the house, if she wasn't there already, which meant Mandy would be calling again. He'd try the best he could to have her wait until he got home before telling her what had happened, but knew that would be impossible. She had to know something was wrong, not only because he hadn't called her before leaving the office like he always did, but because her mother's intuition had always been keener than most.

When Justin called Marj, he didn't give her any specifics other than that something bad had happened and he needed her to be with Mandy until he got home. Marj pushed for more information but Justin shut her down. He felt guilty doing so, but couldn't imagine telling her that Dylan was gone before letting Mandy know. "Please, Marj, just go. I'll be there as soon as I can," was all he could say before hanging up.

As the lights outlining the George Washington Bridge appeared on his left, his eyesight became blurry with tears. The memory of his family of four passing the bridge on their way to spend a fun-filled day in Manhattan filled his mind. Michael had asked how the bridge stood in water.

"The deeper the water gets, the colder it gets," Dylan said. "The bottom is ice and the bridge stands on the ice."

"Cool!" Michael said, staring out the window in awe.

"Dylan, you're terrible," Mandy said. "Michael, don't listen to your brother. Bridges over water this deep use special procedures that allow the pillars to be built into the riverbed. I don't know the details, but I can assure you, the George Washington Bridge is not sitting on giant ice cubes."

Michael smacked Dylan's arm.

"Boys," Justin said calmly, "no fighting. Please wait until we get out of the car."

He was the only one who laughed at his own joke.

And now he held a slight smile, the memory just one of the few he had left of his two sons teasing one another. Images from the past were fading quickly and without Dylan to share them, he worried they'd disappear faster with each passing day.

He jumped when his phone's ring filled the car. Mandy's name appeared on the NAV system display, and he tapped the button on the steering wheel to answer the call.

"Hey," he said.

"Justin, I've been trying you and Dylan for the last five hours with no response from either of you. And now Marj is here. What happened?" He heard her trying to breathe. "Justin, tell me what's wrong."

Justin blinked hard to keep the tears from blurring his vision. "Can this wait until I get home? It should only be another half hour. I promise to get there as fast — "

"No, it can't. You're on speaker with Marj and me, so please say what you have to say."

Justin swallowed and blinked again, the tears running down his cheeks no matter how hard he tried to stop them. He attempted to speak, but his words didn't make a sound. Clearing his throat, he glanced in the rearview mirror. *Get your shit together.*

"Are you sure, Mandy? I'd rather talk with you in person about this."

"What happened to Dylan?" Her voice turned steady and sedate, as if resigned to the fact of what she was about to hear.

He felt a pain in his stomach as if he were about to vomit and pulled onto the shoulder by West 232nd Street. Putting the car in park, he leaned back and gazed at the glowing windows of the apartments to his right. They blurred as his eyes clouded with tears. All he could hope for was that he could get the words out without breaking down.

"It's a complicated scenario, so I can't go into detail right now. My patient, the one with multiple personalities, asked me to meet him late because he had an emergency. He ended up pulling a gun on me. It was more to terrify me than to kill me, but while he was flailing the gun around, Dylan came crashing through the door and scared him. The patient was so stunned, without thinking he just turned around and —"

"No, Justin, no." Her voice trembled through his car speakers. "Please tell me no. Please…"

"Mandy, honey, please hang on. I'll be there in a few minutes."

Silence.

"Mandy? Honey? Mandy, are you there?"

Justin heard rustling on the other end of the line.

"Justin, it's Marj," She spoke softly, as though trying to keep Mandy from hearing what she was about to say.

"Marj, what's going on? Where's Mandy?"

"She's in the living room looking out into the backyard… not saying anything, just staring. Honestly, I think she's in shock. I'm going to her right now and will take care of her best I can until you get here."

Justin wiped his eyes and tried to swallow the golf ball-sized lump in his throat. "Thank you, Marj. I'll get there as soon as I can."

"I'll be here," Marj replied. "And Justin?"

"Yeah?"

"If I had the words to tell you how sorry I am, I'd say them right now. I wish I did, but I don't. My heart hurts too much for the both of you."

Justin hung up without saying another word. He wept until there were no tears left. He then put the car in Drive and got back onto the parkway, a road as dark and desolate as the feeling inside his chest.

CHAPTER 16

This was the first time in years Kyle could remember hugging his father, let alone crying in his arms. His mother stood behind him, rubbing her hand up and down his back.

"I have to call Mandy," she said. "I just can't believe this. I just can't."

Patting Kyle's back, his father let out a sigh that held a faint groan.

"Jen, give her a little time. I'm sure she's in shock and doesn't need us calling her. Kyle said Justin was calling Marj. She stayed with them the last time when…"

Kyle leaned into his father's shoulder, which was already soaked with tears. The reference to "last time" hit him in the chest. He grabbed his father tighter, still reeling from the fact that there *was* a last time and now Dylan's parents would have to go through the same anguish and pain all over again.

"If only... I didn't get on that train." Kyle tried speaking through his sobs. "If I just stayed home and studied... like I should have.... This... this would never have happened."

"Shhh..." his father said. "Don't think like that, Kyle. You had no way of knowing anything like this would happen." He slid his hands from Kyle's back, gently gripped his arms and held him out in front of him. "I don't want you blaming yourself again, Kyle. You weren't responsible for Michael and you're not responsible for this tragedy. Not in the least. Your brother asked for your help and you were on your way to help him. Right now our main focus has to be on helping the Wrights."

"But I did know something like this might happen," Kyle said. He pulled himself from his father's embrace, walked into the living room and fell onto the sofa. His parents followed and sat facing him, each on their own chair on the other side of the coffee table.

"What do you mean?" his father asked. "How could you possibly know?"

Kyle leaned forward and placed his elbows on his knees. He looked first at his mother, then glanced at his father, and then at the empty space between them. He set his sights on the wall, not wanting to see their reaction to what he was about to say.

"Okay, well, everything's going to come out sooner or later, so I'll just tell you now so you'll know what happened if anyone asks." The wall was painted a dirty eggshell color, with an Impressionist painting of flowers perfectly centered on it. "The first thing I have to tell you is that I- I- I'm gay." He held his breath, waiting for a response. Nothing. When he looked at both his parents, their expressions were the same as they had been before he started to speak.

"We had a feeling you might be," his mother finally said. "But we weren't sure."

Kyle closed his eyes and shook his head. "Wait, you both 'had a feeling' but never thought to ask me?"

His father leaned forward, back straight, hands wrapped tightly around the arms of the chair. "We discussed it, but didn't want to invade your privacy. We thought if you *wanted* us to know, you'd tell us when you were ready."

"Well, that just sucks. I've been worried for all these years, thinking you'd hate me if I told you I was gay and now you're just like, 'oh, it's okay.' Damn it, you really should've brought it up to me. You have no idea how hard — "

"How could you think we would *ever* hate you? You're our son. We love you no matter what. We will love you forever, regardless of who you are or who you choose to love."

Just wait, Kyle thought.

"Jesus, okay. We'll deal with *that* whole thing another time. What you need to know right now is who I was in a relationship with and what it has to do with Dylan."

His father fell back in his chair. His mother sat still, her eyes wide open and lips pursed waiting for just another piece of bad news. *Remember, you said you've love me forever.*

"I've been in a relationship with a man named Matthew. But here's the thing, Matthew has multiple personalities. They're called alters. He has four: Frank, Nathan, Matthew and Alex."

His mother's hands fell in her lap and she started to pick at her cuticles. *I guess that's where I picked up* that *habit*. His father was now sitting on the edge of the chair.

"What? What are you talking about, Kyle?"

"Exactly what I said, Dad. I'm sure you've heard about multiple personalities before."

"Yes, I have. I've seen it in documentaries and read news articles, but... wait... you're really telling us you were seeing a man with multiple personalities?"

"Yeah, I am. And just so you know, Matthew had been seeing Justin professionally to get help with his problem."

"Holy crap, Kyle. This is like a movie. A terrible, tragic movie," his father said. He turned to his wife then back to Kyle. "And you've been living it all without telling us about it. I don't know what to say right now."

Kyle pinched the bridge of his nose trying to prevent an oncoming headache.

"Dad, there's nothing to say. Absolutely nothing. If there was, I'd say it myself."

"Okay," his father said. "So this Matthew had been seeing Justin and..."

"Well, the only two personalities I ever met are Alex, who's our roommate, and Matthew, my boyfriend. The story is more complicated than what I'm about to tell you, but on my way to Philly today, I got a call from Matthew. He was afraid that one of the other personalities, Nathan, the one Matthew refers to as 'the mean one,' was going to hurt Justin for trying to get rid of him. I tried to warn

Justin myself, but couldn't get ahold of him. Then Dylan called, so I asked him to warn his father and I would take the first train back from Philly. From what Justin and the detective told me, Dylan barged in while Nathan was waving a gun around. He got so scared, he shot at Dylan. The first bullet missed, but the second one…"

"Killed him," his father finished his sentence. He leaned against the back of the chair and let out a huge sigh. "Wow, Kyle, this is a lot to take in. And I mean *a lot*."

Kyle looked at his mother.

"You still love me regardless who I choose to love?" he asked her.

She walked around the coffee table and sat on the sofa beside him. She placed her arm around his shoulder and kissed his cheek.

"I meant every word I said. Please don't doubt that for a second. And now that I'm hearing all of this, we need to help *you* before we help Mandy and Justin. You've been through so much, I can't even begin to imagine." She hugged him tight. "I'm sorry. I'm so, so sorry my boy. Are you going to be okay?"

An intense wave of sadness moved from Kyle's abdomen to his throat and he laid his head on his mother's shoulder and started weeping. His mother rubbed his back as he tried desperately to come up with an answer to her question.

"I have no idea," he whispered. "I just don't know. All I know…" An intense sob tore through the words he tried to say. "All I know is that Dylan is gone."

He didn't say it aloud, but in the back of his mind he knew this night was going to be the beginning of a lifetime of the deepest imaginable guilt – not only did he lose his best friend's brother, but in some way, he'd also help murder his best friend.

Just another fuckup, another tragic mistake that can never be forgiven.

***

After he showered, Kyle yelled a goodnight to his parents and entered his bedroom – the one in which he'd grown up and spent many lonely yet sometimes enjoyable teenage nights.

He couldn't go back to the apartment. Not yet anyway. He wouldn't be able to be alone in the last place he'd spent time with Dylan. Parsons had been right to send him to his family's home. He needed the comfort of not only his parents, but also familiar surroundings.

His thoughts turned to Matthew and his heart stung. *Where is he? Is he somewhere inside a killer looking for an escape? Is he thinking about me? Does he even still exist?*

Kyle tried to push back against the questions invading his mind. Things were confusing enough without worrying about the man he'd gotten so close to, a man hidden within another who might spend the rest of his life inside a prison or mental institution.

For a quick moment he thought about asking Parsons if he could see Matthew. But would there be even a glimmer of the man he knew as a good and caring person? Or had Nathan taken over completely? The possibility that he'd have to come face-to-face with the killer of his best friend stopped him in his tracks.

No visit. No way. Not yet.

But Matthew is in there. He may be waiting for you right now.

"Stop!" he said out loud. If he couldn't use his mind to fight his thoughts, he'd have to use his words. "Just stop!"

With the still damp bath towel hanging from his neck, he sat on the edge of the bed and glanced around the room. Framed photos filled the bureau and dresser tops, posters hung on the wall, high school baseball and basketball trophies lined the shelves his father had built specifically for showing off his son's talents.

From the day they'd moved in when Kyle was almost five years old until the day he left to live in the NYU dorms, this had been his sanctuary. This room was where he'd hide when things went sour, the place he'd run to when life was going down the shitter and he needed to escape. And tonight it was the same. It was the only place the surreal events of the day wouldn't overwhelm him and he'd be able to catch his breath and try to infuse logic into his thoughts.

As his eyes darted around the room, they were caught by a photo of him and Dylan in ninth grade. With their arms around each other's shoulders after winning a basketball game, they both wore giant smiles. Coach Anderson, a man of little compassion and a lot of envy for the youth he so desperately wanted back, had told them both that morning that if they screwed up on the court during the game, they'd be thrown off the team. He and Dylan cut all of their classes and spent the day at the neighborhood park practicing their assists, jump balls, fast breaks, free-throws and every other move they could conjure up. When the time came to play, they were both at the top of their game. Between the two of them, they broke the school records for a triple-double and helped get the win by double digits.

Kyle stood, grabbed the photo by its frame and looked at it closely. For the first time, he noticed Coach Anderson way in the back by the stands, glaring at the two of them as though they'd just deflated every basketball inside the locker room. Justin, who had taken the picture, knew about Anderson and his constant threats to boot them from the team. Kyle wondered if the genius psychiatrist had waited for just that moment to take the photo. Had he somehow anticipated that in the future, his son and best friend would appreciate the contradiction captured in the photo – two boys headed for a bright future, frowned upon by a man in the background who could only wish he had a second chance at youth? Knowing Justin, Kyle wouldn't put it past him.

Smiling at the thought, he caressed the glass over the photo frame with his fingers. That day felt like a hundred years ago, a lifetime away from the past few hours. The reality of Dylan's death wiped the smile off his face. Kyle turned the frame over. He unhooked the latches on the back and slid the photo out so he could hold it. Going back to the bed, he shut off the light, crept beneath the blankets and curled up in the fetal position. Holding the photo beneath his chin, he closed his eyes and saw nothing but visions of Dylan and the life events they'd shared.

There was only one living person he wanted to talk to at this moment; the one person who would listen, understand and be able to soften the sadness and guilt that filled him. But Justin was suffering his own private hell, a nightmare Kyle couldn't even begin to imagine. So he closed his eyes tighter and prayed to a God he never before acknowledged...

If you exist, please help Justin and Mandy survive this. If you don't exist, I'll try as hard as I can to take care of it myself.

***

"I need to see him." Mandy pulled at Justin's shoulder, using it to try and lift herself out of bed. But the Diazepam and Justin's gentle pressure on her arm made her fall back onto the pillows. "I need to see him, Justin. I need to touch him. To kiss his cheeks. Please, Justin. Please." She struggled to get the words out, the medication making it more difficult with each passing second.

Lying next to Mandy, Justin stroked wisps of hair from her forehead. He took her hand, brought it to his lips and softly kissed it. "You'll see him tomorrow," he whispered, watching her eyelids flutter. "We'll both see him tomorrow, I promise."

Marj, sitting on the opposite side of the bed, held Mandy's other hand against her cheek and wiped her own tears on her shirt sleeve.

After a few more minutes, Mandy's breathing was steady and her eyes completely closed. Justin looked up at Marj and nodded. It was time to leave and let her rest.

When they reached the kitchen, Marj lightly patted Justin's back before sitting on one of the island stools. "Silly question, I know, but how are *you?* You've been through hell today and I want to do anything I can to help."

Justin sat on the stool beside her and leaned against the island. "Honestly, Marj, I don't know *how* I'm doing. And I don't know *what* I'm doing. The whole thing is still so surreal. I saw it happen, but it's like my mind refuses to believe it. It's a horror movie that won't stop playing in my head no matter how hard I try to turn off the projector. It just keeps playing and playing, over and over." He ran his fingers through his hair and then covered his eyes with his hand. "And the thought of seeing him tomorrow, gone, *in a box* for God's sake. I'm not sure I can... I don't think... I just..."

She gently rubbed his arm and squeezed his hand. "Is there someone I can call for you? Mandy once mentioned a Van Sandler or Sunder. A friend and psychiatrist who helped you in the past. Can I call him for you?"

Justin shook his head and cleared his throat, hoping it would help sharpen his focus. It didn't. "Van Sessler. No, thank you. I'm sure I'll be calling him soon, but for now, I just need to be with Mandy and we have to work through this together."

"Can I take care of the arrangements for you? To get Dylan here to Rye so we can plan the... I mean, you know, so Mandy can see him and we can have a service of some kind."

"That would be great, Marj. The coroner said he'd have Dylan at the Graham Funeral Home by ten tomorrow morning. If you could call them and see what has to be taken care of, I'd really appreciate it."

"Anything, Justin. Anything you need, I'm here for you both. I can stay in the guest room so I'm here in the morning when Mandy wakes up."

"Of course," Justin said, his eyes welling up with tears. "I don't know what we'd do without you, Marj."

"Well, you don't have to think about that because I'm here. Since Jack passed, the silence at home is sometimes too much for me. And with what happened today, I couldn't bear to be alone in that house. To be honest, being here to help the two of you will also be helping me."

She stood and kissed Justin's cheek. "You know where I am if you need me. If Mandy wakes up, no matter what time, please let me know. I'll do whatever I can."

They hugged tightly and Justin watched until she closed the guest room door behind her. His legs were weak, his head spinning from not eating or drinking water in what felt like days. He made his way to the living room sofa and lay down so his head fell against the side pillow and he could stare at the blank, white ceiling — the only thing he wanted to see.

"So stupid," he whispered to himself. "How did you not see that?"

He thought back to Nathan shifting the aim of his gun between the two of them. The memory made him feel cold — pain, sorrow and regret coursing through every vein, every fiber of his being. Why would he think that when Nathan spewed his warnings about someone 'getting rid of him and paying for it' he was talking about Frank and not Justin? How did he miss that his life was in danger and a patient like Frank could be a threat to his family?

And then there was Alex.

Mandy cautioned him about the boy, saying there was something off. But he let it slide, thinking it was her imagination or the kid couldn't be as bad as she described.

He remembered his words from their dinner at Le Provencal Bistro: *"One way or the other I'll figure out a way to meet him and see if I get the same sense that there's something up. Can we please eat before the food gets cold?"*

He was so worried about his ruining his dinner, he ignored Mandy's flawless intuition and basically gave a toast to the further destruction of his family. Wasn't he to blame for being so blind? Was the murder of his son proof that he was no longer fit to help other people? What would Van Sessler say? What would anyone say about a man who was supposedly one of the top psychiatrists in the city yet unable to see the forest for the trees? How, in God's name, did he let the trees get in the way?

His eyes burned and he let them close, listening carefully for any sound from the bedroom. He'd given Mandy enough medication to help her relax and sleep, but it probably wouldn't last through the night and he'd have to go back in and comfort her the best he could. But until that time came, he'd allow himself to fall asleep.

As he drifted off, his only wish was that he wouldn't dream. He knew if he did, the nightmares wouldn't be far behind.

CHAPTER 17

It was 6:15 AM when Justin walked from his home office into the kitchen to find Mandy sitting at the table. It was the first time he'd seen her outside of their bedroom since the tragedy had occurred three days earlier.

A half-empty coffee mug sat in front of her along with uneaten bread that looked as though it had been toasted a day earlier. There was no butter or cream cheese in view, just a carton of light cream with drips of condensation rolling down its sides — a sign it had been out of the fridge for quite a while.

"Hi," he whispered, wiping his eyes.

"Hi," she whispered back.

"Why are you up so early? Is the medication not working?"

"I woke up from a dream this morning that I can't get out of my head. It wouldn't let me go back to sleep."

Justin sat down in the chair next to her and placed both hands around one of hers.

"Tell me your dream," he said, kissing her cheek and preparing himself for heartbreak.

"You and I were in the backyard. The trees were in full bloom, the garden brimming with the most vivid flowers I'd ever seen. I remember wondering who planted them, because I knew I didn't. But honestly, within a few seconds I didn't care." She raised her hands in the air as though the plants that had filled her with awe only hours before were standing right in front of her. "They were so beautiful, and their colors were so brilliant, I actually touched them to make sure they were real. The petals were soft as silk, so smooth and delicate, I almost cried at how beautiful they were."

"Sounds lovely," Justin said. His heart was already breaking at the sound of her voice. She was speaking without sentiment, describing without emotion.

"You were at the barbeque. Steak, I think. Yeah, it was steak. The grill marks were black, the outside of the meat looked perfect. Everything was wonderful. The flowers, the food, the sunshine, grass so green it was almost emerald."

She stopped for a few seconds and blinked back her tears. "And then I looked over at the giant maple, the one that Dylan and Michael had the tire hanging from. But there was no tire. No rope. Just Dylan, smiling and holding his arms out to me. He looked more beautiful than the flowers. His skin was rosy and he had those white teeth we saw whenever he'd smile. He wore an off-white shirt and gray shorts. No shoes. No socks. Just my beautiful boy."

Justin's tears rushed down his cheeks, but he wouldn't let go of Mandy's hand to wipe them away. He had to let her finish and release everything she experienced. It was the first step toward healing, no matter how painful a step it was.

"I was also barefoot because I could feel the grass beneath my feet as I ran to him. When I reached him, I touched his face, just like I did the flowers, to make sure he was real. His skin was warm and soft. He continued to smile, almost in a teasing way as though he was silently saying, 'Of course I'm real.' So I hugged him. I cried and I hugged him more. Held him tighter than I ever did in actual life, praying, during the dream, that I'd never have to let go and I could hold him forever. And then..."

Justin waited, but she didn't continue.

"And then what?" he asked delicately, trying to help her along.

She pulled her hand away from Justin and covered her face. With a moan, she started to weep. "I can't..."

"Yes, you can, honey. Tell me, what happened next. Please."

"I... it was... I'm a bad person..." Mandy's words were getting tangled up in her sobs and all Justin could do was rub her back and whisper words of encouragement.

After calming down a bit, she tried to continue. "As I was hugging him and praying, I opened my eyes and looked behind him."

Justin stroked her arm. "And what's so bad about that?"

She took his hand and squeezed it. "I was looking for Michael. I thought he might be with him."

Justin forced a smile though his grief felt like a five-ton weight. "And why does that make you a bad person?"

"Why?" Her voice grew louder. "Why? Because I'm hugging my dead son who was murdered by a psychopath and I'm thinking about his brother! That's why!"

"Shhhh, Mandy." As if she were one of his patients, he said calmly, "Doing something like that is completely natural, in life *and* in dreams. We can talk about that later. I want to hear the rest of the dream."

Mandy grabbed a tissue out of the box on the small table behind her and wiped her eyes. "I was still hugging him and also looking around for Michael. Then I asked him if Michael was with him. He shook his head. 'No, but he's on his way.' I was about to ask him, 'On his way from where?' and that's when he just faded away. Right out of my grasp, into… I don't know. I don't know where he went. He just disappeared. I started to yell his name, begging for him to come back. And I woke myself up, screaming his name and my pillows soaked with tears. I turned over and you weren't there, so I came in here."

Justin pulled his chair closer to Mandy. "I'm so sorry I wasn't there. My phone buzzed and it was Detective Parsons. I didn't want to wake you up, so I went into my office."

Mandy picked up the toast and tapped it lightly against the side of the plate. "What did she have to say?" she asked angrily, as though Parsons was responsible for Dylan's death.

"We'll get to that in a minute. First I want to tell you why the dream you had makes me so happy." He swallowed to push down the growing lump in his throat. "I think you actually *did* see Dylan. You know you had a special connection with him. And I think you had an actual visitation. I believe —" he inhaled deeply to make sure he'd be able to say what he wanted to say without crying. "I believe, with all my heart, he wanted you to know he is well and happy. And he's in a place where one day we will all be together. That's why your dream took place in our backyard. That's why everything was so vivid and beautiful. He was letting you feel what *he* feels and wanted you to know he's okay."

"But why would I ask about Michael? Why would I ruin that moment by asking him about his brother instead of asking about how *he* was? I feel absolutely awful about it. I actually feel guilty."

You feel guilty? My psychopathic patient who should have been institutionalized killed our son. And you *feel guilty?*

"Please, give yourself a break. Why *wouldn't* you ask about Michael? He's Dylan's brother, for God's sake. You wanted to be sure they're taking care of each other."

"Hey," a voice said from the door to the kitchen.

"Hi, Marj," Justin said. "I'm sorry if we woke you."

"No, I was up and heard voices." She looked at Mandy. "It's good to see you up and around, sis."

Mandy rose and slid her chair up to the table. "Well, now your sis is going to take a shower. So that should make you even happier." She kissed Marj on the cheek and headed down the hall toward the bedroom before stopping halfway.

"Justin, you said you were talking to Detective Parsons. What did she say? And why is she calling you at six in the morning?"

"It seems she's always working. She was surprised I answered the phone. Was actually prepared to leave a voicemail."

"What did she want?"

"She wanted me to know that Frank Devlin had his psych evaluation at Bellevue and is in the prison ward until the next step in the process. She said he wanted to see me."

Mandy leaned against the wall. "Justin, please don't tell me you're going to — "

"Absolutely not," Justin said. "For my own sanity, I'm staying as far away from him as possible. We'll make sure he pays for what he's done, but I will not have a one-on-one with him. Never. I just can't do it."

Mandy propped herself up and took a deep breath. "I'm glad to hear that. He deserves nothing but loneliness, despair, regret, and to be put away for the rest of his unnatural life. Please don't comply with any request he ever makes. He should die in hell first."

Justin nodded. "Of course I won't. I would never comply with a request from him."

She turned around and walked into the bedroom. Justin and Marj watched her go and waited to hear the water in the shower turn on.

"I'll make more coffee," he said, picking up the glass pot almost completely filled with cold coffee.

"Thank you," Marj said. "I know she joked about me being happy about her taking a shower, but honestly, it *does* make me happy. It's nice to see her up and around a little." She took the paper towel lying on the table and wiped up a few crumbs of toast. "She doesn't look like herself, Justin. I know it's everything she's been through, but even with Michael... I didn't see Mandy *disappear* like this. She almost looks like a different person."

Justin couldn't think of a response. Instead, he mechanically poured the water into the coffee maker reservoir, the grounds into the filter, slid it into place, put the pot on the burner and hit the "on" button.

"I'm sorry," Marj said. "Here I am talking to you about my worry for Mandy and you're going through the same thing. I'm so sorry, Justin."

Justin sat across from her at the kitchen table and leaned back as the coffee maker started to gurgle. "No apologies necessary. This is a very strange time and frankly, I'm in a daze. I feel like a walking zombie and right now I think it's better that way. I don't want to feel. I don't want to attempt to understand. I don't want to wonder if there's a universal plan that for some reason involves taking my sons from me. I don't have the energy or the will."

He stood and made his way back to the coffeemaker. "Right now, my priority is Mandy and figuring out how we're going to get our lives back. We have friends and people like Van Sessler who can hopefully help get us through this in one piece. Mandy is an extremely strong woman. Shocks like this can break the exterior, but who she is deep inside remains."

He took two mugs out of the cabinet and filled them both with coffee. As he put them on the table, he looked out the window into the backyard. A breeze moved the bare branches and, for a split second, he could've sworn he saw Dylan standing in front of the giant maple. Justin squinted, hoping to focus his view, but there was nothing there but a giant tree trunk and dead leaves floating over its thick roots.

"You okay, Justin?" asked Marj.

He nodded. "Yes. I'm fine," he said, sitting down. He poured a teaspoon of sugar into his coffee and stirred in some cream. "I think the main issue will be getting over the injustice of what's happened to our family. The 'What did we do to deserve this?' question. I know I'll never find the answer, but that doesn't mean I can stop asking."

Marj used the paper towel to blot her tears. "Oh, Justin. How I wish I had the answers for you. No two people should have to endure what the both of you have. I never had much faith. And now I have none — in God *and* in the human race."

Justin took her hand. "Marj, keep trying. I know it's hard to do right now. Trust me, I know. But the majority of people are good. So please, don't give up on everyone else. It will only make you bitter and angry. And we need your sweet smile and soothing words right now."

Marj bowed her head. "I know you're right," she said. "And I will do what you're saying... for you, Mandy and for myself."

Justin tried with all his might to believe his own words and quell the rage growing inside him. He'd done it before when Michael was taken and he'd have to do it again. He had no choice. Mandy was counting on him and she was the only person left in the world who he cared about disappointing.

He took a sip of coffee and leaned back, his head splitting and heart aching. His eyes welled with tears when reality struck like someone taking a baseball bat to his chest. In those few seconds the uncertainty of his future became clear: the question wasn't so much whether he could support Mandy, but if he would be able to save himself.

EPILOGUE

H ow do I look?" Mandy asked, standing in the hallway just outside the bedroom door as though getting ready to walk the runway.

Justin turned to her from the news on the big screen TV. A midnight-blue Amalfi silk tank showed off her tanned skin and fell over a flowing pleated skirt. Her black suede stiletto sandals finished the outfit in a way only Mandy could carry off. Although she looked much thinner than the last time she'd worn the outfit, he was ecstatic she was wearing it at all.

"Absolutely beautiful," he said. "Stunning, as always. Are you ready for your first day back?"

Mandy walked into the kitchen and refilled her coffee mug. She leaned against the island, took a sip and looked out the giant windows into the backyard.

"Thanks to you, I think I am. I have to try living again and deal with my feelings as they come up. You, Van Sessler, Marj and everyone else are only a phone call away." She took another sip of coffee and smiled. "All on speed dial, of course, just in case."

"They're on my speed dial, too." Justin returned the smile. "Honestly, I'm not sure where we'd be without them."

"I'm not too sure either." Justin could tell by the slight quake in her voice that she was fighting back tears. She cleared her throat and pursed her lips. "I hope I'm at the top of that speed dial list."

"Always," he said. "Always." He walked over to her and kissed her on the cheek. "You're just going in for half a day so you can slowly get back into things, right?"

She nodded.

"Promise me," he jokingly demanded.

She pecked him on the lips. "I promise."

As Justin sipped his coffee, he heard his cellphone ring. He walked into the living room, where the phone sat on the side sofa table. It was Detective Parsons.

"Good morning, Detective," he said, signaling for Mandy to join him. "You're on speaker with Mandy and I."

"Good morning to you both," Parsons said.

"Good morning," Mandy replied.

"What's up?" Justin asked.

"Have you been watching the news today?"

"It's on in the background. We haven't been paying much attention to it. Why?"

"Well, with Devlin's trial finally starting next week, it appears he and his lawyer are looking to score some points, maybe take some time off the prison term he'll most likely get."

"How do you mean?" asked Justin. "What did he say?"

"Seems out of nowhere, he suddenly remembered being molested as a kid by a man in Pennsylvania. Said his uncle would pretend they were going on vacation but instead would bring him to this guy's house where they would – damn, how do I say this – where they would take turns with him."

Justin looked at Mandy. She closed her eyes and turned away. She didn't want to feel any compassion for Devlin, he knew that, and hearing this kind of news could only make it more difficult for her. He thought about taking Parsons off speaker, but didn't want Mandy to feel excluded.

"Do you know who shared this piece of information?" Justin asked. "Was it Frank?"

"Honestly, Dr. Wright, half the time, I don't know which one is talking, which one is lying or which one, if any of them, is trying to help. I leave that to the professionals."

Justin remembered Nathan telling him about the trips to Pennsylvania and the 'sharing,' so unfortunately he didn't believe this was a lie. "I'm just not sure why he would put this information out now. What does he get out of it? Sympathy? A reason for his actions? A lighter sentence because of a jury's compassion?"

"Well, that's why I'm calling. There's more to this Pennsylvania guy than molesting one boy. When they found him — "

"Justin!" Mandy said urgently, pointing to the television. "Look!"

He turned toward the TV. Staring back at him was the huge mugshot of a man who, due to premature baldness, wore a horseshoe-shaped head of hair To the right was live aerial footage of blurred figures being led out of what looked like a compound.

"Mandy, why does that guy look so familiar?"

He picked up the remote and turned up the volume.

"Alfred Dingle of Eagletown, Pennsylvania has been arrested for the abduction of ten children, ranging in age from eight to fifteen, some of whom he's held in the basement of his compound for more than seven years. Police are not providing names of the minors until their family members have been informed. More to come on this evolving story."

He pressed the "mute" button on the remote, his insides shaking, and made his way toward Mandy. No. It can't be. How is this possible?

"Detective, I have to call you back," he said, hanging up the phone and tossing it onto the sofa.

"Justin." Mandy took hold of his hand and squeezed tightly. "That's the man who took the photograph of us at the Empire State Building. The stranger on the observation deck."

"Oh my God, you're right! He took the photo we have in the bedroom! That's why he looks familiar."

Mandy leaned against him for support. His own legs were so wobbly, he worried they'd both be lying flat on the floor within seconds.

Before he had time to think through his next move, his cell phone, still sitting on the sofa, started to ring.

The sound pierced his skull. He hoped it wasn't Parsons again. Not now. Not in the middle of this devastating news. He tried to ignore it but the shriek of the ringtone persisted and it took all the energy he had not to scream back.

"Damn it!" he whispered under his breath.

He let go of Mandy's hand and bent over to grab the phone. When he looked at the display, his legs buckled and he fell onto the sofa. Mandy immediately sat down beside him and grasped his arm. Before she could ask what had happened, he saw her glance at the phone in his hand.

He watched her eyes fill with tears. Her stunned expression, he assumed, probably no different than his own as they both tried to grasp what they were seeing:

The phone number he'd kept active "just in case." A photo from seven years ago. Beneath the photo, the name Michael.

His hand trembling, he gave the phone to Mandy and kissed the tear running down her cheek.

"I think it's for you," he said.

THE END?
Absolutely Not.

Read the Prologue for BOOK 2
starting on the next page...

JUSTIN WRIGHT SUSPENSE NOVEL

BOOK 2

"JADED"

PROLOGUE

The room was pitch black.

So black, in fact, the boy's eyes hurt as he tried to focus them. It was impossible to see anything — not even his own hands when he held them up to his face.

Was he even in a room? Maybe he was in a basement, a cave, maybe he was in a motionless vehicle. Wherever he was, there was a hard floor beneath him and no sound but his beating heart and the stuttered gasps of his breath.

The air was stagnant, as if there was no ventilation. And it stank, an odor reminding him of the day he found a decomposing field mouse in the wall of his bedroom. It had somehow made its way in but apparently couldn't get out and for two weeks his bedroom reeked of a rotting rodent. He'd had to sleep in his brother's room until the stench had faded.

He slowly stretched his arms out into the darkness in front of him. Nothing. He moved them to his sides. Still nothing. Then he circled them behind him. Emptiness, nothing but space. With the darkness and silence filling every one of his senses, he hesitated to move from where he was. If he tripped, fell and hurt himself in some way, he'd be in a shitload of trouble. What if he broke a bone or sliced his leg on a sharp object? He might not even know he cut himself and could bleed out before he realized it.

Crawl! he thought. *Crawl along the floor on your hands and knees — head down to protect your face. One hand, one knee in front of the other until you reach a wall, an object or see some kind of light.*

As the boy got on all fours, the air around him started to stir. Like a slippery, shapeless creature, the coal-blackness felt as though it had its own spirit that gently glided up and down his body. It eventually found its way into his ears, his nose, his eye sockets and every other bodily orifice and pore it could find. To his surprise, the slithering energy spread warmth throughout his body and provided some unexpected comfort. Not knowing what it was or its ultimate goal, he surrendered and let it do with him whatever it wanted.

Once the presence flooded his entire body, he slowly lifted himself so he was almost squatting, sitting on the back of his calves, back straight as a board. With his eyes looking dead ahead, a shadow appeared out of the black, its color the slightest shade lighter than the darkness surrounding it. At first he couldn't tell what it was. Without shape or form, it moved closer until he could distinguish the outline of a person. The energy that had invaded him helped keep him calm as the person he now recognized to be a man edged nearer.

Way in the distance behind the man, he saw a white spot of light. Then the man held out his hand and the boy's feeling of calm turned to hopelessness. He realized the only way to make it to the light was to take the hand and let the man lead him.

And so he did. Each step stirred more churning in his stomach; soon he'd be out of this darkness, soon he'd be somewhere else.

As the spot of light grew larger, the boy saw movement. He stared through the opening, unable to figure out if what he saw were people, animals, or maybe even swaying trees. But for certain, this new world had light, more than the darkness fading behind him.

Still holding hands, he and the man reached the opening. There the boy had to use his free hand to shield his eyes from the brightness. The movement he had seen was from children, at least a dozen of them, ranging in age anywhere from six to sixteen. They were running around a yard, some kicking soccer balls, some jumping rope, while others had climbed on play sets with slides, rock walls and swings that seemed to reach the sky.

The screams of excitement and laughter made him smile. Although most of the children looked familiar, he drew a blank when trying to remember their names or where he might've seen them before. Wanting to join in on the fun, he tried running toward the playset, but the man beside him squeezed his hand and he couldn't move. He looked up and chills ran up his back.

It was him.

The screams of delight from the other children turned to horror-filled shrieks. Some of them ran under the playset house. Others hid behind the trees. There was no way out of the yard, no break in the fence, no gate to open.

The man led him further into the yard and little by little, the shrieks turned to cries. Though the man was still far away from them, they wept, not bothering to dry their tears or hide their terror.

The boy looked up at the man, who was now smiling down at him, crooked yellow teeth crowding a mouth too small to hold them. He tried pulling his hand away, tugging so hard he thought his arm might get pulled out of the shoulder socket. But the man wasn't letting go. He simply squeezed the boy's hand tighter until his smile became a laugh and then a roaring cackle that echoed throughout the yard.

He continued to tug, trying to free himself from the man's grip. It was no use, the man was too strong. The boy was ready to scream from frustration and fear. The man bent down and swept the damp hair across his forehead.

That's when his eyes jolted open and he found himself lying on a sofa, looking into the blue eyes of a rosy-cheeked nurse. Her smile radiant as sunshine, her tiny diamond nose ring sparkling like the brightest of stars, she brushed the hair away from his forehead and touched his cheek with the back of her index finger.

"Hi, Michael. I have good news," she said, her voice as soft as a whisper. "Your parents are here."

If you'd like more information about
new book announcements, events and other news, just visit:
www.RobKaufmanBooks.com

Other books by Rob Kaufman

One Last Lie

A Broken Reality

The Final Step

The Perfect Ending

In the Shadow of Stone

JUSTIN WRIGHT SUSPENSE SERIES

Altered

Jaded

Avenged

Scared

Deceived

Revealed

Made in United States
Orlando, FL
21 December 2024

56301964R00157